ZACHARY
AND THE DRAGON EMPEROR
YING

Also by Xiran Jay Zhao

Iron Widow

ZACHARY YING

AND THE DRAGON EMPEROR

YING

XIRAN JAY ZHAO

MARGARET K. McELDERRY BOOKS
New York London Toronto Sydney New Delhi

MARGARET K. McELDERRY BOOKS
An imprint of Simon & Schuster Children's Publishing Division
1230 Avenue of the Americas, New York, New York 10020

For information about special discounts for bulk purchases, please contact Simon & Schuster Special Sales at 1-866-506-1949 or business@simonandschuster.com.
The Simon & Schuster Speakers Bureau can bring authors to your live event. For more information or to book an event, contact the Simon & Schuster Speakers Bureau at 1-866-248-3049 or visit our website at www.simonspeakers.com.
Interior design by Karyn Lee
The text for this book was set in Alkes.
Manufactured in the United States of America
0322 FFG
First Edition
10 9 8 7 6 5 4 3 2 1
Library of Congress Cataloging-in-Publication Data
Names: Zhao, Xiran Jay, author.
Title: Zachary Ying and the Dragon Emperor / Xiran Jay Zhao.
Description: First edition. | New York : Margaret K. McElderry Books, [2022] | Series: Zachary Ying ; 1 | Summary: After his augmented reality gaming headset is possessed by the spirit of the First Emperor of China, twelve-year-old Chinese American Zack Ying is compelled to travel across China to steal an ancient artifact, fight figures from Chinese history and myth, and seal a portal to prevent malicious spirits from destroying the human realm.
Identifiers: LCCN 2021030444 (print) | LCCN 2021030445 (ebook) | ISBN 9781665900706 (hardcover) | ISBN 9781665900720 (ebook)
Subjects: CYAC: Spirits—Fiction. | Spirit possession—Fiction. | Good and evil—Fiction. | Magic—Fiction. | Mythology, Chinese—Fiction. | Chinese Americans—Fiction. | China—History—Fiction. | LCGFT: Novels.
Classification: LCC PZ7.1.Z516 Zac 2022 (print) | LCC PZ7.1.Z516 (ebook) | DDC [Fic]—dc23
LC record available at https://lccn.loc.gov/2021030444
LC ebook record available at https://lccn.loc.gov/2021030445

To my family,
who didn't take this writing thing seriously at first,
and then not even after my first book deal,
but finally did after this one

How to Get Superpowers
by Reading Wikipedia

ZACK HAD LEARNED TO STOP OPENING THE LUNCHES HIS MOM packed for him in front of his friends. He didn't eat them anymore either. He loved his mom's cooking, but his friends always wrinkled their noses as if the pungent sauces and spices hit them like a physical wave. Of course they made a big deal out of how the one Asian kid in school had the "weirdest" food. Ugh, he hated that this was a stereotype.

"Why care what others say?" His mom had been baffled when he'd begged her to just make him sandwiches. "My cooking is way tastier than slices of meat slapped between bread!"

She wasn't wrong, but she didn't understand the problem. Zack had finally gotten a steady friend group after going to a different middle school than his few friends from elementary; he didn't want to risk getting left out again. Yet no matter how many times he told his mom she didn't need to cook him full-on Chinese meals, she never listened, because "where would you get your nutrition?" And whenever he'd come home with his lunch uneaten, even with the excuse that he'd been practicing fasting for Ramadan, her scientist side would activate, and she'd unleash yet another lecture about the daily amount of protein and healthy vegetables a twelve-year-old boy needed.

It was easier to just pretend he'd eaten them.

Ignoring the stab of guilt to his heart, Zack hurried down the empty hallway with his lunch box tucked under his arm like he was smuggling something illegal. He stopped in front of a row of color-coordinated trash bins and unzipped the lunch box. The smell of stir-fried green beans and beef slices heaped juicily over rice exploded through the air. It made his mouth water, and he couldn't help but eat a few sauce-soaked pieces with the chopsticks packed to the side, but he stepped back as he remembered the smell might stick to his hair and clothes. Plus, he didn't want someone to catch him eating near literal trash bins in a hallway. The last thing he needed was another reason for the other kids to call him weird.

He popped open the compost bin.

"Whoa, kid. Are you really letting all that food go to waste?"

Zack startled at the voice, so close it was practically in his head. It was deep and gruff like a teacher's, yet when Zack looked around the hallway, there was no one else around.

He set his lunch box on the lid of the paper-waste bin and checked his phone. No sudden notifications or apps that had opened or anything. He dug out the other device in his pockets that could've made a sound—his augmented reality portal-lens from XY Technologies. He slid it on over his eyes. Its clear interface spanned his vision as a single long lens. Transparent neon widgets for stuff like the time, temperature, and weather popped up along the edges of his view. But he'd gotten no new notifications there, either.

"Hey! Do you play *Mythrealm* on that?"

Zack jumped. This time it was for sure a real person speaking. Though instead of a deep, gruff voice, it was another boy. Another *Asian* boy, coming down the hall with a shy smile. The shiny floor glistened like a path of light beneath him.

Zack couldn't help his shock. This part of town was so white that he'd been the only Asian kid all through sixth grade. He wondered if the boy was just here for summer school, or if he'd stay for the fall.

"Who doesn't play *Mythrealm*?" Zack composed himself and pressed his voice low, as he always did when talking to someone new, because otherwise the first impression they got was that he looked and sounded like a girl. Even short hair and baggy clothes didn't help when he was so scrawny. Still, he smiled a little. He loved being able to make friends through *Mythrealm*. It'd been a long time coming. The game—and XY Technologies' portal-lenses in general—had blown up about three years ago, but that had also been when he and his mom had to move out of New York because she could no longer afford it, so she couldn't afford to get him a portal-lens then either. *Mythrealm* did have a phone app version, but the controls were much more cumbersome, so nobody wanted to play with the kid who had to use their phone exclusively. Only after

Zack's mom had surprised him with a portal-lens on his birthday last year had he finally been able to play for real, make friends through it, and even earn a little money from trades on the secondary market—which was how he could afford to buy school lunches every day instead of eating what his mom had packed. "I'm even on the school team," Zack added. "That's why I'm here. Get some classes outta the way in summer, and there's more time to prep for tournaments in the fall."

"That's awesome! Wanna add each other?" the boy said while opening the *Mythrealm* app on his phone. His accent sounded like Zack's mom's, which meant he was probably also from mainland China, speaking Mandarin Chinese as a first language.

Zack's excitement slowed into caution, as it always did when he met another kid from China. There was a chance that politics would get between them, considering that Zack's mom had to flee with him from the Chinese government when he was just a baby. Most Westerners thought of Chinese people as all having the same background and same beliefs, but that couldn't be further from the truth. Zack was often frustrated that English labeled them all as "Chinese," while in Mandarin there was a clear difference between *Huárén*, someone of Chinese descent, and *Dàlùrén*, someone from mainland China. *Huárén* had been migrating all over the world for centuries, maybe millennia. Back in New York, his mom's Chinese friends had been mostly from Taiwan, Malaysia, Singapore, and other Southeast Asian countries—those who were *Huárén* but not

Dàlùrén, and thus were more likely to be as against the mainland Chinese government as she was.

It wasn't that Zack had to stay away from all fellow mainlanders. After all, his mom had friends from there, too. But he first had to figure out if the boy was gung-ho about the Chinese government—the way some kids here believed the American government was all good and powerful without questioning it—before getting too close to him. It was an awkward question to ask right away, though, so Zack just flashed a hopefully natural-looking smile and opened his own *Mythrealm* profile on his portal-lens, which was connected to his phone app.

"So you're Zachary Ying, right?" The boy held up the friending QR code on his phone screen. "I'm Simon Li."

"How'd you know my name?" Zack frowned as he pointed a finger beneath the code, which made his portal-lens scan it. A thin neon square closed around the code and flashed, then Simon's profile popped up in Zack's view. He tapped the floating friend-request button.

"A teacher told me!"

Zack blinked fast. He didn't know how to feel about that. He could guess what had happened—Simon must've dropped into summer school for some August classes, and a teacher must've told him to find Zack, as if they should automatically be friends just because they were both Chinese. It was another sharp reminder that when people looked at Zack, Chinese was all they saw. *Ha-ha, of course the two Asian kids found each other,* he could already imagine the other kids saying.

A familiar exhaustion weighed down on Zack. He was tired of being singled out because of how he looked, which had gotten so much worse after moving to Maine. Back in New York, people were so diverse that his race was hardly a huge deal, but here, it was like he walked with a glaring sign saying FOREIGNER. He didn't get it. He was as American as any other kid in his classes. He couldn't even speak Mandarin besides a few basic phrases. Why couldn't people see past his face?

"So is your family name the same Ying as the First Emperor's?" Simon turned his phone back toward himself. His thick bangs seriously needed trimming; they were so long that they basically hid his eyes.

"The what?" Zack took off his portal-lens and smoothed out his own hair, which his mom always complained was too messy.

"The First Emperor of China. Everyone calls him by his title, Qin Shi Huang, but his real name was Ying Zheng. Is your Ying the same as his Ying? I mean, there are a couple of different family names that are read as Ying, but his is really rare. 'Cause, you know, most of his kids were killed when his dynasty fell. But if your Ying is his Ying, you're probably from a surviving lineage!"

"What are you talking about?" Zack's own last name didn't sound like a real word anymore.

Well, it never sounded like a real word. He had no idea if it meant anything. Besides, he hated it. He'd been teased all his life about how it made his name sound like a verb. *Zacharying*. Past definitions included "running out of breath faster than anyone else in gym," "acting like a girl when you're a boy," and, of course, "bringing weird food to school."

"You don't know who the First Emperor of China is?" Simon recoiled. "Wow, what is going on in American schools? He, like, invented China! That's a big deal, even for world history! By 221 BCE, he had conquered the Seven Warring States and declared himself—"

Oh God. This was too much. *Ha-ha, of course the two Chinese kids are nerding out about ancient Chinese history together,* Zack imagined other kids saying again.

"Listen, uh"—he cut Simon off—"speaking of history, I actually have that class right now. And I told the teacher I'd only be at the bathroom for a little while. I'll see you around, okay?"

"Oh. Okay." Simon whipped his bangs out of his eyes, which caught the gleam of his phone screen. "You should search up the First Emperor of China, though. He's pretty cool. I'll send you a link!"

"All right. Thanks." Zack snatched his lunch box off the paper-waste bin lid.

"Wait, were you gonna throw that food out?" Simon pointed.

"What?" Zack laughed a little too stiffly. He slapped the compost bin shut. "Of course not. I was throwing . . . something else out."

"Kid, you care way too much about what other people think."

Zack jolted, then looked around as cold sweat broke under his shirt and jeans. That voice definitely didn't come from his phone or portal-lens.

"What's wrong?" Simon's gaze turned weirdly piercing.

"Um. Nothing. Just . . . bye." Zack shuffled away.

When he passed the bathroom, he briefly thought of flushing his lunch down a toilet, but he couldn't stomach the idea of doing *that* to his mom's cooking. At least compost went somewhere valuable. Or so he told himself.

Maybe the voice was his conscience.

But since when were consciences so loud?

Once Zack got back to history class, he sat down with his friends to continue their project on Alexander the Great.

"Welcome back. Had fun?" quipped Aiden from across the small round table, twirling his tablet pen with a lazy grin. He was the captain of their *Mythrealm* team, and Zack's heart had an embarrassing tendency to beat faster around him. Not only was Aiden absurdly tall, his short blond hair was always impeccably styled.

"I got held up by this random new Chinese kid, actually," Zack muttered, averting his gaze from Aiden's pale blue eyes. "You guys heard anything about him?"

"Why are you asking us? You're the one who's also Chinese," said Trevor, another member of their *Mythrealm* team. He had shaggy brown hair and wore the same weatherworn hoodie year-round. Or maybe it was two twin hoodies that he switched around. Theories differed.

"That doesn't mean I know anything about him!" Zack spluttered. "That's why I'm asking!"

Trevor's hands shot up in defense. "Sorry. Don't sue me."

Zack tensed back a sigh, not wanting to seem so sensitive that he'd get offended at a single comment. After checking to make sure Ms. Fairweather was busy helping another group, he scrolled on his phone under the table. Simon had already sent him a message on *Mythrealm* and a link to an article about the First Emperor of China. "This kid's kind of intense. He said a whole bunch of stuff about some emperor and made me add him on *Myth—whoa.*"

"What?" Trevor peeked over at Zack's phone, which was open to Simon's *Mythrealm* profile. It showcased six favorite virtual myth creatures in Simon's collection, visible to friends only. All of them were maxed rank and extremely rare.

Trevor's jaw dropped as well. "Is that an Exalted level ten hydra?" he exclaimed, drawing looks from a nearby table. "And an *Exalted level ten Chinese dragon*?"

Zack shot a nervous glance at Ms. Fairweather, ready to pocket his phone. Luckily, she didn't seem to have heard.

"Are you serious?" Aiden snatched the phone from Zack. "Dude, I've been needing an Exalted version of that! How much is it worth now?"

Trevor did a quick search on his own phone, then looked up with a mind-blown expression. "About two thousand dollars on *Mythrealm Exchange.*"

"No way that kid could've caught all these on his own." Aiden's wide eyes reflected the glow of Zack's phone. "His family must be rich!"

"Well, duh, he's an international student." Trevor shrugged in almost a defeated way. "They're all rich."

"Zack isn't rich," Aiden said. "His mom works at Target."

Heat scorched Zack's ears, but he tried to keep his tone unbothered. "I'm not an international student. And my mom works at UMaine, too."

"Well, my sister says these crazy rich Asians are all over UCLA, wearing Supreme and driving BMWs and Porsches." Trevor huffed. "More like University of Caucasians Lost among Asians."

Aiden choked out a laugh. "You are so not allowed to say that."

"We're friends with Zack! We get a pass, right?" Trevor nudged an elbow at Zack, grinning.

"Uh—" Zack didn't know how to answer that. He just reached to take his phone back.

"Dude, you need to actually become this kid's friend." Aiden waved the phone in a way that prevented Zack from getting it. "You gotta borrow this dragon for me."

Zack drew his hand back as casually as possible so he wouldn't seem desperate for his phone. Aiden would prank him by keeping it longer if he sensed it.

"Ugh, you weakling. These boys are no true friends."

Zack sucked in a sharp breath. What *was* that voice? How was it speaking right in his head?

"Zack?" Aiden leaned closer. "Did you hear me?"

"Oh, um . . ." Zack hesitated. Whenever Aiden said "borrow," he never meant the part where you gave the thing back. A few months ago, when walking near a pond with *Mythrealm* open on his portal-lens, Zack had captured a super-rare level 5 boto, a shape-shifting dolphin from South American myth. The next day, Aiden had "borrowed" it. He still had it. "Come on," Zack said. "He's never gonna let me borrow a two-thousand-dollar creature."

"If his parents are letting a twelve-year-old—is he also twelve?—have that, that amount of money is obviously nothing to his family. Besides, it's not like we could lose it."

"You already have a level ten Chinese dragon, Aiden. It does the same thing."

Exalted *Mythrealm* creatures were only different aesthetically, having a fancier design that spawns with a one-in-ten-thousand chance.

"But it's not *Exalted.* Look, I'm running my Water-type roster for the next regionals. If you don't get this for me, my Chinese dragon will be my only creature that's plain."

"No one's gonna expect you to have an Exalted one," Zack pleaded. Unlike Western dragons, Chinese dragons controlled water, not fire, and were by far the most powerful Water-type creature in *Mythrealm*—and thus rarer than rare.

"But imagine their faces if I do show up with it! It would make our rep forever." Aiden stared into Zack's soul with his striking blue eyes, making Zack's skin grow uncomfortably warm. "Come on, dude. Be a team player."

Zack bit his lips together. It didn't look like Aiden was going to back down, and he didn't want Aiden to hold a grudge against him. He couldn't lose his friends and go back to being the weird kid eating alone at lunch. "Fine. I'll talk to him."

A dazzling smile broke across Aiden's face. He pointed at Trevor with his chin, then bumped Zack on the shoulder. "We'll come with you. Give you some moral support." He placed Zack's phone back in front of him. "Tell him to meet us after school."

"Um. Okay."

When Aiden said "us," Zack didn't know he meant them, Trevor, plus three other boys on their team also taking summer classes.

"Zack!" Simon laughed nervously in the looming shadows of Zack and his five teammates. They were at the school's back entrance, right near the turf and running track. "Did you read that link I sent you?"

"Not yet. Sorry." Zack scratched the back of his head. He didn't like how it looked, them crowding around Simon, but saying something like *Don't worry; we're not here to beat you up!* seemed like it'd make everything worse.

"So, Simon." Aiden slipped on his portal-lens. "Zack tells me you have an Exalted level ten Chinese dragon." He strode toward the running track as he spoke, and everyone followed, equipping themselves with their own portal-lenses. *Myth-realm* players never wasted time standing around outside. They were always on the move, collecting the virtual creatures and in-game items that spawned everywhere.

"I—I didn't tell him that. Not deliberately." Zack adjusted his portal-lens to hide his guilty glance at Simon. "I just showed them your profile. Because of how impressive it is."

"Yeah, it really is impressive." Aiden peered sideways at Simon. "Listen, I don't know how the tournament circuit works in China, but over here, we have a regional one in two weeks. I'm running my Water roster. I would really appreciate it if you would let me borrow your dragon."

"Oh, uh—" Simon clutched the straps of his schoolbag.

"Come on. You'd be doing me a huge favor."

"Um . . ." Simon stopped walking, shoes scuffing the red-paved track. "That dragon is pretty important to me. I don't know if I'd feel comfortable lending it out."

Aiden halted as well, spinning toward Simon with his hands in his jean pockets. "Relax, we'll give it back right after."

Simon glanced up at the group. He was taller than Zack, but shorter than Zack's five teammates, so they seemed to be bearing down on him. Just when he looked about to stutter out something else, he suddenly squeezed his eyes shut as if hit with a wave of pain. A strong wind blew over, rustling everyone's hair and skimming a raindrop across Zack's portal-lens. Zack flinched, but the material of the lens was so water-resistant that moisture slid right off, and no water mark lingered.

When Simon opened his eyes again, there was something completely different about him.

"I'm not giving you my dragon," he snapped with shocking

force. He raised his chin and straightened his back. His stare turned as sharp as knife edges under his thick bangs.

Aiden bristled. Zack exchanged bewildered looks with the others, relieved to find he wasn't the only one who had noticed Simon's change. As the wind blew Simon's hair out of his eyes, he looked strangely familiar, yet Zack couldn't figure out from where.

Aiden recovered and said, "Why? Are you actually coming to the regionals with the dragon or something?"

"It doesn't matter," Simon said. "You're not getting the dragon, and that's that."

Chills shivered across Zack's shoulders. He was awed by Simon's audacity, the confidence he was summoning despite being surrounded by six other boys. Where had it come from? More and more raindrops plummeted from the sky, streaking across Simon's portal-lens, yet he didn't even blink.

A scowl scrunched up Aiden's face, then he relaxed his expression and leaned down slightly. "Are you staying here past the summer? Wouldn't you want to join our team?"

Zack had never heard someone "chuckle" in real life, but Simon made a sound pretty close to how villains did it in movies. "Team? This game isn't even played in teams. You call yourself a team because you pool your resources and knowledge. I have more of that than all of you combined. Why would I downgrade?"

"Wow!" Aiden lurched back. "Didn't think you'd be such an arrogant little jerk."

Simon laughed again. "It's just a silly game. Don't take it so seriously."

Lightning flashed across the school grounds, glinting in Simon's eyes. Aiden's fists clenched. Panic burst through Zack's chest.

He darted in front of Simon just as the shove from Aiden came. Aiden's palm smashed into Zack's collarbone, jarring him against Simon. Simon stumbled a step back, steadying Zack by his shoulders.

"Dude, stop!" Zack said to Aiden, surprising himself with how firm he sounded. Fear instinctively recoiled into him, but a few murmurs of agreement from his other teammates gave him the courage to go on. "If he doesn't want to give us the dragon, he doesn't have to. This is going too far. You're making the team look bad."

"No, *you're* making the team look bad." A wild intensity bloomed in Aiden's eyes. "You've always made it look bad. I never wanted you on it!"

Before Zack could process the shock of hearing that, thunder crashed and rumbled in the distance. Aiden snatched Zack by the arm.

"Give me that dragon!" Aiden shouted at Simon while shaking Zack. His grip was so painful that Zack gasped, terrified that his bones might actually break. "Transfer it to my account right now, or I'll hurt him!"

Variations of "Whoa, man!" erupted from their teammates. Trevor made a grab for Aiden's elbow.

"Stay out of this!" Aiden smacked Trevor with his free arm.

Trevor went sailing out of the track. He landed in the inner turf with a thud and a scream of pain.

Zack was so stunned he couldn't breathe. The cries of his three other teammates reached him distantly, as if through a tunnel. They ran to help Trevor while casting horrified glances over their shoulders. Another flash of lightning blanched their faces. It was now raining so thickly that the tips of Zack's hair plastered to his scalp. He didn't understand what was going on. No matter how much of a jerk Aiden could be, he would never do *this*.

This wasn't him.

"You have ten seconds!" Aiden yelled at Simon, fingers crushing Zack's arm. A yelp shot out of Zack's throat.

Simon said nothing. He stared intently at Zack, as if expecting something to happen.

"Dragon! Now!" Aiden kept demanding.

"Zack," Simon said, deathly calm, "in 221 BCE, the First Emperor of China unified the Seven Warring States and founded the Qin dynasty, the first imperial dynasty of—"

Aiden twisted Zack's arm. Zack screamed. How could Simon be rambling about Chinese history right now? *"What are you—"*

Zack choked on his words upon catching sight of Aiden's face in his periphery.

Aiden's eyes were glowing completely fluorescent green, and a *Mythrealm* tag hovered beside his face.

TAOTIE (TA-OW-TYEH)

Dark Type

Origin: Chinese

A malevolent creature of greed with the body of a goat, the fangs of a tiger, the hands of a human, and eyes under its armpits. It will eat whatever it sees, even if it means stuffing itself to death.

No matter how Zack moved his head, the tag's indicator ring encircled Aiden's rain-splattered face. Not only that, but an energy meter trailed above the tag. And Zack's own energy meter appeared at his bottom right. Just like the interface during a *Mythrealm* battle.

Simon went on in a rush of words. "The Qin dynasty set up a government system that'd be used for the next two thousand years. The First Emperor built the Great Wall and the Terra-Cotta Army, and—"

With an almost animalistic howl, Aiden switched his grip from Zack's arm to Zack's neck, lifting him into the air. Zack screamed again while kicking uselessly against Aiden's legs. What were the others doing? Were they just standing on the turf and gawking? Zack tried to pry at Aiden's grasp, but his strength was pathetic compared to Aiden's. It had always been.

If only Zack were stronger. If only.

Simon let out an exasperated sigh. "Zack, *click the link I sent you!*" he yelled over Zack's shrieking while taking out his phone.

A new message from him popped up on Zack's portal-lens.

Simon Li: READ IT.

Wheezing, Zack double-tapped the air where the transparent notification appeared. It opened to his chat history with Simon. He aligned his finger with the link and tapped again. A webpage flew open on his portal interface.

Qin Shi Huang, birth name Ying Zheng, was the first emperor of a unified China. He was born in 259 BCE—

As he skimmed the summary, something happened to him. His senses retreated into himself, as if plunging into water. Aiden and the whole chaos of the situation faded to darkness. A shadowy figure in heavy black robes appeared in Zack's mind.

"Finally! Be my mortal host, boy, and I will do everything in my power to grant you your greatest desire," the figure said in the same low, gruff voice Zack had heard earlier. *"So, tell me: What is the one thing you wish most direly for?"*

Aiden may have faded out of Zack's awareness, but Zack's heart still thrashed with panic. "I want to be stronger," he blurted. "Make me stronger!"

The figure burst into echoing laughter, then rushed at Zack

like howling wind. "That's what I like to hear!"

Before Zack could scream again, reality blew back into his senses. But everything was dimmer, duller. Aiden was still clutching him by the neck, yet Zack's arms hung limp at his sides. He couldn't move them.

Zack heard a growl rip out of his own throat, even though he'd had no intention of making a noise like that. A string of words that sounded vaguely Chinese, but not any dialect Zack recognized, rasped from his mouth. In his utter confusion, he caught how his energy meter dropped a huge chunk.

Then everything slowed down.

Literally.

In vivid detail, Zack saw the deepening grooves of Aiden's contorting expression, the lashing of his tongue, and the individual flecks of spittle flying out of his mouth.

As if controlled by someone else, Zack's arms shot up at normal speed and wrenched Aiden's fingers from his neck. When Zack dropped to the ground, the rainwater under his soles splashed out from the red track in slow motion, like two watery crowns. He tried to turn and run, but his body still wouldn't respond. It cleared a distance from Aiden with several backward steps, then the flow of time coursed back to normal like a restarted train. Aiden looked disoriented for a second, grasping at the air where Zack used to be. Then he snarled and charged toward Zack.

Zack's arms swung out and slammed downward.

At once a storm descended.

A downpour of water struck the track like a million tiny bullets, wave after wave after wave, so loud he could barely hear Aiden's hollering and so thick he could barely see their teammates freaking out on the turf. Everyone else was drenched within seconds, yet Zack remained dry. The rain swerved around him like a wet, ghostly aura. He felt his fists clench and curl upward, as if lifting two heavy dumbbells. The ground water swirled up like a twister around him.

Zack's mind went blank except for one thing: *Unlike Western dragons, Chinese dragons controlled water, not fire.*

To his rising horror, a network of black lines darkened across his arms. Like veins, except straighter and more angular. Despite not getting wet, a coldness seeped into his bones. His energy meter drained steadily. His hands drew inward with a massive effort he only faintly felt, then made the motion of throwing a baseball.

The frothy twister of water around him hurtled toward Aiden as a single shooting stream. It splattered on and on into Aiden's chest, making him stagger and stumble.

Zack's body stepped forward calmly. Bolts of lightning shot down around him as he walked, each coming with an earth-shaking clap of thunder, charring craters into the track. The air practically hummed, charged with the smell of burning rubber. His every hair rose on its end.

What the heck is happening?

All Zack wanted to do was scream and run and hide, yet his body refused to obey. His black-lined fingers splayed to the sides. The rainstorm gathered into orbs of churning water beneath his palms.

His hands slammed the orbs together and thrust the combined water forward. It caught Aiden's head and trapped it, swirling around it like a sphere of liquid glass. Flailing, Aiden tripped over his own feet and fell. He rolled over the wet track and onto the turf, but the water wouldn't let his head go. His energy meter dropped rapidly.

Fresh terror surged through Zack.

Stop! he tried to yell, but the sound wouldn't come out anywhere. His black-lined hands extended before him like claws, moving in circles that matched the water sphere's motion. Aiden grasped for his throat, hands splashing into the water, but it was useless. His energy meter drained to its last quarter.

Zack had a bad feeling about what would happen if the meter hit zero.

Stop! Stop it! He struggled for control over his body.

"Back off, kid!" came both out of his mouth and in his head.

The voice in his head was the same one that had been haunting him all day.

Zack was sure, then. He was being possessed. The voice was using his body to kill Aiden.

Be my mortal host, it had said.

Oh God, what had Zack agreed to?

He'd made a terrible mistake. This wasn't what he wanted!

Stop! Stop! Stop! he mentally shrieked over and over.

His hands and the water sphere faltered a little.

"*Kid, shut up!*" the voice snapped.

Zack refused. *Stop! Stop! Stop! Stop!*

"*No, you are going to—*"

Stop! Stop—

"Stop!" The word finally broke free from his mouth.

Zack swore his breath came out like black mist for a moment before the world sharpened. His senses crashed back to their full depths. The sphere of water collapsed, leaving Aiden choking for air. His energy meter stopped draining, almost depleted.

Zack's legs buckled. His knees hit the wet track, his previously dry jeans soaking instantly. The storm weighed down his hair and drenched his skin like a shower. The black lines faded from his skin, and so did the bone-biting coldness.

Messages appeared on his portal-lens, having no sender's name.

: NO.

: WHAT HAVE YOU DONE?

The rain leveled off to a drizzle. Dark green smoke curled out of Aiden's mouth. It briefly took a monstrous shape before unraveling in the air. His energy meter vanished.

Zack's breath came in short, hyperventilating spurts. He braced against the track, vision swinging, nausea tiding in his belly.

Another message came. But this time it bore a name.

Qin Shi Huang: YOU TRULY DON'T KNOW WHAT YOU'VE DONE, BOY.

How Not to Win a
Battle Using Soup

ZACK RAN HOME.

He thought he heard Simon calling after him, but he didn't turn back. He didn't want to stay there for another second.

His sneakers scuffed and pounded over wet sidewalks. He scrunched up his schoolbag's shoulder strap so the bag wouldn't keep thumping against his hip. Suburban houses flew past him. For once, he didn't drag this trip out to harvest as many *Mythrealm* items as he could before they stopped spawning after dark. He didn't care about any of that anymore.

When the strange messages wouldn't stop coming, he deleted the *Mythrealm* app from his phone and portal-lens. He considered throwing his portal-lens into the street altogether, but one thought about how long his mom had saved up to buy it for him, and he couldn't bear it. He shoved it into his schoolbag instead.

He made it to the side door of the basement suite he and

his mom lived in. His hands shook so hard it took him several tries to tap in the right pass code for the smart lock. Once he shoved his way in, he ditched his bag on a chair near the kitchen table like it was a ticking bomb, then bounded for his room and slammed the door behind him.

He sank to the carpet, back hitting his bed frame. A dreary slant of light cut through the narrow window that peeked aboveground. For a small eternity, he sat with his face in his trembling hands, struggling for air. His teeth chattered, and his soaked clothes clung to him like frost. He wiggled out of them, but the wet coldness remained so uncomfortable that he had to go take a hot shower.

The moment he turned on the showerhead, the sight of the jetting water stopped him dead. The memory of himself gathering rain into orbs of water while striding between striking bolts of lightning flashed back to him. A prickle raced up his scalp. He stared at the water as it gradually steamed up, then stepped into the shower stall and cautiously moved his hands around.

Nothing happened. Nothing stirred in him in response to the water beating down on his body, except a sharp pain when it turned too hot. Hissing, he wrenched the temperature down. He didn't feel anything that suggested he could . . . control the water.

Had everything been a dream? A hallucination?

Simon and his teammates could tell him. Maybe some of them had even caught a video with their phones.

But that wasn't *Zack* controlling the water. Not *him* trying to drown Aiden.

Oh God, what if they thought it was? What if they reported him as a superpowered murderer?

Zack scrambled out of the shower, grabbed a towel, and hurried back to his room to dig his phone out of his damp pants. His wet feet soaked the carpet further.

No new posts from his teammates. No internet mob flooding his notifications. A relieved sigh heaved out of him, and he sat down on his bed, toweling himself.

But he tensed back up, because his teammates were *too* silent.

What happened after he left? Was Trevor okay? Was Aiden? Why hadn't he stayed to make sure?

Zack berated himself for running away without figuring things out. Yet when he opened his messenger app, his thumbs hovered uselessly. He couldn't muster the courage to text any of them.

Wimp, he thought, curling up beneath his covers.

demonic possession

   spiritual possession

   first emperor of china

Huddling in his bed, Zack paused on the search results of that last term. There was a bunch of news about how there'd been a recent earthquake near the emperor's massive, mercury-filled mausoleum. Too freaked out to continue, Zack closed the page without tapping anything. Listening to the info Simon had blabbed out and reading the link he'd sent was how Zack had lost control of his body.

The searches about possession hadn't been any help either. They'd been all about psychiatrists trying to debunk it or Christian-centric possession stories. He was pretty sure his case had nothing to do with those. No, he'd been possessed by . . . the First Emperor of China?

He wanted to laugh off that idea. It was ridiculous. That kind of stuff only happened in movies.

But he couldn't deny what had gone down on that track. In that storm. The storm that his body had controlled.

Tell me: What is the one thing you wish most direly for?

Make me stronger.

Had he accidentally made a *deal* with the emperor? A monkey's-paw wish, the kind that came true in the worst possible way? He'd read a short story about that in English last year. But how could something like that happen in real life?

Zack scrolled mindlessly on his phone, watching videos of people doing silly things and telling silly stories, laughing occasionally like a robot without really feeling any better inside. Only when the newest promo video from XY Technologies popped up did he really pay attention. It was a teaser for the latest generation of portal-lenses, X6, releasing later this year. But it wasn't the new functions and incredible specs that snagged Zack's mind, but the person talking about them over a chill, futuristic-sounding beat: Xuan Jihong, aka Jason Xuan, founder of XY Technologies.

He was everything Zack wanted to be. Looking at him talking about revolutionary display pixels and unprecedented battery life, with his movie star looks, sharp suit, and glinting, expensive watch, Zack felt worse about doing nothing but cowering in his bed. Jason had also lost his father when he was a baby, though he'd had it even tougher than Zack, having grown up in rural China. But he had studied so hard and won so many coding competitions in his teens that he'd received a full-ride scholarship to MIT. There, he developed his idea of portal-lenses into reality, then founded XY Technologies to create features and games for them. By age twenty-four, he was a millionaire. Now, ten years later, he was a billionaire leading the tech and gaming worlds, so prolific that he was instrumental in convincing the Chinese government to drop some of their strict video gaming restrictions.

In every interview with him that Zack had watched, Jason gave credit to his mom for devoting her life to raising him and teaching him both discipline and innovation. Just like Zack's mom, who'd been a biochemical engineer back in China but had to work mostly retail jobs in America while raising him alone. Yet, for the longest time, she'd never made him feel like they were struggling. He'd been so much happier when he'd been little, when he hadn't realized his mom had been lying on those nights when she would make him dinner but not eat anything herself because she had "already eaten." Other kids had been simpler back then too, not noticing or caring that Zack's clothes and shoes were never new, or that he watched free documentaries on YouTube instead of the newest Netflix shows, or that he and his mom never went on any vacations or ate at any fancy restaurants. When she had free time and the sun was shining, she would pack some food and take him for a picnic in Central Park, and that had been enough for him.

A wave of hot shame rolled through Zack as he remembered how he had pleaded and begged for a portal-lens before his ninth birthday, then how his mom had burst into tears the night before it, saying how sorry she was that she couldn't get it for him without worrying if they could make rent, and that she wasn't even sure they could afford to stay in New York. That had been the night Zack had realized he couldn't be like other kids anymore, that he had to get straight As and stay out of trouble and never add more to his mom's worries.

This was why Zack never told his mom about his issues making new friends every time they moved, first from New York to Maine when he was in third grade and then to a different neighborhood after he graduated elementary school. He didn't want her to regret any decision to make her own life easier. She was able to get a part-time position in the labs at UMaine, the first step to picking up her science career again, and they were much less strapped for money. Even though the basement suite they now lived in was still a basement suite, it was roomier than their apartment in New York and quieter than their first home in Maine.

After hearing Jason Xuan's story in fourth grade through a YouTube documentary, Zack had learned to code. He'd been making more and more complex games, though he wasn't brave enough to put them online yet. He didn't dare dream of having a rise like Jason's, but he at least wanted to go to MIT too, and make enough money to give his mom the life she deserved. No more cramped apartments in shady neighborhoods, no more basement suites, no more picking up shifts in stores where customers yelled at her for things she had no control over.

Zack was so lost in his dreams for the future that the clatter of the front door almost startled his soul out of his body. He lurched up under his covers. He'd hardly noticed that the rainy daylight had waned from his window.

"Zack?" his mom called out.

"Yeah?" He rushed to flip on his light switch.

But it was too late. She would've noticed the darkness of their suite as soon as she'd walked in, hence the concern. She knocked on his door. "You feeling okay?"

"Yeah, was just taking a nap!"

"You stay up late playing video games again?"

"No! I—I was just really tired today. We studied a lot of . . . history."

Before this day, Zack never got why comic book characters who got superpowers always had to hide them. Now he knew. He understood. He *related.* How was he supposed to *begin* explaining what'd happened without sounding out of his mind?

"Ah, okay." His mom's slippered footsteps shuffled away from his door.

That got him off the hook temporarily, but after a while of pots and pans clanging in the kitchen and noises of sizzling oil and him pacing his room aimlessly, his mom called him out to dinner.

Jason Xuan wouldn't hide in his room.

Zack took a deep breath, released it, then got dressed. Pretending to be too tired to eat would only worry his mom more. The aches that intensified with his every movement reminded him of the bruises on his arm and neck, so he pulled on a turtleneck. Thankfully, the lingering chill from the storm made the sweater less suspicious. Turtlenecks could always be justified in Maine.

Once he stepped out of his room, Zack immediately shut the door after himself. The basement suite was so small that the smell of his mom's cooking stuck to everything it touched. He could never risk leaving his door open during dinnertime. Even his mom had to change out of her Target uniform whenever she cooked after a shift there.

Their kitchen table was right near the suite entrance. Eyeing his schoolbag like it was cursed—and his portal-lens may well have been—Zack sat down at his bowl of rice in the only other free chair. He'd always wondered why his mom put exactly three chairs out. He suspected the third was an unspoken stand-in for his dad, who'd been executed in China when Zack was a baby for "acts of terror," which were really just him speaking up against the government's oppression of Uighur Muslims and other minorities. Zack had never asked for a confirmation, though. As strong-willed as his mom was, his dad was the one thing she couldn't talk about without breaking down into tears.

For dinner, she'd made stir-fried eggs and tomatoes, pan-seared fish with plenty of soy sauce, and seaweed-and-egg-drop soup. Zack's lunch box sat beside the dishes, open and incriminating.

"Ying Ziyang"—his mom pointed at it—"you didn't eat your lunch again."

Zack bristled at his Chinese name. His mom only used it when he was in deep trouble. Distracted by the Simon situation, he'd forgotten to take another washroom break during class to compost his lunch. "Sorry, Mom, wasn't feeling up for it. Got something from the cafeteria instead."

"Got what?"

"A . . . garden salad." Zack couldn't lie about his very few options. Since he was only supposed to eat halal meat, prepared according to Muslim traditions, he could only get vegan stuff from the cafeteria.

His mom's brows squeezed upward. "How much nutrition can a garden salad have? You need to eat more than that. You're a growing boy."

"I know, Mom. I just didn't have much of an appetite today."

"You sure you're not sick? Are you cold?" She eyed his turtle-neck, tone softening, then put one hand to his forehead and the other to her own, checking for a fever.

"I'm fine." Zack pulled back, though discomfort stirred in him at the lie.

He wasn't fine. Nothing close to it. He wished he could tell her everything, but she'd never believe him without proof. She'd think he was watching too much anime again. He subtly moved his hand near the soup, hoping it would spurt over the brim or something. Nothing happened.

After a slight pause in which his mom pierced him with her best interrogation glare, she asked, "Did you get a bad grade?"

"No! Definitely not!"

"Then what's wrong?"

"It's nothing. Seriously. I'm not—" Zack's schoolbag caught his eye. In its gaping opening, his portal-lens flashed like a distress beacon.

He squashed the bag closed.

"Almost forgot I have a whole bunch of homework to do tonight!" He forced out a laugh when his mom glanced between him and the bag. He dragged the bag closer and fished out his small laptop for good measure. His mom had no issue with him doing homework at dinner; his room was too small to have a desk, so the kitchen table was the only solid surface he could use his laptop on. Hopefully it would get her to drop this conversation.

Just when he opened his laptop beside his rice bowl and searched for a random file to read, a harsh knocking came at the door.

Zack and his mom exchanged a quick glance; then she rushed to her room to put her hijab on while he went to answer the door first.

After he turned the handle, a cold gust of night air poured in, smelling like wet dirt and concrete. He looked up to find their landlord, Mr. Lansbury, and his son Nathan. Nathan was only a year older than Zack, but he was a lot bigger and always had a mean look on his face, so Zack usually did his best to stay out of his way.

"Is—is something the matter, Mr. Lansbury?" Zack gulped. A landlord visit was never good. And why did he come with Nathan?

"Yes," Mr. Lansbury said. "I'm afraid we cannot let you live here anymore."

Ice plunged into Zack's stomach. "*What?* Why?"

"Because you are a vessel that must be destroyed."

A heated force blasted into Zack. He tripped and fell, landing harshly on his hand. Pain detonated through his arm and hip.

"Zack!" His mom lunged from her room, scarlet hijab wrapped securely around her head.

She reached him just as another hot ripple warped through the air. She screamed as she hit the floor, limbs jerking unnaturally, as if pulled by something invisible. At the door, Nathan was making the pulling motions. Somehow, without contact, he was dragging Zack's mom across the floor.

"Mom!" Zack latched on to her ankles, but the force was too strong. Hot winds blew into his face out of nowhere. They were being attacked by something he couldn't see. If only he could see it—

His bag buzzed again and again on its chair, the wood conducting the vibrations. He swore a muffled voice came from it. He barely made out what it was saying over his mom's screams: *"Kid! Put me on!"*

As his mom thrashed under the invisible force, Zack had nothing left to lose. He lurched for his bag, fumbled out his buzzing and flashing portal-lens, then slid it on.

The buzzing and flashing stopped.

"Finally!" the gruff voice said, clear and real and outside of Zack's head for the first time, coming from the bone conduction speakers in the arms of the portal-lens. "You've made matters very difficult for me, kid!"

When Zack looked back at his mom, a gasp jetted from his mouth. He could now see glowing, blurry red sashes tangled around her limbs. They led back to Nathan, who was tugging on them. Whole spools of more sashes swirled and floated like neon mist around Nathan's arms and torso. His eyes were entirely a radiant, demonic red, while Mr. Lansbury's were blazing green. Energy meters hovered near their heads.

But this wasn't like *Mythrealm* after all. In *Mythrealm*, your energy meter resets after every battle. Zack's meter, at the bottom right of his view, hadn't. It was still the amount he'd had after the Aiden fight, less than half full.

"They're being possessed by demon spirits!" The voice that may or may not have been the First Emperor of China intensified in Zack's portal-lens speakers, pressing against his skull. "I shall lend you my power—*use the soup!*"

Zack darted his hand toward the bowl. This time, when he willed the soup to move, it did. It bulged and curled like a huge, smooth worm. His energy meter drained even more, and an uncomfortable coldness surged through him from his portal-lens, but he had no time to think about it. He just made the motion of hurling the soup at Nathan.

Some of it whipped against Nathan's face, but most of it splattered over the table and floor. Nathan reared back but didn't let go of the glowing sashes.

Looking Zack dead in the eye, Mr. Lansbury crouched low and raised a hand over Zack's mom's face. Wisps of green light gathered into a hazy form in his grasp, a form that kind of looked like a tiny Asian-style tower—a pagoda. A curl of luminous breath emerged from his mom's shrieking mouth and slithered into the mini pagoda. She stopped struggling, eyes glazing over in the dull light of the suite.

"*No!*" Zack screamed with all the air in his lungs. He hurled the empty soup bowl at Mr. Lansbury. Nathan casually deflected it with a flick of his hand. Zack had to dodge it before it shattered against the wall behind him. He tried to control the puddles of soup on the floor, but there was pathetically little of it, and he couldn't even get that to rise much.

"Give me more power!" he begged the voice in his portal-lens.

"Get more water!" it yelled back.

Zack floundered for the kitchen sink. Maybe if he turned on the tap, he could—

Nathan's sashes caught around his legs. This time, when Zack collapsed, he landed on his elbows. It hurt so much that his whole body went rigid, and a cry rasped out of his throat, but it was nothing compared to the dread pounding in his chest.

Nathan dragged him closer. Mr. Lansbury tilted the green pagoda toward him.

Just as Zack's terror spiked to a maximum, someone outside shouted something he didn't understand. A boy's voice, charged with a man's confidence.

Nathan and Mr. Lansbury jolted one after another, as if struck by something in their backs. Red and green smoke spewed from their respective mouths. Their bodies wobbled, then fell splat to the floor on either side of Zack's mom, revealing a figure in the darkness beyond the door.

It was Simon, holding a tall bow that looked to be made of the same neon red mist as Nathan's sashes. Behind his portallens, his eyes shone entirely bright red.

3

How Video Game Nerds Can Be Trounced With Ancient Chinese Military Tactics

TRANSPARENT, LUMINOUS ARROWS JUTTED UP FROM NATHAN'S and Mr. Lansbury's backs. They vanished like red vapor after a moment, and so did the sashes around Zack's legs. He scrambled to his feet and grabbed the plate of stir-fried eggs and tomatoes, about to chuck it like a Frisbee.

Simon's hands shot up in defense. The red glow left his eyes. His bow dissolved like windblown smoke. "No, calm down— I'm on your side!"

"My side?" Zack gasped for air. "What is my side—*what is going on*? Mom!" He threw the plate down, greasy egg bits shuddering onto the table, and dropped beside her. He shoved Nathan aside to check on her, putting a finger under her nose. To his overwhelming relief, she was still breathing. "Mom, wake up." He shook her gently. Her face stayed dull and sullen, framed by her red hijab. "Wake up. *Please.*"

"That's no use. The demons have captured her spirit." Simon stepped into the suite and shut the door behind him, cutting off the cold, shrill winds. His chest heaved deeply, breaths labored. Something that looked like a *Mythrealm* tag hovered beside him, showing his energy meter at less than a quarter, yet the info beneath the meter was nothing like a *Mythrealm* creature's.

TANG TAIZONG

"Emperor Taizong of Tang"

Real Name: Li Shimin

Lived: 598–649 CE

Cofounder of the Tang dynasty, considered the golden age of ancient China. Righteous jerk who thinks he was sooo much better of an emperor than the rest of us.

Zack blinked at the bizarre tag, then at what Simon said. "Captured her spirit? What does that mean?"

Simon dropped to one knee beside the unconscious bodies. "He's bound her spirit to his and escaped. To get it back, you'll have to join us on our mission."

"Who—*what* are you?"

Simon hesitated before saying, "I know this will be hard to believe, but I am the spirit of an ancient Chinese emperor known as Tang Taizong." He touched his chest. Zack couldn't tell if Simon was messing with him, but he truly sounded like an adult despite his boyish voice. His English was suddenly as American as Zack's as well—had Simon been faking an accent before? "I'm using this boy, Simon Li, as a mortal host to interact with the material world. This is possible because he's a descendant of mine, just as you are a descendant of Qin Shi Huang, the First Emperor of China."

"I'm a *what*?"

"Precisely what he said," grumbled the voice in Zack's portal-lens. "You are an eighty-eighth-generation descendant of mine."

With sweeping polygons like a virtual construct being rendered, a young man took shape beside Simon—or Not-Simon, apparently.

"Wow. That actually worked." The young man stared at his virtual hands. Though his mouth moved as he spoke, his voice still buzzed from the portal-lens speakers behind Zack's ears. He looked like someone out of the Chinese palace dramas that his mom's friends would watch when he'd be over at their apartments after school, waiting for his mom to get off work. Heavy black robes draped from the young man's body, and he wore a headdress like a college graduation hat, except with bead curtains at the front and back that left trails of shadows over his face. The dark circles under his eyes were the worst Zack had ever seen, like he hadn't slept in thousands of years. Yet his gaze was deathly sharp, like the reason he hadn't slept was because he was plotting mass murder. A *Mythrealm* tag floated beside him, as well.

QIN SHI HUANG
"The First Emperor of China"

Real Name: Ying Zheng

Lived: 259–210 BCE

Glorious unifier of China. Built the Great Wall, commissioned the Terra-Cotta Army, standardized Chinese writing and measuring systems, invented the "Huangdi" emperor title that all you losers used for the next 2,133 years. Also secretly sealed the biggest portal between the spirit and mortal worlds so malicious spirits would no longer roam the lands and cause conflict. DIDN'T KNOW MERCURY WAS POISONOUS, SO STOP ASKING HIM ABOUT IT.

Zack's mouth popped open. He moved his portal-lens up and down over his eyes. The young man and tag appeared in his portal view only.

Not-Simon angled an amused look up at the young man, adjusting his own portal-lens. "Huh, so you can appropriate the AR technology to appear without draining your host's energy? That's an unexpected upside to this catastrophe, I guess."

"Yes, yes." The young man who was apparently the First Emperor of China kept checking himself out, spinning in place. "Jason Xuan may be a pain to deal with, but his inventions are a marvel."

What's this about Jason Xuan? Zack wanted to ask, but he couldn't make himself speak when his brain was still trying to process the scene before him.

Not-Simon snorted, oblivious to Zack's turmoil. "Aren't you

about two thousand years too old to take your teenage form, though?"

"It's less intimidating to the boy than appearing as an adult." The First Emperor placed his hands on his hips, floppy sleeves swallowing all hints of his fingers. "He clearly needs considerable convincing to accept me."

"I doubt anybody could be convinced to accept *you*."

"But I cannot believe he . . . he expelled me! If I didn't bind to this intelligent eyewear instead, our plans would have been foiled!"

"They still might be." Not-Simon's expression turned more serious. He rose to his feet. "It doesn't seem like you can channel much power into him from the device, can you?"

They were doing that Adult Thing where they were talking about Zack as if he couldn't hear, despite looking right at him. Zack glanced rapidly between them. He couldn't believe this. Supernatural beings—*ghosts*—really existed, and here were two of them.

He *wouldn't* believe it if his mom wasn't unconscious beside him.

"*Why didn't you come earlier?*" he finally choked out, interrupting their banter. What he really wanted to do was shout it, but all his screaming had ruined his voice.

Stunned, Not-Simon took a second to react. "I would have if you'd answered my messages!"

"We've been trying to get your attention for *hours*," added the First Emperor.

"I—" Zack pressed his fingers into his temples, head sagging. He really, really, really shouldn't have run away. He should've stayed with Not-Simon and figured everything out. Why did he have to be such a coward?

"Listen, kid—*this* is what happens when you ignore us." The First Emperor pointed at Zack's mom. "There are forces at work beyond your understanding. If you want to retrieve your mother's spirit, you must do exactly as we say. Or her spirit will dissolve, and you will lose her forever."

Horror seized Zack's heart like an icy claw.

"Wh-what do I have to do?" He grasped his mom's hand. It was so cold. He could barely handle looking at her face, at how she wasn't grinning or frowning or arching an eyebrow at him like usual. She just looked . . . *empty.* He had to keep a hand on her ribs to make sure her heart was still beating. He was beyond disbelief; he just wanted her back.

"You have to come with us to China," Not-Simon said. "That's where the main trouble is."

"*China?* Why? Isn't the demon right here?" Zack gestured at Mr. Lansbury. The spilled soup soaked and crawled into his polo shirt, making a wet, darkening patch across his side.

"The demon itself is long gone by now," Not-Simon said. "It's hard to explain. But, speaking of—" He dug a glass spray bottle out of his schoolbag. He twisted the spray cap before spraying Nathan and Mr. Lansbury in the face.

"What's that?" Zack blinked.

"Diluted Meng Po broth." Not-Simon shook the bottle.

"What broth?"

"You haven't heard of Meng Po broth? The broth that all spirits must drink before reincarnation so they'll forget their past life?"

"No?"

Not-Simon quirked a brow. "Your mom isn't very big on telling you Chinese myths, is she?"

"No, she likes sci-fi stories more." Zack clutched his mom's hand tighter, thinking of the old sci-fi shows she'd watch with him on their computer as they ate dinner, things like *Star Trek* and *Ultraman.*

"Well, this is a diluted version of Meng Po broth. At this concentration, a single spray just makes someone forget the past hour. These two shouldn't wake up with any memories of being possessed. I did the same to your classmates. Now they're just confused about why they suddenly found themselves soaking wet on the field. There's no way to explain the lightning damage to the track, but we can let the people here come to their own conclusions. Oh, and that kid who got possessed is fine, by the way."

"Okay." Zack supposed he should be relieved, but he was too overwhelmed to think about Aiden. He just wanted to skip to the part where his mom woke up and the first thing out of her mouth was if he finished his homework, and everything was normal again. "But what's this about going to China? I can't. They killed my dad for speaking up against the government!"

Not-Simon shared a long, awkward look with the First

Emperor before saying, "I understand your fear, but we can protect you. We have many more resources in China."

"Then why didn't you protect my dad?"

"We didn't have the resources *then*," the First Emperor snapped. "It took a while for us to regain a foothold in the mortal world."

"Zachary," Not-Simon said in a much gentler tone than the emperor, "what happened to your father was horrific and unforgivable, but you must remember that the Chinese government does not represent our people. It acts with its own agenda, an agenda the average citizen has no control over. And most of those average citizens would never think of hurting you."

"So you guys want to take down the Chinese government?" Zack reflexively lowered his voice.

"Well—no. We don't interfere with mortal affairs. Only spirit ones."

"And such is the entire point," said the First Emperor. "Throughout history, the influence of spirits has only ever made the world more chaotic. They possess regular folk and amplify their darkest desires, like that boy Aiden and his greed. Which is why, two thousand and two hundred years ago, I—"

A siren wailed through the night, warping closer.

Not-Simon opened the front door to peer outside, letting in a whistling draft and a louder siren sound, then shut it to face Zack again. "We'll explain more later. Your neighbors must've called the police, so you need to get your story straight. Say this was an armed robbery. Your mom was attacked. I—Simon—was over playing *Mythrealm* with you. She screamed for us to not come out, so we both huddled in terror in your room. We heard your landlord and his son come down to help, but they got knocked out as well."

"I—I'm supposed to explain *this* to the police?"

"It doesn't have to be coherent. Just act terrified and confused at any detailed questions. We'll take care of the rest." Not-Simon shut his eyes. A spasm passed his face, and his hair stirred with a sudden wind. The floating tag beside him changed.

SIMON LI / LI SHUDA
Tang Taizong's host. 12-year-old boy from Shaanxi, China.

Zack abruptly figured out why Simon looked so familiar.

"Wait, Li Shuda?" He shot to his feet. "As in *Shuda Li, the* Mythrealm *world champion*?"

Simon's eyes stuttered open, and suddenly he was moving and speaking like an awkward kid again, his Mandarin accent returning too. "Oh, yeah. That's me. That's my Chinese name. Here." He swept his bangs out of his eyes and made a more stern expression. His face instantly matched the posters Zack had seen of Shuda Li. He usually had his hair gelled up and looked like he was ready to kick anyone's butt with his virtual creatures.

"You . . . you . . . you're that kid who beat out hundreds of thousands of adults," Zack stammered. "You won *five million dollars.*"

Simon let his bangs go while lowering his head, looking especially guilty with the police sirens approaching. "I didn't. I mean, it wasn't me who won all those battles. I like the game, but I'm nowhere near world champion level. Tang Taizong was the one battling. He was a genius strategist who helped his dad reunite China when he was only twenty. So he, um, had no problem trouncing a bunch of video game nerds."

Zack slumped down next to his mom again, head throbbing as it became split between freaking out over her and trying to make sense of the boy standing before him. "Wait—did the *kidnapping* have anything to do with this?"

Zack had watched the drama go down live. It'd been one of the most exciting things to happen on the internet: Shuda Li had been disqualified from the finals for not showing up in time, only to turn up on his own livestream with proof that he'd been kidnapped and had barely escaped. The whole finals arena and millions of stream watchers had gone berserk, demanding XY Technologies delay the finals until Shuda could make it there. Zack had spammed quite a few #LetShudaPlay hashtags into the chat.

"Right, that was Jason Xuan trying to stop me from winning. He realized I was an emperor host. He's also the reason we entered the championship. Besides the money, I mean. Which we did need. We were mainly there to investigate XY Technologies. It's a long story. But just think of me as Simon Li, not Shuda Li, okay?" Simon pleaded.

"Jason Xuan *knows* about this . . . this . . . ?" Zack gestured wildly at Simon, lost on how to describe this situation.

"He more than knows," the First Emperor cut in. "He's a host himself for the source of all our problems. We'll explain everything later. Right now, you must focus! Law enforcement incoming!"

A muscle twitched under Zack's eye. He couldn't do anything but hold on to his mom's hand, praying she'd suddenly wake up and brush this off, like she did her toughest days of work. Or that this was just a nightmare, and *he'd* bolt up in his bed any second.

Neither of those things happened. There was only the weight of her hand in his, chillingly cold, chillingly real. Not cooking him delicious food or pointing out scientific phenomenon to him or fussing over his messy hair anymore.

Oh, he'd have no problem acting terrified and confused for the police.

4

How the Creation of China Was Exactly Like American Idol

ZACK NEVER THOUGHT HE'D BE SO UPSET DURING HIS FIRST TIME flying first class on a plane.

He wasn't just in the first-class seating area but a private cabin with two single beds and its own bathroom. He sat on one bed against a pile of fluffy pillows, while Simon sat on the other, commenting on a Chinese historical documentary playing on a big screen above the foot of their beds. Light shifted on Simon's face in the dim cabin like they were in a theater. Zack was supposed to be paying close attention, yet he couldn't. He tried, he really tried, but he couldn't.

Last night, at the police station, he'd blubbered through the robbery story fed to him by Not-Simon—or Tang Taizong, as he had to get used to calling him, along with Qin Shi Huang for the First Emperor. Halfway through, Zack had started crying so hard that he could barely catch his breath. The police had then backed off on grilling him about why a bunch of robbers would target a random basement suite, or what the robbers looked like beyond "they wore ski masks."

"Wow, you're such a good actor!" Simon had said afterward.

Zack hadn't been acting.

His mom had been rushed to a hospital, where the doctors had declared her to be in a coma, though they of course couldn't figure out why. Just when Zack had been about to say no to the police asking if he had any other living relatives, a tiny prompt on his portal-lens—which he'd kept on with the excuse that it had a prescription—had told him to say "yes, officer, an aunt in China named Yaling Sha."

He was pretty sure his mom didn't have a sister, but he'd gone with it. The message had come with a phone number that he'd passed to the police. He didn't know what kind of conversation had happened over the phone, but an hour later he had a plane ticket booked for Shanghai, China. The police had taken him home so he could pack his things, then driven him through the towering forests of Maine to the Portland airport. Zack suspected there'd been some magic involved for them to act that quickly. Or maybe they just hadn't wanted to deal with an orphan overnight.

No, he chided himself. *Not an orphan.*

"I still don't get how this is supposed to help get my mom's spirit back," he cut Simon off mid-commentary, fed up with the mess in his head.

Simon paused the documentary by double-tapping the air in front of his portal-lens, which he'd connected to the screen by Bluetooth. He looked like he wanted to say something but couldn't figure out the words. He really wasn't the cool-and-collected Shuda Li from the championship livestreams, which made Zack feel a little less surreal about being around him. If Shuda was "real," so to speak, Zack wasn't sure he could've met him without fainting. He still blushed sometimes remembering the promo pictures of Shuda that he had saved to his phone during the championship. Zack had scrambled to delete the pictures on the ride to the airport.

"You need a stronger connection to Qin Shi Huang's legend magic to pull off the mission," Simon finally said, angling his face away in the distant screen light, looking slightly guilty. Zack could barely hear him over the roar of the plane engines. "Which means a stronger connection to the cultural consciousness of him."

Frustration welled up in Zack. "What even is that?"

Simon straightened in his bed, eyes glistening behind his portal-lens. "Okay, so there are legends basically everyone in a culture knows. Like Americans and their Batman and George Washington. For us in China, it's Qin Shi Huang and Tang Taizong. We all know who they are and the legendary stuff they did. Them being in the minds of so many people for generation after generation is what makes their spirits so powerful. But they don't have a place in *your* mind. That's why Qin Shi Huang couldn't bind properly to you."

"Precisely." Qin Shi Huang emerged in Zack's portal view with a glimmering sweep of polygons, hovering above the beds. "This eye device of yours had more of a connection to me than you by virtue of the data about me that it could access on the internet. It was a miracle that I discovered its computational pathways were complex enough to host my spirit before I fell back into the underworld." He gazed up in thought. "Actually, I am quite impressed with what I'm finding in here."

Zack had to once again take a moment to process how things like this were part of his life now. "Then why didn't you pick someone else to possess?" he accused. He bet he and his mom wouldn't have been attacked if Qin Shi Huang had chosen differently.

"Because you're the one I incarnated a piece of my spirit into, and therefore the only anchor point I could use to pull myself back to the mortal realm." Qin Shi Huang folded his arms. His wide sleeves met like black curtains in front of his chest. "If I kill you and start over, it'll take at least another twelve years for a new host to grow into any semblance of usefulness. I do not have time for that."

"Well, I'm sorry!" Zack blurted. "I'm sorry I'm not Chinese enough for this, when nobody told me I needed to know so much about Chinese culture until *yesterday*!"

His raspy voice shook and cracked. He wasn't sure who he was angrier at, them or himself. The airplane walls quivered behind his pillows from the turbulence outside.

"Calm down, kid," Qin Shi Huang said. "This is about your personal connection to me, not about you being Chinese enough. Which is not something that can be measured. You claim Chinese heritage. That makes you Chinese. Knowledge of me is just one small part of Chinese culture, which is vast and different across the world, wherever Chinese people are.

Why do you think I can speak American English? It's because of Chinese Americans like you and your mother, who surely thinks of me as a cultural legend."

"But she never told me about you."

Qin Shi Huang's expression twitched. "I can't help that some people have no appreciation for history! But if she grew up in China, she's heard of me for certain. Pity that the approach she took to keeping you safe is prioritizing your assimilation into American culture instead. Not an approach I agree with, but there's no changing the past. Believe me, I didn't want to do this mission on this tight of a timeline either. Simon here was supposed to transfer to your American school in the autumn and gradually introduce you to the necessary knowledge. We were supposed to have many more years before having to embark on our mission. But a recent earthquake changed everything. It critically loosened the portal to the underworld that I had built my mausoleum over. Now we have a mere fourteen days to reinforce the portal plug I had made."

That didn't sound good.

"Or what?" Zack sat up straighter. "What would happen?"

"Well, first of all, the demon who has your mother will grow powerful enough to utterly consume her spirit. No heaven, hell, underworld, or reincarnation for her. Just gone."

The bottom dropped out of Zack's world, as if the plane had plunged hundreds of feet.

"And the spirits of the Chinese underworld will flood into the mortal realm," Simon added, expression haunted, but

Zack's mind stayed frozen around the terror that his mom's spirit might get *consumed* when the afterlife was apparently an assured thing.

"How do we stop this?" Zack said in a rush of breath. Anxiety crawled like ants in his gut. "How do we reinforce this portal plug?"

The words felt like nonsense in his mouth, but if this was the way to save his mom, he had to know.

"Before we delve into that, show me something." Qin Shi Huang pointed at a glass of water on a wall-mounted tray beside Zack's bed. "Try to control that water. Get it as high as you can."

Coldness seeped into Zack's body from his portal-lens, like ice water splashed over his face. With the hesitance of still not really believing he could waterbend, he lifted his hand before the glass, willing the water to rise.

It did. But not by much.

"Higher!" Qin Shi Huang commanded.

Zack hissed through clenched teeth. He strained the water higher until spots speckled his vision, then he had to let go. It collapsed back into the glass with a small splash.

"As I thought," Qin Shi Huang grunted. "With me merely possessing this device, you can't channel enough of my magic to put up a proper fight. And you certainly can't use it as well as I do."

Hot shame flared into Zack's face. "Can we redo the possession deal?"

"The deal? Oh! Right, me promising to make you stronger in exchange for using you as a host. That wasn't a magical deal. It was simply a promise of honor, one I remain happy to fulfill. Heaven knows you need it."

Zack couldn't even argue. If he were stronger, if he weren't such a wimp, he wouldn't have run away and cowered in his bed and given the demons the opening to attack.

"But no," Qin Shi Huang continued. "I'm afraid I'm permanently bound to this device the way I should've been permanently bound to *you*. However, it's still possible to improve our spiritual connection by improving your knowledge of my legend." He gestured backward at the screen. "Has this documentary given you a good grasp of it?"

It was paused on an actor's depiction of him, raising a glinting sword in what looked like a shadowy, firelit palace chamber. The actor, bearded and buff, looked a lot older than how Qin Shi Huang appeared to Zack.

"Um . . ." Zack strained to gather the fragments of facts that had made it through his storming thoughts. "So you were a prince born in the middle of a lot of wars. When you were only thirteen, you became the . . . king of Qin?"

Qin Shi Huang huffed. "Let me put it in terms you can more readily understand. About three thousand years ago, there were over a hundred states in the lands that would become China. Three legendary dynasties had claimed sovereignty over them all, but they were mere figureheads. After the states stopped respecting those figureheads, they descended into a knockout competition like one of your American reality TV shows. They gradually swallowed each other up over the three-hundred-year Spring and Autumn era before whittling down to a top seven, also known as the Seven Warring States. That round of finals continued for another two hundred years before I defeated them all in a rapid-fire ten-year campaign. Yes—I won Ancient Chinese American Idol." Qin Shi Huang recoiled. "Ancient Chinese Idol? Whatever."

It was a lot of info, yet all Zack could think to ask was, "How the heck do you know what *American Idol* is?"

"Chinese Americans, remember? No reason Chinese culture and American culture can't overlap. Back in *American Idol*'s heyday, George Washington made some of us watch it with him." Qin Shi Huang shook his head. "Its entertainment value greatly plummeted after Simon Cowell's departure."

". . . Who's 'some of us'?"

"Me, Alex—"

"Alex?"

"A conqueror from Europe. Macedonia, was it?"

"*Alexander the Great?* You're friends with *Alexander the Great?*"

"You know him, but you don't know me?" Qin Shi Huang scoffed.

"He's—he's Alexander the Great! I was literally just doing a presentation on him for history class!"

"And I am Qin Shi Huang, the First Emperor of China! Unlike Alex, I actually achieved my goal of conquering all the way to the Pacific Ocean! He's a decent lad, though. I taught him how to play mahjong. He and I and Ram and Genghis get together and enjoy a few games every few decades."

The names deciphered themselves in Zack's head. "You play mahjong with *Alexander the Great*, *Ramses the Second*, and *Genghis Khan*?"

"How do you know *all of them* except me? I am as much of an A-list conqueror as any of them!" Qin Shi Huang spluttered, then put his fingers to his temples, just under his headdress. His eyes squeezed closed, and his demeanor mellowed. "Ah, it's not your fault. *Zhèxiē báirén zhēnshì de.* Such nonsense that children in China are bombarded with Western legends and history, while children in the West are taught nothing beyond the typical Europeans, the occasional Egyptian, and maybe Genghis Khan."

"Maybe you're not as A-list as you thought," Zack mumbled.

"You listen here!" Qin Shi Huang whipped his finger toward Zack. "I am the only conqueror in any history to have eliminated all possible enemies and had my governing system persist for over two thousand years. I ruled over my entire known world! I literally ran out of places to take over! The only reason I get snubbed on these conqueror lists is because my empire is still a single country! Can *they* say that?"

"Why aren't you telling him the part where your dynasty fell apart in just fifteen years?" Simon suddenly quipped.

No, with that confident tone, relaxed grin, and smooth English, it wasn't Simon. Tang Taizong had taken over. Zack wondered what happened to Simon when he did, if Simon's mind would retreat into his body and lose all control of it, becoming a spectator to his own existence, like what had briefly happened to Zack. Zack shuddered. He was torn between being glad that couldn't happen again and feeling guilty, because if he hadn't kicked Qin Shi Huang out, the demons probably wouldn't have stood a chance at taking his mom.

Qin Shi Huang swiveled his glare onto Tang Taizong. "Why don't *you* tell him the part where you picked your meekest son as your heir because you believed he was kind and gentle and wouldn't kill his brothers like you did, not realizing that he'd have an affair with one of your concubines while you suffered on your deathbed, and then that concubine ended up usurping your dynasty and becoming the only female emperor in our history? Why don't you go ahead and tell *that* story, huh?"

Tang Taizong's grin faltered. "None of that was *my* fault!"

"Don't test me, Taizong." Qin Shi Huang held up a palm, looking pointedly away. "I am eight hundred years older than you. I watched your entire life play out. I have more dirt on you than you will ever have on me."

"Whatever. *I* still created the golden age of China. Most diverse and tolerant era ever. Hashtag *TangDynastyBestDynasty.*" Tang Taizong made the hashtag gesture with his fingers.

"Hash—" Qin Shi Huang grimaced. "You've been in the mortal realm for far too long."

Tang Taizong flashed a smirk. "Sorry, stuck in a twelve-year-old's body."

Rolling his eyes, Qin Shi Huang turned back to Zack, who felt like his brain was melting from this conversation. "But it's true. I only ruled China for twelve years, then my dynasty collapsed three years after I passed into the beyond. It wasn't surprising. I'd made a lot of enemies, both mortal and supernatural. Though the part about plugging the underworld portal is one achievement you won't find in history books. I did my best to erase the portal's existence from record. The less it's believed in, the less power it has. And that is where I get my bad reputation for burning books."

"Please." Tang Taizong snorted. "As if you didn't burn certain books just because you wanted to control your newly subjugated masses."

"I kept backups in my imperial library! Xiang Yu was the one who erased those from existence when he burned down my palace."

"Oh sure. Blame *Xiang Yu*."

"He really did—!"

"So what exactly is your magic?" Zack asked to keep them on topic. "Why can you control water? And . . . time? Or is it superspeed, like the Flash?" Zack recalled a lot of lightning shooting down.

"The Flash?" Qin Shi Huang blinked. "Oh, right, you and your American gods."

"No—uh, the Flash is a superhero, not a god."

"Same thing. Superheroes are just American myth. They haven't been passed down long enough to take spiritual form, but if they last another few centuries, I reckon I'll be playing mahjong with Bruce Wayne on the same ethereal table as George Washington."

"*What?*" Zack shot to a new level of disbelief. "But superheroes aren't actually worshiped as *real.*"

"Then what's Comic-Con, huh?"

Zack had no good response to that, so he just mentally filed this under Things to Stop Questioning About the World Now. "Okay, but did you also have these powers in history?" he asked, because he would've paid a lot more attention to the documentary if it had showed Qin Shi Huang controlling water, summoning lightning, and slowing time.

"No, I was a regular person in my mortal life. I mostly relied on the cooperation of my ancestors in the underworld to plug the portal. But after I transcended my physical flesh—"

"He died taking mercury pills that he thought would make him immortal," Tang Taizong said.

"So did you!" Qin Shi Huang yelped without looking at him.

"Allegedly! Sources differ!"

"You know what you did! So *as I was saying*"—Qin Shi Huang bugged out his eyes at Zack—"in death, my spirit became tied to the Chinese cultural consciousness as a legend. As the tales and beliefs about me grew wilder over decades and centuries and millennia, I gained astonishing abilities. Legend magic is fickle, however. Sometimes you can bend it to your will, such as me creating my time-slowing magic out of the various legendary assassination attempts against me. But other times, you are at its mercy. I used to be able to raise and crack the earth with a whip because of a legend believing I built the Great Wall that way. Now, that legend has fallen into obscurity, and I am more associated with dragon abilities, such as controlling water and summoning storms. I owe this in particular to a popular video game called *Glory of Legends* that depicted me with those abilities."

Zack balked. "You can get powers from a video game?"

"Of course," Qin Shi Huang said. "It compels an entire new generation to think of me as having dragon abilities, thus adding to my legend."

"The game is that popular? I've never heard of it."

"Are you kidding?" Tang Taizong chimed in. "*Glory of Legends* is a consistent top grosser in the Chinese gaming market. But unlike *Mythrealm*, it didn't add in Western elements for the international release, so it tanked overseas. *Tsk.* Guess Chinese history isn't that interesting to Westerners."

"Right. *Mythrealm*." Zack tensed up. "What's up with it? Is it . . . real?"

Qin Shi Huang answered, "Not in the sense that every creature in it is a real spirit. However, the widespread exposure of their legends has certainly made the real spirits out in the world more powerful."

"Then how come my portal view looks like a *Mythrealm* battle when we fight spirits?"

"Ah, that. I've simply appropriated its interface design. I must admit, it's very convenient and user friendly. Much easier for me to subconsciously convey information to you via the widgets than to shout updates at you every other second."

"Oh." Zack couldn't tell if he was disappointed. It would've been cool for his favorite video game to be real.

On the topic of disappointment, he knew it was past time to ask another question that'd been eating away at him, no matter how much he didn't want to hear a negative answer.

"And what about Jason Xuan? You said he's . . . also a host? He's not evil, is he?"

Tang Taizong clenched his bedsheets. "Jason Xuan is the chosen host of the Yellow Emperor, a legendary ancestor of the Chinese people. We found this out after we grew suspicious of XY Technologies and joined the *Mythrealm* championship to investigate it."

"As if the company name itself wasn't a big enough hint." Qin Shi Huang rolled his eyes. "It clearly stands for Xuanyuan, one of the Yellow Emperor's names. We believe he guided Jason Xuan into creating XY Technologies, then sent dreams to the masses to influence them to buy Jason's products and games."

"*What?*" Zack lurched to rip his portal-lens off.

"No!" Qin Shi Huang lunged toward him, virtual figure glitching into the bed. "You must keep that on to stay connected with me. The device itself is fine. I've checked every aspect of its programming and disabled anything that could allow XY Technologies to track us with it."

Zack dropped his fingers from his portal-lens but remained

spooked. "But why would the, um, Yellow Emperor want people to play video games?"

Qin Shi Huang drifted above the bed again, forcing Zack to crane his head to look at him. "Games can subtly change the way people see the world—especially AR games, which blend make-believe with reality. Take *Mythrealm*, for example. By influencing people to hunt down mythical creatures in augmented reality, he essentially makes the creatures 'real' to them, and thus the spirits of those creatures become stronger as well. Strong enough that together, they could shatter the portal plug if we don't reinforce it in fourteen days."

"Why fourteen days exactly?" Zack tilted his head at the repeated mention of that number.

"The seventh lunar month will begin then." Tang Taizong was the one who answered. "In traditional Chinese culture, it's the Ghost Month. Normally, only the most legendary of spirits such as ourselves can slip into the mortal realm, but during the Ghost Month, all spirits are believed to have the ability. The flood of them trying to escape the underworld at once this time could rupture the portal plug altogether. Then they'd rampage through China, possessing people and polluting their minds. The chaos could plunge China into war, which would be disastrous with your modern weapons."

Zack swallowed hard, throat drying. This sounded so outlandish that he couldn't believe *he* was being demanded to do something about it. He was always last pick for teams in gym!

"Indeed," Qin Shi Huang said. "And since the creature

spirits will have the Yellow Emperor to thank for their new strength—and because being a good beast tamer is part of his legend—he thinks he'll be able to control them as his personal army. He's too arrogant."

So he's like the pot to your kettle, huh? Zack would've said if he'd been braver. "But what does he need an army for? If he's the ancestor of the Chinese people, why would he doom us?"

"Because he believes his children have gone astray, of course, and that he needs to discipline them. You can't deny that you modern humans have done a terrible, disappointing job taking care of your planet. Problem for him is, his spirit may be vast and ancient, but it's scattered across the realms since people simultaneously believe him to be a divine ancestor and yet a dead mortal. Even when he's adapted into video games— which Jason Xuan has tried plenty of times—he's never popular. An all-powerful ancestor is simply too boring compared to more colorful legends like mine. And when the games try to give him more personality, people often reject the depiction of him. Only by having the portal be free-flowing can he gather himself into a concrete existence, which he appears to want to do with Jason Xuan as his host."

"Isn't he already possessing Jason?"

"No, right now he can only *influence*, not *possess*. Like the difference between me speaking to you versus taking over your body. He can whisper to people in their dreams, when their minds are closest to the spirit realm, but can't quite follow them back to the real world."

Zack's heart sank. First Shuda Li, now Jason Xuan. He couldn't believe two of his idols were big, fat, supernatural lies. "So do we have to take down XY Technologies?"

"No," Qin Shi Huang said. "No point, and no time. Even if the company went bankrupt tomorrow, people's memories of the creatures wouldn't fade. Our only option is to strengthen the portal plug. I'm working on adjusting my original plan. Simply do everything I say, and we can still win, despite these numerous setbacks."

Zack didn't like the sound of that, but his mom's spirit was on the line. He winced at the memory of how lifeless she looked, hooked up to all those machines in the hospital. It was so easy to imagine a coffin lid sliding over her ashen face.

Fear twisted deep inside Zack. He couldn't lose her. He *could not*. She was his only family. Where would he even go if she were gone? Foster care?

No.

He couldn't imagine that future. He didn't want to. If it took pulling off this mission to get her back, then he'd do it.

He would do anything.

5

How to Get Rich and Famous by Renting Your Body to a Dead Emperor

ZACK DIDN'T KNOW WHERE HE WAS. IT SEEMED TO BE A HUGE palace chamber. Licks of flame provided the only lighting, gleaming faintly off dozens of thick bronze pillars wreathed with dragons, which soared into the darkness above.

"*My child . . .*" A voice floated past his ears, no stronger than a breeze.

Startled, Zack looked around. A metallic chill hung in the air, seeping into his flesh and bone. He shivered.

"*. . . he's . . . lying . . .*"

Zack suddenly got the sense to look up. An elaborate bronze throne was on a raised dais ahead, shrouded in shadow. A silhouetted figure sat on it, wearing a familiar headdress with bead curtains. For some reason, terror streaked through Zack like lightning.

"*. . . he . . . mother . . .*"

The voice was saying something important, something he knew he couldn't miss, yet its words muffled at the most critical intervals. As Zack looked around, he realized he was standing on a long metal platform over a pool of dark water. Something white drifted in it. When it rose closer to the surface, two gaping black sockets stared back at him.

A skull, framed by a red hijab.

Chills shocked through Zack.

"He is a tyrant, and he always will be!" the voice warped in anguish. *"Don't fall for his lies, my child . . . he—"*

"Zack! Wake up!"

Zack's eyes jarred open. Simon hovered beside him, shaking his shoulder.

"Come on, we're landing." He sounded underwater. "We have to buckle up."

Zack pinched his nose and popped his eardrums. The airplane engines howled back in full force. He was covered in cold sweat.

"Did you have a bad dream?" Simon eyed Zack's drenched hairline.

"Um—" Zack jerked back at Simon's closeness, cheeks warming, and wiped his forehead with his arm. He must've had a terrifying dream, but as he tried to remember it, his mind drew a blank. "I don't remember."

"Oh. If you do, definitely say so. Qin Shi Huang should've given you some protection against the Yellow Emperor trying to influence you through dreams, but you never know. Chinese spirits communicate through dreams a lot. It's called *tuōmèng.*"

"Tuōmèng," Zack repeated in a murmur, the syllables foreign in his mouth. A language that was supposed to have been his mother tongue but wasn't. His mom never spoke it with him because she didn't want him to have an accent when speaking English. He never learned because he never wanted to.

He was about to land in a country that was, by all means, foreign to him. One where he wouldn't understand any of the language or customs. One that had killed his dad and forced his mom to flee with him to another continent.

After he and Simon strapped themselves into the huge leather seats on either side of the beds, Zack spent the descent with his eyes squeezed shut. The fear of ending up like his dad spiked through him, but the thought of a demon tearing his mom's spirit apart was far worse.

For her. He would tough this out for her.

The moment Zack stepped off the plane and into the tunnel-like boarding bridge, heat swarmed every inch of his body. He sucked in a sharp breath. Having spent the past three years in Maine, he was no longer used to weather this hot. Sweat practically soaked his T-shirt and pants after just the short walk through the bridge.

Thankfully, the airport buildings were air-conditioned. The shiny floors reflected hundreds of lights across the ceiling. A soothing lady's voice announced things in multiple languages overhead. Since he and Simon were unaccompanied minors, security officers helped them get their luggage and then escorted them through Chinese customs. Zack had no idea how his visa was being handled, but he thought it was best to not rouse suspicion by asking questions. He prayed nobody would discover he was the son of an executed dissident. His mom had legally changed his name from Ying Ziyang to Zachary Ying when they'd gone to America—maybe that was enough? He felt like he had a secret identity in a terrible way that had nothing to do with the superpowers he could barely use.

While the adults sorted it out, Zack couldn't help but gawk at everything in the airport. The last time he'd seen this many people in one place had been during his and his mom's last New Year's in New York, when they'd gone to see the ball drop in Times Square. (Which had ended up being very disappointing and very cold. Zack had better memories of drinking hot cocoa with his mom while sharing a blanket and laughing at themselves after finally making it home through sludge and snow.) The masses of travelers chattered loudly and hauled their luggage in such giant packs that personal space didn't seem to be a concept.

And most people looked like him. For the first time in three years, nobody was eyeing his every move or doing double takes on him. He felt so . . . normal.

Yet it was an illusion. He couldn't understand their language. He didn't know the legends and history they knew. He was an impostor. A fraud.

A terrorist's son, he imagined the airport officers hissing before dragging him off to a "re-education camp" the government of China would insist was nothing but Western propaganda.

But it wasn't as if he'd been safe in America, either. Last year he had tried out this Ask Me Anything website. The first anonymous question he'd gotten was *How does it feel, being a terrorist's son?*

He'd frozen in his chair for several minutes, thinking the Chinese government had gotten to him, before he realized it must've been someone who'd seen his mom drop him off at school, and *she'd* been the one they'd been referring to.

"You okay?" Simon took sudden notice of Zack as they stood at the marble counter of a customs officer.

"I . . ." Zack breathed in short spurts. He couldn't get enough air to answer.

"Hey, it's gonna be fine." Simon smiled. "You're *home*."

Am I? A quiver came over Zack's heart. Could he ever find a place where he truly belonged, when he was so different from the typical American, the typical Chinese person, and even the typical Muslim?

When the customs officer finally gave back their passports, she said something to them in Mandarin with a dark look in her eye.

"What? What is it?" Zack asked Simon in a frantic whisper, gripping his suitcase handle.

Simon turned to him with a troubled expression, shutting his passport like a book. "Her daughter's a big fan of mine."

A laugh tumbled out of Zack in sheer, crashing relief. "Congratulations?"

"I'm just glad she didn't ask for a selfie or something," Simon muttered as they dragged their luggage onward. "I totally don't have the Shuda Li look on right now."

Traveling with a celebrity. Now that was a different kind of weird, and a much easier one to deal with.

"Oh, and heads up," Simon went on, "there's a third member of our team. She's here to pick us up. And she's the host of, um, Wu Zetian herself. So beware."

"Who's that?" Zack asked, gut twisting tight again with the dread of being in an alien world. "Simon, I don't know these names you drop."

"Right! Sorry. You know that concubine Qin Shi Huang was yelling about? The one who was married to Tang Taizong, but got with his son on his deathbed and then usurped her way into becoming the only female emperor in Chinese history? That's her."

"Oh. Wow."

"It's okay—don't be too scared. Her host is also twelve like us, 'cause the emperors incarnated a piece of their spirits at the same time twelve years ago. She's called Wu Mingzhu, or Melissa Wu."

"Does she speak English?"

"Oh yeah, pretty well. We both go to an international school in Shanghai."

Zack let out a small sigh of relief. Simon may have a noticeable accent, but he didn't have any problems understanding Zack, so hopefully she would be the same.

The arrival gate came up ahead, lined and packed with

people behind metal barriers. Except instead of holding signs with names on them like in the movies, virtual letters and characters hovered over their heads. Mostly in Chinese, but many other languages too, visible in the Common AR Field that portal-lenses could connect to. Another thing Zack had noticed was that almost *everyone* wore a portal-lens, not just young people, like how it was in America. And they were making a lot more practical use of them. In fact, he rarely saw phones being pulled out. People in every direction spoke into the mic that could swing down from the portal-lens's left arm, and they swept through virtual windows in front of themselves, which appeared in Zack's portal view as blurry, transparent boxes. He must've auto-connected to a Wi-Fi to be able to see them—or maybe Qin Shi Huang had connected to one for him.

By what was probably also Qin Shi Huang's meddling, the virtual signs vanished down to a single one in bright magenta that said ZACK & SIMON. The instant Zack caught sight of the ponytailed girl beneath it, he knew she must've been the one Simon was talking about. She dressed very adultlike for a girl their age. She wore a chic white dress, matching platform sandals, giant pink sunglasses shaped like cat eyes, silver hoop earrings, and several rows of intricate silver bracelets, and hauled a massive, expensive-looking purse over one shoulder.

She gave a small shriek when she saw them. Once they got past the gates and barriers, she strode up to them, arms wide, ponytail bouncing. Her platform sandals made her considerably taller than both Zack and Simon. "What's up, losers?"

Her perfume reached them before she did. Zack had to admit it was very nice, a warm combination of vanilla and berries. A bootleg *Mythrealm* tag appeared beside her.

WU ZETIAN
"Empress Wu"
Real Name: Wu Zhao (or so she made up herself)
Lived: 624–705 CE
The only woman to become a full-fledged emperor in China's history. Usurped the Tang dynasty to found the Zhou dynasty for 15 years, before returning the throne to her son. DO NOT MESS WITH UNDER ANY CIRCUMSTANCES.

"Niáng-niang!" Simon spluttered. "Are you sure you should be out in the open like this?"

Niáng-niang: my lady. A translation appeared at the bottom of Zack's portal view.

He wondered the same thing. On the plane, the emperors had told him that after they landed, they could only emerge when necessary or in the charm-protected condo they were using as a base, or else their spirit signatures might attract enemies.

"Relax, there are way too many newly arriving people here for anything to sense me. I couldn't resist meeting Qin Shi Huang's host personally." With a wild grin, Wu Zetian nudged her sunglasses downward and peered at Zack over their top edge. "Oh, he really is a gorgeous boy."

Zack's mouth slipped open at the sight of her eyes. They were so pretty. So, so pretty. He usually didn't feel anything around girls, yet flutters rose in his belly like butterflies taking off.

Then she moved her sunglasses back in place, and the feeling vanished. It left him reeling, blinking fast.

"See? He's not immune to my charm magic. I *told* Taizong I should've been the one to fetch him, or this fiasco would've never happened."

The daze winded Zack so much, it took him a second to notice that a scowling woman with a partially shaved head had come up behind Wu Zetian. The woman crossed her bare arms, which poked out of a sleeveless jean jacket. She had the biggest biceps he'd ever seen. He got the sense that she'd torn the sleeves off her jacket herself. Maybe with her teeth.

"Um—" He sidestepped toward Simon.

"Oh, right." Wu Zetian pointed a hand over her shoulder at the woman. "This is Yaling, our henchwoman. She's the one who posed as your aunt over the phone and got all the paperwork sorted out."

"H-henchwoman?"

"Yeah, she's great! Gets the job done without asking any prying questions. Five-star reviews from so many gang leaders and local crime lords." Wu Zetian flashed two thumbs-up.

Zack's gaze flitted between the people moving past them as she said that, afraid someone might call the police or some- thing. But she was in a twelve-year-old girl's body and speak- ing English, so no one seemed to pay her any mind. "But—but why do you have a *henchwoman*?"

She frowned, her neatly penciled brows only half visible above her sunglasses. "How else are we supposed to get any- thing done? We can't do everything in the bodies of children, even with charm powers like mine."

"Does she know about the supernatural stuff?" Zack pressed his voice low, eyeing Yaling cautiously.

"Pretty sure she thinks we're a bunch of rich kids playing around," Wu Zetian leaned close and whispered back with a mischievous grin. "We wipe her memory whenever she sees something truly unscientific. But even if we miss an incident, nobody would believe her if she tried to tattle. Which she wouldn't. That's what makes her worth the money."

Zack shuddered. This had to be breaking at least a dozen moral codes. What was he getting himself into?

"Now, come on!" Wu Zetian spun on her platform sandals. "We're going to have so much fun!"

Unlike the contrast between Simon's awkward shyness and Tang Taizong's smug confidence, the real Melissa Wu acted exactly like Wu Zetian. Seriously. Zack saw no difference in their demeanors whatsoever. The only visual distinction was that Melissa didn't wear sunglasses to keep her charm magic in check. Though she bragged that she still had a minor level of it, since she was born with a piece of Wu Zetian's spirit. She reminded Zack of one of those popular girls who always hung out with a flock of friends and spammed heart emojis on each other's selfies. The kind of girl he used to love playing with in elementary school before he started worrying about what other kids would think of him, being in a friend group like that when he was a boy.

"I already have a lot of fans online for my makeup and hairstyle videos, but once we finish this mission, Wu Zetian says she'll help me become one of the top-billed pop stars in China," Melissa smirked, talking to Zack and Simon over the back of her seat on the Shanghai Metro. Yaling sat beside her, watching a palace drama on her phone, featuring fancy ladies sobbing in elaborate robes and hairdos. The train rumbled and rattled them into the city proper. Concrete and underground lights blurred past the windows. "That was my wish. What was yours?"

"Oh, um . . ." Zack was suddenly too embarrassed to say that it was to "get stronger." He clung to his suitcase for dear life. The train was more crammed than any New York subway he'd been on. He and Simon had to balance their luggage in the tiny legroom in front of their seats. Their flight had landed during rush hour, which was apparently so bad in Shanghai that even suffering the metro would get them to their base faster than driving. The people in the aisle beside them leaned over them like trees while scrolling on their phones. It seemed like this was the one place everyone could agree that the excessive gesturing needed to browse on a portal-lens would be a nuisance.

"You didn't get a wish for being a host?" Melissa moved to sit on her knees, folding her arms over the back of her seat. Even her high, airy voice was barely audible over the train announcements and people practically yelling into their phones. "Mine was to get out of my village and be pretty and famous. Simon's was to get rich."

"To get money for my family," Simon clarified, raising a finger. "Enough to pay off our debts and never worry about my little brother's medical bills again."

"Well, they won't. Not with all that—" Melissa peered at the train full of bystanders, then leaned in and stage-whispered, *"Mythrealm money."*

"Yeah, but all they want to do is buy condos and keep the rest in the bank." Simon puffed out his cheeks. "They're still mad at me whenever I spend it."

"Like on a private first-class cabin on a flight from America to China?"

"Z-Zack and the emperors needed to talk!"

"Sure, sure." Melissa mussed up Simon's hair.

"Hey!" He ducked away.

"What? Scared I'll make you look too cool and expose your secret identity? Oh my God, *video game champion here, everybody*!" she fake yelled under her breath, then beamed at Zack. "So, really, what's your wish?" She made a frame with her fingers and looked at him through it. "You could be a Chinese pop idol too, you know. You have the look."

"I do?" Zack flushed.

"Hasn't anyone ever told you you're a very pretty boy?"

"Pretty isn't a good thing for a boy to be." He bowed his head. He would much rather have a sharper and more angular face, like Simon's.

Melissa scoffed, dropping her hands. "Who said? Americans? Forget them and their tough-guy obsession! In Asia, pretty boys are all the rage! I swear, I will put a lip tint on you, and you will look great!"

When Simon laughed and smiled at that, Zack's blush deepened, heating to his ears. His hands curled over his suitcase. "Um, thanks, but I think I'm just gonna wish to get my mom's spirit back. That's all I want now."

Simon's and Melissa's grins stiffened and faded.

"Though a lot of money would be nice," Zack mumbled out of the side of his mouth. He didn't want to make them feel bad by being all mopey.

Melissa snorted. "I'm sure Qin Shi Huang can find a way to get you that."

"So do your parents know about . . . ?" Zack glanced between her and Simon.

"No." Simon sighed. "It was a condition of the emperors granting our wishes. They said our families would only worry too much and get in our way if they knew the truth."

"They don't even live in Shanghai." Melissa's shoulders sagged a little. "The only way to keep them safe is for us to stay away from them. Our enemies can't pinpoint their spirits if we aren't around them. My family's back in my mountain village in Hunan. Which is a province, if you didn't know. Simon's is in Shaanxi. They think we got scholarships to our boarding school in Shanghai. Which we kinda did. It was just that Tang Taizong gave us . . . considerable help . . . with our applications."

"But for the summer, they think we're filming a TV competition that doesn't let us have phones," Simon mumbled. "Saves us from having to lie to them about where we are every night."

"Won't they expect to watch that competition soon?" Zack asked.

Melissa shrugged. "We'll just say it got banned from airing. It happens all the time."

"Right," Zack muttered. "Tyrannical government."

"Whoa, shh!" she hissed, eyeing the other passengers. "Don't say stuff like that in public!"

A brighter swath of light ripped past the windows. A sudden commotion boiled through the train. Voices rose. People pressed against the glass, looking out with concerned frowns.

Zack slapped his hands over his mouth.

No. No way. Was that one comment really about to get him in trouble?

"What's happening?" Simon sat straighter.

"Is it what I said?" Zack yelped.

"No, we didn't stop at the last station." Melissa scowled at the windows, then looked down with a wild glint in her eye. "There's an enemy spirit on board."

6

How to Lose Friends and Alienate People

"WH-WHAT DO WE DO?" ZACK'S FOCUS WHIPPED LEFT AND right.

"Check if it's true. Come on!" Melissa leapt from her seat and squeezed through the train full of murmuring, rubbernecking people.

Simon blew out a calming breath before wiggling out of his own seat. He asked Yaling to watch their luggage, then offered Zack his hand.

Zack took it, heart skipping at the hint of Shuda Li in Simon's tense expression. Zack was totally not ready to battle after the disaster last time, but he trusted Simon. Simon had to know what he was doing after going through that whole championship while being sabotaged by Jason Xuan, right?

They stumbled after Melissa. Unfortunately, they were at perfect elbowing level for most adults. They received plenty of whacks to the face before making it to the control booth at the front. The train ran automatically, so there was no one inside.

But a spooky red glow emitted from the equipment beyond the small window.

"Oh, the system's deeefinitely being possessed," Melissa exclaimed under her breath, sounding way too excited about fighting a demon on a cramped, out-of-control subway. Especially given how scared of the government she was a minute ago. She put her fingers to her temples and closed her eyes for a few seconds, then said, "Wu Zetian says it's probably a demon sent by the Yellow Emperor's influence, but we should be able to take it down by ourselves."

"We'll need room to battle, though." Simon grimaced at the people pressing against them, also trying to see into the control booth.

"I got this," Melissa said. "Cover your eyes!"

"Do as she says," Qin Shi Huang commanded from Zack's portal-lens. "Trust me!"

Zack pressed his hands over his portal-lens at once.

"Rì yuè dāng kōng!" Melissa whispered.

Like the sun and moon in the sky! came a subtitle for Zack, the digital letters showing against his palms.

A blinding flash of light went off beyond his hands. People screamed. More elbows jutted against him.

"Shì gè zhàdàn!" Simon shouted.

It's a bomb!

The screams got sharper and more panicked, filling the train car. The pressure of people left Zack's side. Footsteps stampeded away.

He dropped his hands in time to see Simon igniting a small plank of wood with a lighter. Then he threw it after the people, who stumbled and piled over each other to get away.

"Whoa!" Zack shrieked.

"It's okay—I can control fire because of Tang Taizong's depiction in *Glory of Legends*." Simon flashed his hands open as if casting a spell. The wood burned much slower than normal, though it gave off plenty of smoke. Simon's energy meter—or *qi* meter, as the emperors insisted it was called—appeared. It trickled down slowly from the almost full bar he'd recovered during the flight. The emperors had explained that *qi* was the Chinese term for the vital energy that moved all things. If someone's meter hit zero, their body would become too weak to hang on to their spirit, and they would die. "This is just a smoke screen to keep them from coming back. But this means you two will have to handle the battle!"

"How?" Zack cried, then coughed as smoke invaded his lungs.

"I told you; I got this!" Melissa said, then continued in some form of ancient Chinese, *"Qiè néng zhì zhī, ránxū sānwù, yī tiěbiān—!"*

I the concubine can tame it if I had three items. First, an iron whip—!

Her *qi* meter dropped a big chunk before continuing to drain. Trails of misty white light flowed past her hand. They gathered into a bright, blurry whip, which she grasped tightly.

"What's going on?" Zack yanked down his portal-lens mic

while coughing some more. "Was that a spell? An incantation? That's a very weird incantation!"

"We can access our most powerful magic by invoking our most famous legends," Qin Shi Huang explained. "Wu Zetian's blinding flash comes from the name she invented for herself after declaring herself emperor. It was a brand-new Chinese character read as 'zhào,' but it means 'like the sun and moon in the sky.' Her weapon comes from . . . this one time she claimed she could tame this untamable stallion owned by Tang Taizong. But she said it in a very awe-inspiring way when she was only fourteen, so everyone remembers the story."

The spirit whip in Melissa's hand sharpened in Zack's view the moment Qin Shi Huang explained the context, looking more like glowing glass than a vague blur. Melissa lashed the conducting booth's door with the whip. The door shuddered but didn't break.

"If it will not obey upon being stricken with the whip, then I shall bludgeon its head with an iron hammer!" she chanted in ancient Chinese in much fewer syllables than Zack's subtitles. Her *qi* dropped another fraction. Her whip morphed into a spirit hammer.

"Wu Zetian's exact words from back then," Qin Shi Huang said. "The quote is so famous that when she or her host recites it, they can access the three different forms of her weapon."

Melissa's brows tensed in concentration. Her *qi* depleted faster as her hammer beamed brighter, turning from transparent to opaque. She smashed it against the door. Its small glass window shattered into a million glinting pieces, and its metal crumpled like paper.

"Okay, seeing what you mean by awe-inspiring!" Zack's voice screeched up an octave. "But what about you? Us? Do we have a signature weapon?"

"We do, but it has a very annoying summoning condition. The girl can handle this! She's been trained in using Wu Zetian's magic."

Melissa ripped the battered door off its hinges. "Show yourself, demon!"

A pained cry tore through the wobbling train car. "No, please!"

Zack froze. It was his mom's voice.

"Help . . . help me . . . ," she sobbed from inside the glowing train console.

He rushed forth. "Mom—!"

Melissa's spirit hammer turned transparent again. She swung it into the console. It phased through the metal panel like an illusion, not dealing any damage, yet Zack's mom screamed in anguish. Her red light flickered.

"No!" Zack tackled Melissa by her waist.

They hit the wall of the control booth before tumbling to the floor in a tangle of limbs. She yelled something to him, but all he could focus on was his mom's tortured crying.

A giant message pierced bright orange through his view.

Qin Shi Huang: THAT'S NOT YOUR MOTHER, THAT'S A

WANGLIANG, A TRICKSTER DEMON WHO CAN IMITATE VOICES.

Zack threw off his portal-lens. It was blocking his vision. His mind seemed to be swimming through murky water, and all he could think about was his mom. Her red light swelled, beckoning. He wrestled against Melissa to keep her from hurting his mom again. Voices drifted in and out of his ears like a malfunctioning radio.

"—don't hurt him!"

"Then how am I supposed to—"

No matter how Melissa thrashed against him, Zack clung to her legs. A frustrated growl warped from her throat, followed by another. *"Rì yuè dāng kōng!"*

The brightest flash he'd ever seen struck his vision raw.

Yelping, he let go of her to clutch his stinging eyes. Her clothes rustled as she got up; then her thick-soled footsteps pounded away from him. A whole universe of spots and sparks popped behind his eyelids. It took him several seconds to bear the pain of peeling his eyes open. Even then, he couldn't see much except gold specks. Tears leaked down his face. More pained cries spurted from his mom, raking down his heart, yet he couldn't do anything about it.

When his vision finally started to bloom back in, he saw Melissa swinging her transparent hammer over and over into the console. The hammer phased through the hardware but pulsed against the red light until the light ruptured from the console. It morphed into a phantom form of a monstrous little boy with black skin, red eyes, huge ears, and overly long arms that ended in sharp claws. With an echoing wail, it scattered away.

The murkiness cleared from Zack's head.

That wasn't his mom; why the heck did he think it was? She was in a hospital in Maine!

Melissa turned around, glare slashing into him. Her eyes shone a cold, blazing white.

Uh-oh.

Zack flinched against the wall. She stomped up to him and crouched low.

"Do you know what the last part of Wu Zetian's stallion-taming quote is?" She held her spirit hammer above his face. Coldness sighed from it like a block of ice. "'If I bludgeon its head with a hammer, and it still refuses to cooperate, then I shall slit its throat with a dagger.'" The hammer sharpened into a dagger, glinting white on one edge. "'So, tell me: Are you fit to dirty my dagger?'"

"Hey, Mel, that's too much." Simon walked in and pulled Melissa back by her shoulder.

"Didn't you see what happened?" She shook his hand off. "His spirit isn't even strong enough to have immunity to basic demons! If this isn't fixed, things like this are gonna keep happening! How are we gonna get anywhere without worrying?"

"I know, I know, but blaming him won't help." Simon kept his voice soft. "Plus, bigger mess to worry about—" He gestured at the wider train car.

The fire and smoke had vanished. The other passengers, so stunned they seemed catatonic, clustered as far away from them as possible, as if they'd been tilted and spilled to the other end.

Melissa grunted, letting go of her hammer. It misted away. She thrust her hand into Simon's bag with such force that he doubled over; then she took out a spray bottle. "Fine. Let's get memory wiping."

She marched off between the empty seats while raising the bottle. The passengers shrieked and tensed further against each other.

Simon picked up Zack's discarded portal-lens. Qin Shi Huang's furious voice crackled in its speakers. Zack hugged his knees tightly.

Simon gave Zack a sympathetic look, then put the portal-lens in his own bag. "Probably best to let him cool down for a bit. It's, um . . . it's gonna be okay." He placed his hand beside Zack on the floor yet didn't touch Zack. "We'll fix this."

Will we? Zack couldn't help but wonder.

Simon strode after Melissa, leaving Zack on the floor, heart pounding against his rib cage like a small, trapped animal.

7

How the Qin State Unified China By Turning Itself into an MMO

"So." Qin Shi Huang's virtual form floated in the fancy living room of Simon and Melissa's condo. "We direly need to strengthen your spiritual connection to me."

Huddling on a red wood sofa padded with beige cushions, Zack carved his hands through his hair. He peered outside the floor-to-ceiling windows. A breathtaking view of Shanghai, lit up with the million neon lights that only a world-class big city could have, glittered beyond the glass. A gauzy mist—or maybe just smog—hung over the city, hazing the lights and smearing the tops of the highest skyscrapers. The streets glowed like orange tunnels between a jungle of buildings. The Huangpu River—labeled by his portal-lens—cut through it all like a thick serpent, reflecting the lights in puddles of neon.

So this was China. Shanghai, China. The most populous city of the most populous country on earth. Zack didn't know what he'd expected, but it was simultaneously so similar yet so different from New York that it left him disoriented, like he'd been dropped into an alternate dimension. If he remembered the few stories that his mom would tell about his dad correctly, this had been where they'd gone to university and met each other. He wondered what it'd been like to see this city through their eyes. If his dad had ever regretted risking all the light and glamor to speak up for the voiceless. If his mom had ever regretted having to leave it behind forever. Had they ever looked at this very condo building, not knowing that one day their son would sit in it, screwing up a supernatural mission to save China? Would they be proud of him for trying at all, or angry that he was putting himself in so much danger?

Melissa sat on a different couch, hugging her knees and not looking at Zack. He hadn't realized how badly he'd messed up the battle until he'd put his portal-lens back on and saw that her *qi* had dropped to about a third left. He'd apologized to her so many times on the way here, but she wouldn't speak to him. Her face was shaded with rectangular shadows; the living room's chandelier was hung full of peach-wood tablets with Chinese characters written on them, which could supposedly ward off demons.

But not all of them, Simon had warned.

And Zack's spirit was so weak that he'd be at the mercy of any who made it in.

He shrank against the couch. Fake as they'd been, his mom's pained cries haunted him. What if they failed this whole mission because of him? Was her spirit suffering in the demon's clutches? He was too scared to ask.

"Show me more documentaries," he said, head low. Maybe if he'd paid more attention to the one on the plane, he would've had a stronger connection to Qin Shi Huang's magic. "I'll watch them all."

"That won't be enough." Qin Shi Huang rubbed his virtual chin in thought. "Right now, the most efficient thing you could do would be to touch something that was important to me during my lifetime. In traditional Chinese belief, the spirit—or soul, it doesn't matter what you call it—is divided into many parts, classified as either *hún* or *pò*. *Hún* are the lightweight and ethereal parts, which ascend away from the body after someone's passing. *Pò* are the heavy and corporeal parts, which stay in the mortal realm, because they have to be bound to something. How it works in reality is that every passing moment, a mortal sheds a little bit of their *pò*. The more value they attach to something, the more of their spirit lingers on it. Since you were born with a piece of my spirit, if you come in contact with an artifact I cherished, you could absorb the portion of my *pò* on it."

"You mean something like the Terra-Cotta Army?" Zack thought of Qin Shi Huang's famous army of life-sized clay soldiers. Even when he'd known nothing of Qin Shi Huang, he'd known about those.

Qin Shi Huang huffed. "Those weren't actually important to me. The only reason you're all so impressed is because you haven't dug up the rest of my mausoleum."

"It's true," Simon chimed in from the other end of Zack's

couch. Zack tried not to think too much into why Simon was sitting so far away from him. "If you look in the history books, there's not a single mention of the Terra-Cotta Army. The descriptions of the mausoleum were all about the star chart made of glowing gems in the burial chamber's ceiling, the ever-burning lamps filled with mermaid oil, and the replica of China with mountains made of bronze and rivers of mercury. Lots of mercury."

"So we're going there?" Zack asked.

"Eventually, the plan is to go there," Qin Shi Huang said. "However, there's one item right in Shanghai that I cherished deeply: the measuring vessel of Shang Yang." He raised a hand as if offering something. A wave of polygons conjured a virtual, rotating device above his palm. It looked like a rectangular rice scoop made of heavily tarnished metal. "This represented the standard measurement of one weight unit in Qin, then all of China after my conquests. Currently, it's on display in the Shanghai Museum."

"So we're gonna go there and ask them to let me touch it?" Zack raised both brows, hopeful, though a bad feeling bubbled inside him.

"Of course not," Melissa finally spoke up. "It's a priceless artifact. To have any hope of touching it, we'd have to sneak in. Duh." She leapt to her feet. "Let's go."

"Now?" Zack recoiled against the couch.

"Of course. These protections aren't foolproof." Melissa pointed at the chandelier full of peach-wood tablets. "How are we supposed to sleep if we're worried about the Yellow Emperor influencing another trickster demon to come make you kill us or something?"

"But shouldn't you stay here and rest?"

"Please." She marched toward the door and tugged open the coat closet, revealing a row of fashionable coats, jackets, and ponchos over several shelves of shoes. "As if I would miss out on a museum heist!"

"You wouldn't happen to know anything about Shang Yang, would you?" Simon asked Zack on the drive to the museum. They sat together in the back while Yaling drove. Melissa had called shotgun to no challengers. Cruising alongside multiple lanes of other cars, they passed under elevated stacks of twisting and winding concrete roads, lit a spooky sci-fi blue at the bottoms. Shanghai was a lot more enthusiastic about LEDs than New York.

"Just assume I don't know anything about anything next time, Simon." Zack flashed a weak smile.

"All right. Well, if you're gonna get power from his artifact, you'll have to understand its significance. So I guess I gotta tell you about him." Simon double-tapped the air in front of his portal-lens to open a new window. Then he raised his hands to typing position. A virtual keyboard appeared beneath his fingers. He typed something into the search bar. "He was the guy who made the Qin state so powerful that just a hundred years later, Qin Shi Huang was able to conquer all of China. He did it by basically turning the country into a . . . what do you call those big online games again? Games like *World of Warcraft*? Sorry, forgetting the English."

"MMOs? Massively multiplayer online games?" Zack rested his elbow on the car window. Ribbons of city light streamed outside, almost in time with the Mandarin hip-hop thumping from the radio.

"Yes, he basically turned Qin into one of those!"

"What's with all these video game comparisons?"

"Hey, we are a proud gamer nation!" Simon scrolled through the search results hovering in front of him. "Qin had ranks and everything. Twenty of them. You leveled up by turning in the heads of enemies you defeated in battle. The higher you ranked, the more land and servants you got."

"Seriously?"

"Yup. Supposedly, the armies of other countries would see Qin soldiers charging at them with severed heads dangling from their belts. They became an unstoppable war machine in just decades, all because of Shang Yang's reforms." With two fingers, Simon moved a virtual picture toward Zack. It was a half-bust, white stone statue of a stern-looking man in a brooding pose.

"Is that him? He looks mean."

"He was. Well, he was *strict*. His laws were so intense that Qin was basically the world's first police state. If you knew your neighbor committed a crime, yet you didn't report it, you'd be punished along with them. He even died because of his own laws. When the old king who liked him died and a new king who didn't like him took the throne, Shang Yang tried to run away from Qin, but no inn would let him stay anonymously because of his own law that inns had to check all travelers' identification slips, so he soon got caught and executed. He's the reason that whenever Chinese people think 'Qin,' we think 'strict and ruthless.' Fun fact: the Fire Nation in *Avatar* was partially based off of them."

Zack gaped. "Are you telling me I'm spiritually bound to real life Fire Lord Ozai?"

"Pretty much. Except, you know, if Ozai had actually conquered everything. And was a waterbender. And . . . well, no genocide."

"Ohhhh boy." Zack sank lower in his seat. His seat belt strained against his stomach. His portal-lens suddenly felt heavy as a brick over his nose.

"But anyway, there was a reason for the strictness. Before Shang Yang came along, Qin had been wasting away at the very west of China because lazy nobles had all the power and riches, so the peasants saw no point in working hard. Shang Yang changed everything by following a philosophy called 'legalism.' It was all about how the law is the most important thing, not bloodline or background. So he may have been strict, but he was strict to *everybody* under equal terms. He shattered the privileges of the rich nobles and made it so no matter what you were born as, if you could make Qin stronger, you could have a good life. Qin became the land of opportunity.

Peasants from other countries were obviously super intrigued about this, and Qin lured them in by promising them plenty of extra perks if they came."

"That kind of sounds like America." Zack looked at the bust of Shang Yang in a new light.

"America in theory." Simon raised a brow. Patches of neon swiveled across his face from all kinds of flashy signs in front of stores and buildings. "I'd say the immigrants to Qin had a better chance of achieving the Qin Dream than people nowadays with the American Dream."

Zack wished he could refute that but couldn't. Not when his highly educated mom had been working mostly retail for a decade now.

"Plus," Simon continued, "unlike the rest of the world, America still won't use the metric system! That is so not what Qin would've stood for. Part of legalism is that a state can only be strong when it has clear standards everywhere, so Shang Yang standardized all measurement systems in Qin. Qin Shi Huang later pushed the same standards across China." Simon flicked over what looked like an academic analysis picture of the vessel. Lines of ancient Chinese text from its sides and bottom were magnified and highlighted.

Two translations appeared for Zack, telling of how they commemorated what Shang Yang and Qin Shi Huang had done respectively. A sudden nostalgic feeling hit him, pumping his heart faster. Maybe the piece of Qin Shi Huang's spirit inside him was resonating with the text.

Simon went on. "Qin Shi Huang usually gets all the credit for unifying China, but he knew he couldn't have done it without Shang Yang's work a hundred years before. He was such a big fan of Shang Yang and legalism that he also standardized all the currencies across China then, and the width of the roads so carriages would stop running into problems, and the Chinese script so communication became way easier. Honestly, these standardized systems are probably why China kept coming back together no matter how many times it shattered into civil war. You hear about empires built by Alexander the Great and Genghis Khan and Napoleon, but where are they now? China is the only one that lasted. And it's all because of what this vessel represents."

Simon looked extremely proud of this, yet Zack couldn't help but feel a little unnerved by all this talk of "standardization." Whenever an empire or country pushed for everyone to be the same or do the same, there were inevitably those who suffered because they couldn't help but be different. And Qin Shi Huang's China didn't sound like a place that tolerated difference.

With Zack's track record of being different, if he had been born back then, would Qin Shi Huang have allowed him to live?

Zack debated whether to ask this out loud, but swallowed his words in the end. This wasn't the time to start an argument.

"Wow." He just remarked at the picture of the simple-looking

Shang Yang vessel. Knowing its backstory really did make a huge difference to how he saw it. "Man, Simon, how do you know so much history?"

Simon shrugged. "Most people in China do. History's really important to us. These were, like, my bedtime stories."

"Your bedtime stories were about mean law dudes and people cutting off the heads of their enemies for level-ups?"

"Yours weren't?" Simon gave Zack a confused look.

Zack didn't know how to respond before Simon laughed and said, "Okay, fine, Melissa and I probably know a lot more than the average Chinese kid. We had to study up to make our magic stronger. Besides, I'm from a scholar family. My mom's a history professor, and my dad's an archaeologist."

"Whoa, wouldn't they be stoked to meet the spirits of real emperors?"

"They would." Simon's gaze drifted beyond the front window. More LEDs outlined distant skyscrapers in the haze ahead. "Oh, man, they would. But I can't break my promise to Tang Taizong to keep him a secret."

"What would happen if you did? Are you under some kind of magical pact? Would he . . . hurt you?" Zack hesitated in asking, nervous that Tang Taizong might pop out and throw hands, but Simon had said that the emperors usually weren't watching everything through their eyes. To keep their spirit signatures as low as possible, they hibernated like closed laptops, only to awaken when Simon and Melissa called to them in their heads. Then they would either emerge shallowly to give advice as mental voices or to take over altogether if Simon and Melissa could no longer handle the situation.

"No, there's no magical pact, and I'm not doing it 'cause I'm scared of being punished. I legit owe him big-time." Simon bowed his head, twirling his thumbs. "My little brother has cerebral palsy. My family struggled for years to keep up with our medical bills until Tang Taizong got me all kinds of opportunities with his smarts. It's only right that I repay him by doing this mission perfectly."

Zack hummed, nodding. No wonder Simon was fine with going along with this demon-fighting, museum-heisting madness. He was doing it for his family, too.

Zack nudged his head toward Melissa and whispered, "What about her? Is she really risking her tlife just to become a pop star?"

"Mel?" Simon blinked, then smiled while snorting. "I'm pretty sure she'd risk her life for fun, even if there was no promise at the end."

Melissa whipped around, seat belt tugging at her shoulders. "I can hear you, you—"

Something rammed into the side of the car.

Screams spurted out of them all. The impact choked Zack against his seat belt. Yaling swerved the car, its tires screeching. Car horns blared behind them.

Someone dressed in all leather despite the warm summer night kept chase beside them on a motorcycle. His eyes shone white through his helmet's dark visor.

"Oh no, that man is being possessed by Jing Ke!" Qin Shi Huang's voice rose in Zack's portal-lens.

A tag appeared.

JING KE

Lived: ?–227 BCE

Assassin who went down in legend because Qin Shi Huang was the one he tried to kill, even though the assassination failed. Posed as an envoy from the Yan state, claiming he wanted to present key maps to Qin Shi Huang in surrender. Actually hid a poison-soaked dagger in the map and whipped it out while Qin Shi Huang was distracted by the geographical details. Chased him around a palace pillar before Qin Shi Huang finally pulled out his very long sword and retaliated. Do not imagine this as a scene out of Tom and Jerry.

"The Yellow Emperor really knows exactly who to send to piss me off!" Qin Shi Huang said, pissed off.

The Jing Ke–possessed man revved his motorcycle. Swinging away then back, he slammed again into the car, shattering the window beside Zack. Glass shards ruptured over him. He yelped, shielding his head.

Yaling slammed her foot on the gas pedal. With a *vroooom*, the car lurched forward faster. Warm, gritty wind poured against Zack's face, gagging him with the smell of gasoline.

They rushed right toward a collision with the car ahead.

"No, no, no!" Zack shrieked.

Yaling jerked the steering wheel to the side. They narrowly avoided the car, screeching to the next lane. A louder symphony of long honks blasted through the night. Simon screamed with Zack, then suddenly stopped.

"*Xuánwǔmén zhī biàn!*" he choked out.

Coup at Xuanwu Gate! came the subtitle.

A chunk of his *qi* meter drained away. With tongues of red light like flames, his spirit bow whooshed to life in his hands.

"That bow comes from Tang Taizong shooting his brothers during his infamous coup for the throne," Qin Shi Huang hastily explained, causing the bow to appear clearer to Zack, turning from mist-like to a texture more like molten metal. "Its spirit arrows are powerful, but always reflect a portion of the pain they deal back to its shooter."

Simon unbuckled his seat belt with shaky fingers, then leaned across Zack to aim an arrow out the window. The wind blew his hair back, making him look more like Shuda Li than ever. As he pulled his radiant bowstring, his elbow dug into Zack's chest, making Zack wheeze.

"Sorry!" Simon blurted, but didn't relent in his movements.

The spirit bow's heat baked against Zack's face. He strained to get a glimpse of what was happening outside. Jing Ke came up in the rear window, weaving through honking and screeching cars.

Just as Simon loosed an arrow, Yaling had to swerve into

another lane. Simon tumbled against the back of the driver's seat.

"This isn't going to work!" He steadied himself while grimacing at what must've been the arrow's recoil pain. "We're not going to lose him in Shanghai traffic!"

"We're almost to the museum," Melissa said. "We can get there on foot—Yaling, pull to the curb!"

With another tire-squealing turn through a gap between cars, Yaling did so. Simon and Melissa popped their doors in sync, then leapt onto the wide sidewalk with an agility that suggested they'd done stuff like this before. Zack stumbled to follow them across the polished pavement, which glistened with neon from the signs around storefronts. Startled pedestrians staggered back, shouting in concern, their faces bathed in electronic light.

Jing Ke rode toward the sidewalk as well, cutting in front of furious drivers. He raised one hand like a claw. White spirit daggers shot out of his palm like a meteor shower.

Zack cried out as one slashed through his shoulder. It didn't break flesh or draw blood, but pain burst through him where it hit, and his *qi* meter dropped a fraction.

The daggers kept coming like white lasers. He reminded himself to ask later if the different colors of *qi* meant anything, because there'd been no pattern so far. Nothing that indicated friend or enemy.

With a growl, Simon threw Zack behind him and loosed a red spirit arrow at Jing Ke. Zack's heart stuttered at being protected like this. The arrow whizzed on a perfect trajectory, yet curved away at the last second, as if repelled by a magnetic force.

"*Aiyah,*" Simon hissed through his teeth. "Tang Taizong says his arrows can't hurt him!"

The bow dissipated from Simon's hands, and he tugged Zack into a sprint down the sidewalk. Freaked-out bystanders scrambled out of their way.

"Seriously?" Zack bumbled through virtual ads that danced and shifted in his portal-lens' Common AR Field. "Why not? I thought Jing Ke was a failed assassin!"

"Yeah, but his story is so popular that he's become much more powerful in death. Part of the assassination legend is that when it happened, the strict Qin laws against moving through the throne room without permission prevented any officials from helping Qin Shi Huang. Which means you're the only one who can vanquish Jing Ke!"

While he explained this, Melissa lagged behind and activated her flash bomb power. Even though Zack didn't bear the full force of it, he winced as it gleamed off the buildings nearby like lightning. Screams erupted all around them. The people ahead, who had turned to gawk at the commotion, clutched their eyes in agony. Cars screeched and rear-ended one another. The spirit daggers stopped darting toward them.

Jing Ke had crashed into another car.

"That won't stop him for long!" Melissa warned while catching up.

"Yeah, so—" Simon looked at Zack while bolting past the temporarily blinded masses. *"Wáng fù jiàn!"*

Bear your sword, my king!

"Bear your sword, my king!" Melissa shouted as well. *"Bear your sword, my king!"*

Qin Shi Huang spoke up. "When Jing Ke was chasing me around the pillar, I couldn't get my sword out of its scabbard at first because it was built more for ceremonial length than functionality. I had to be reminded by my officials to draw it over my back. *This* is the annoying summoning condition—I need others to keep chanting for it. Now imagine this! Imagine how badly you need your sword while being chased by an assassin!"

"Isn't that literally what's happening to us?" Zack cried.

"Then you should be plenty inspired!"

"Bear your sword, my king!" Simon and Melissa chanted over and over as they barreled through neon auras and virtual ads of dancing mascots and beautiful people holding up products.

A length of coldness grew against Zack's back. He looked over his shoulder. A long black spirit sword appeared behind him.

But when he went to grab it, his fingers passed through it, no better than grasping smoke.

"Kào!" Qin Shi Huang exclaimed. No translation came, but it sounded like a bad word. "You can't even channel enough magic to sustain the sword's construct!"

"Ummmm, sorry?"

"Then we have to get you to that museum, fast!" Simon charged toward a rack of rental bikes. With his portal-lens, he scanned a QR code on three of them in turn. Green dots of light blinked alive beside the codes. The locks over their wheels sprang open.

"Get on, but don't put your feet on the pedals!" he said.

Zack clambered onto the one next to him. Copying Simon, he perched his feet on the bike frame, his knees scrunching close to his chest.

"Zhāo líng liù jùn!" Simon called out once Melissa straddled the third.

The Six Steeds of Zhao Mausoleum!

A phantom whinnying breezed past Zack's ear. Red spirit forms of horses appeared over the bikes, then seemed to absorb into them.

"Jià!" Simon leaned back, making the front of his bike lift off the ground.

"Whoa!" Zack snatched the handlebars tighter as the bikes careened out of the rack by themselves and then blitzed down the sidewalk.

THE SIX STEEDS OF ZHAO MAUSOLEUM

Tang Taizong's six most prized warhorses. Were immortalized as stone sculptures in his mausoleum. But he can only summon four at most now, because two of the sculptures were broken up, stolen by American smugglers, and brought to the Penn Museum at

the beginning of the 20th century. (GIVE THEM
BACK, AMERICA.)

The warm night air blasted into Zack's face. They went so fast
that he couldn't keep track of what they passed anymore, just
bright signs and shocked faces. The pedals spun into blurs. He
desperately kept his feet out of their way. His stomach surged
toward his throat. He'd never been on a motorcycle, but he
was pretty sure this was how it felt to ride one.

Streams of red light connected their three bikes. As Simon
turned his bike into a side street, Zack's and Melissa's followed
automatically. The sound of phantom galloping stormed
through Zack's mind. He could only grip the handlebars like
they were his sole anchor to reality.

Which, at this point, they pretty much were.

8

How Chinese Sherlock Homes and Chinese Leeroy Jenkins Can Help a Museum Heist

THEY STORMED THROUGH NARROW ALLEYS AND EMPTIER, darker streets. Streets where most storefronts were shuttered with metal curtains and only a few shone open, spilling slabs of light onto the pavement. They zipped past the occasional street food vendor or people sitting outside on stools, fanning themselves with giant woven fans. All kinds of smells ripped past on the roaring wind, delicious fried goods one second and sewage the next.

Thankfully, they got to the Shanghai Museum before the speed and wind broke Zack in half. They rode up a ramp beside its front stairs and stopped before its glass doors. Zack's legs wobbled like noodles when he got off his bike. Every cell in his body quivered with lingering energy, like he was the Flash fresh out of the Speed Force. His butt throbbed from how hard he'd been clenching the seat.

Sitting in front of a huge plaza, the museum had a design like a pot with a handle on top. Actually, on closer look, its roof had several handles, one facing each cardinal direction. If giants existed—and Zack was starting to suspect they did—they could probably lift the whole building up and go.

"S-so how are we getting past the security systems?" Zack's teeth chattered like he'd touched a live wire.

"*We* can't." Melissa flipped her hair over her shoulders. It had fallen out of the tight bun she'd made before the drive and been blown to twice its volume, like she was ready to be on a magazine cover. "But Wu Zetian can summon someone who could. Cover me."

She folded her hands like she was praying and mouthed *Wu Zetian.* That seemed to be an optional flare of drama, because Simon never did it when calling Tang Taizong to take over.

Wu Zetian's virtual tag appeared as she opened her eyes in Melissa's place. She raised her hand in front of herself. Colorful panels appeared before her, looking suspiciously like the cards that represented your roster in *Mythrealm*—except instead of myth creatures, they each had a watercolor painting of a person in ancient Chinese garb. Zack couldn't tell if the panels were spiritual or virtual. Either way, he wouldn't be able to see them without his portal-lens. With a flick of her hand, the cards scrolled past in a blur. She tapped and paused on a particular one, then splayed her fingers in front of it.

"By the command of your emperor—" Wu Zetian's eyes beamed bright white. "Arise, Di Renjie, detective of legend!"

Wind gusted in front of her, billowing her loose jacket and long hair. Zack shielded his eyes from the dust that slipped past his portal-lens but gasped when a network of white lines lit up across her body. They shone brilliantly on her bare face, neck, and hands, and mutedly under her clothes, especially her black leggings.

"What's happening to her?" he raised his voice over the wind. He vaguely remembered a similar kind of network crawling over his skin during the Aiden battle, except his lines were black.

"Her *qi* meridians are lighting up!" Simon explained, shielding his portal-lens as well.

"Meridians?"

"The network that carries our *qi* through our bodies! It's what traditional Chinese medicine like acupuncture is based on, and this means she's conducting her *qi* really, really hard. The emperors can summon subordinates from their dynasty if they're also legendary, but it takes a lot of *qi* to fuel the magic."

The wind turned into strokes of white light, gathering into the form of an ancient Chinese official. He wore a round, bulging hat with two drooping flaps near his neck. The bottom of his belted tunic billowed above his boots. A tag appeared beside him.

DI RENJIE

"Judge/Detective Dee"

Lived: 630–700 CE

Famous chancellor who served under Wu Zetian.

Managed to stay morally upright in a court terrorized by her secret police. One of the only people who
could stand up to her. Frequently serves as the protagonist of Chinese detective stories. Is basically the
Sherlock Holmes of China.

Di Renjie opened his ethereal eyes. The wind died down,
though a faint thread of light connected his chest to Wu
Zetian's. With the grace of a cloud, he fell to his knees before
her and prostrated himself with his hands flat on the ground.
"May my emperor live for ten thousand years, ten thousand
years, ten thousand upon ten thousand years."

Wu Zetian gave the first warm, non-smug smile that Zack
had seen on her. But her eyes and meridians were still lit up,
and her already low *qi* meter shrank steadily. "It's been a while,
Chancellor Di. Let's not waste time—take care of this museum's security system for us, will you? I'm sure you can crack it."

"As Your Majesty commands." Di Renjie sat back on his
knees and nodded, then morphed into a curl of white light
and burrowed into the museum beside its glass doors. Wu
Zetian grunted, swaying on her feet. A shining link remained
between her and the wall.

Just as Zack waited in anticipation of what would happen,
the growl of a motorcycle picked up in the distance.

"Oh—" He glanced toward it, eyes going huge. Jing Ke had
found them after all.

"Renjie, hurry!" Wu Zetian slapped the wall.

Nothing.

The growl grew louder and closer, echoing across the plaza. Zack spun in a panic, then went to try the glass doors.

"Wait—" Simon held him back by the elbow. "Trust Di Renjie."

"But—"

Lights beamed on in the museum. The glass doors slid open by themselves.

Zack, Simon, and Wu Zetian bolted in.

The atrium looked more like a fancy hotel lobby than a museum, cutting through the building's four floors. The full moon loomed over a huge skylight in the ceiling, which looked like half a transparent soccer ball.

"I must stay here. You two go on." Wu Zetian backed against the wall beside the doors, peering out. The glowing white thread from her chest remained connected to the wall. Her brows furrowed with strain.

"Won't Jing Ke get you?" Zack exclaimed over his shoulder.

"I'm not the one he wants. Besides, he wouldn't fight us in a museum."

"Really? He wouldn't?"

"Yeah, he knows better!" Simon ran ahead of Zack. "Every artifact in here is a priceless part of our heritage."

"But you still must hurry!" Wu Zetian called after them between heavy breaths. Her meridians ebbed in brightness. "I can't sustain Renjie for long. If I fail, the alarms will go off instantly!"

As Zack followed Simon across the atrium, Qin Shi Huang flitted through a series of windows on Zack's portal-lens and brought out the museum's augmented tour. Pulsing labels like ANCIENT CHINESE SCULPTURE GARDEN, CHINESE SEAL GALLERY, and NO. 2 EXHIBITION HALL floated in and out of Zack's view across the building's four floors.

A Chinese Minority Nationalities' Art Gallery on the top floor gave him pause. Bitterness curdled in him. Funny how places like this pretended to be proud of "minority nationalities" like him and his family, while the government was locking so many of them up, "re-educating" them, and executing them in real life if they dared speak up.

Not a lot of Americans knew this, but China's population wasn't homogeneous. It had at least fifty-six ethnic groups. The biggest and most dominant one, Han, was what most people thought of when they heard "Chinese person." But Zack's family wasn't one of them. They were Hui, a minority people with Islamic heritage, descended from Silk Road traders. The government had gotten less and less accepting of Muslims across the years, and Zack's dad had been jailed and executed for speaking up.

Calming himself down for the sake of not losing his mom as well, Zack went with Simon into the Ancient Chinese Bronze Gallery, right on the first floor. The room full of glass displays lit up as they hurried in, dim and somber. Chills rose across Zack's arms. The instinct to be respectful crushed down on him, as if his ancestors were watching and judging through the dark, tarnished bronze vessels.

His portal-lens marked out each artifact with a slowly turning ring and a label of its name and era. His belly flipped at how old some of this stuff was. He passed a wine vessel so intricate it looked like a real mythical creature turned to bronze by magic, except it was from the LATE SHANG DYNASTY (13-11TH CENTURY BCE)—over three thousand years ago. Over three thousand years, and yet it had survived for him to lay eyes on it.

Simon skidded to a stop at a display case built into the wall, showcasing multiple small bronze artifacts. Zack felt a pull to it and knew Shang Yang's vessel was among them. It was so plain compared to the daggers and crossbow bolts it was displayed with, yet his portal-lens encircled the vessel with a second ring, golden and pulsating, marking it as one of the museum's most prized treasures.

"Oh my God," Zack breathed. "There it is."

"I know, right?" Simon checked over the glass blocking them from it.

"Do we have to smash the case?" Zack eyed it, a tight feeling pinching his heart.

"No, better to not mess up the other artifacts or leave a trace that we were here." With a hard blink of his eyes, Simon's virtual tag changed to Tang Taizong's. "I've got my own legendary subordinate to summon," Tang Taizong said, the sudden cockiness to his tone giving Zack whiplash compared to Simon's demure one.

Tang Taizong let his own roster cards appear. He swept through them before settling on an armored warrior with a huge, messy beard. "By the command of your emperor—" His eyes blazed red. "Arise, Cheng Yaojin, brash warrior of legend!"

Wind picked up out of nowhere, stirring his hair. His meridians flushed like lines of lava under his skin. He pressed his hand against the glass. With licks of fiery light, the warrior gathered partially into form inside the display. His tag came with him.

CHENG YAOJIN
Lived: 589–665 CE
Warrior who contributed much to the founding of the Tang dynasty and Tang Taizong's coup for the throne. Served under the first three Tang emperors. Famous in folklore for showing up out of nowhere to save the day or disrupt whatever was going on. Star of the popular saying "Then Cheng Yaojin suddenly showed up halfway through," used to describe unexpected disruptions to plans. Can be considered the Leeroy Jenkins of ancient China.

Zack briefly wondered who Leeroy Jenkins was, then remembered it was a really, really old internet meme about a guy who ruined a meticulously planned *World of Warcraft* raid by charging in headfirst while yelling his own name. Had Qin Shi Huang been checking out internet memes while in the portal-lens?

"Yo, boss!" Cheng Yaojin looked down and around the case, having just his head and one arm. The rest of him smeared out like red mist, connected through the glass to Tang Taizong's chest. "Aw, man, this is a tight fit."

"Listen, Yaojin, we need Shang Yang's measuring vessel. That scoop thing." Tang Taizong pointed, speaking slowly. Zack got the sense that Cheng Yaojin was not as smart as Di Renjie. "Just grab it and jump out with your teleporting power."

"Sure thing, boss! It's this one, right?" Cheng Yaojin pawed around for the measuring vessel.

"Be very careful!"

"I got it, I got it!" His spirit hand closed around the vessel's thick handle. His fingers turned more opaque. *"Bànlù shāchūgè Cheng Yaojin!"*

Then Cheng Yaojin suddenly showed up halfway through!

He vanished, then reappeared outside the display case, form more complete. Zack staggered a step back.

"Here, boss." Cheng Yaojin held up the vessel. The smell of rust drifted into Zack's nose.

"Seize it!" Qin Shi Huang commanded near his ear.

After a split second of hesitation about touching something so precious, Zack took it with both hands.

An unnatural coldness surged into him through his fingers. A breath shuddered out of him. His knees wobbled and buckled. Images fluttered behind his eyes. A first-person view of pale hands examining the vessel, tracing the inscription on its side. Wavering light from an oil lamp reflecting off its bottom, which was still blank.

Out of nowhere, a hot pulse of tears broke from Zack's eyes. It hurled him back to reality. He found himself on the floor, clutching the vessel to his chest. Startled, he touched his wet cheeks.

"I—I think I just saw one of your memories," he said in disbelief.

"Excellent." Qin Shi Huang huffed. "That means this worked."

"Your Majesties," Di Renjie spoke up through the museum speakers. "Her Majesty is running direly low on *qi*!"

"Yaojin!" Tang Taizong commanded.

"Yeah, yeah, put it back. I got it, boss." Cheng Yaojin motioned to take the vessel from Zack. Zack felt a resistance against giving it up but knew it belonged in the protective case.

The moment he passed it over, Cheng Yaojin invoked his legend again. He teleported back into the case and laid the vessel down exactly like before. Then he grinned and flashed a thumbs-up with his single hand.

Tang Taizong released him. As Cheng Yaojin dissipated, Tang Taizong teetered with a huge breath of relief. His red meridians faded. He composed himself the next second, glare sharpening. "All right, let's go!"

They dashed back the way they had come. Near the doors, Wu Zetian leaned in anguish against the wall, meridians flickering. Sweat shone on her forehead. Her *qi* meter was close to running out.

"Good luck, Your Majesties," Di Renjie said through the overhead speakers. The doors opened.

The moment they raced out of the building, Wu Zetian released him. As her meridians dimmed, she crumpled, almost collapsing to the ground. Tang Taizong caught her at the last second, supporting her.

The museum's lights went out, better revealing Jing Ke at the bottom of the stairs leading into the plaza. He seemed to have been waiting there the whole time.

Tang Taizong whipped his attention to Zack. *"Bear your—"*

A shock wave swept through the air, shattering the glass doors behind them. Alarm lights switched on in the museum, flashing red. A cagelike gate slammed over the entrance.

"Oh boy!" Zack yelled, but couldn't hear himself. He couldn't hear the emperors, either, though their mouths were definitely chanting *Bear your sword, my king!* It wasn't working. No sword appeared behind him. The only thing he could hear was a sad guy's voice singing over a slow instrument. To Zack's shock, he knew the song was in ancient Chinese, and he could understand it without subtitles.

"Oh, how the wind blows over the cold Yi River. Oh, how the brave heroes go where they shall never return."

On a closer look, someone was standing behind Jing Ke, back to his back, arm moving over a glowing instrument. Wave after wave of visible sound pulsed out from their direction, preventing Zack from hearing anything else.

Qin Shi Huang: OH, NOT GAO JIANLI.

GAO JIANLI

Lived: ?–? BCE

Jing Ke's musician friend who had sent him off to the assassination with a famous mourning song at the Yi River. Tried to infiltrate the Qin palace and complete the mission after Jing Ke died. Got his identity busted before he could make an attempt. However, because he played the lute so well, Qin Shi Huang let him live as a court musician under the condition that he be blinded. Tried to kill Qin Shi Huang anyway by filling his lute with lead and taking a swing at Qin Shi Huang's head, but missed. Probably because he was blind.

Jing Ke raised both arms. White spirit daggers shot out of his palms, even more aggressively than before. Zack zigzagged to dodge them, but many caught him, eating at his *qi* meter. He stumbled and doubled over from the pain, mouth springing open with a silenced scream. The new security gate prevented him from running back into the museum, leaving him wide open. He ran toward a pillar a little ways ahead, one of the two that held up a glass-and-concrete canopy over the entrance. Jing Ke and Gao Jianli sidestepped to another angle to get him. He darted around the pillar to evade the daggers, feeling a wild sense of déjà vu, though Jing Ke would definitely not make the same mistake of coming up the stairs to do a direct chase, as he did over two thousand years ago.

Tang Taizong summoned his spirit bow and tried to shoot at Jing Ke and Gao Jianli, but his arrows deflected away like before. Wu Zetian dashed down the stairs, spirit whip shining in her hand, but the farther she got, the harder the sound waves kept her back.

Baring his clenched teeth, Tang Taizong dissolved his bow and fumbled a lighter and a piece of wood out of his messenger bag. He set the wood alight, the orange glow of the flame dancing over his face. Combined with his shining red eyes, it made him look like a demon. He hurled the wood through the museum's security gate and spread his hands like a magician. The flame flared brighter.

Sprinkler water gushed down from the ceiling, splashing on the floor in foamy puddles. Zack hoped every display case inside was watertight—they should be, right?

Tang Taizong gestured frantically at Zack, and Zack knew what he wanted him to do. Still bearing the pain of the spirit dagger hits, Zack waved his arm at the museum, willing the water to come to him. It did, flooding out through the gate. An opposing, straining force clenched inside him, cold as slush, but excitement rushed over it. Pretending he was a waterbender—well, he *was* a waterbender!—he heaved the water down the stairs with a thrust of his arms. There wasn't enough to knock the assassins down or away, but it caught them off guard. The onslaught of spirit daggers veered wide. Gao Jianli's singing went out of sync with his lute playing, and the sound waves weakened. Zack and Wu Zetian both took the chance to charge down toward them. Swinging his hand, Zack lurched the water against the assassins' legs over and over, like tides slapping two rocks at the shore.

Qin Shi Huang: CLOSE YOUR EYES.

Zack did. Wu Zetian used her blinding flash.

When it was safe to look again, the assassins appeared more distraught than ever. The spirit daggers flew even more erratically. Zack could now see that Gao Jianli was playing a green spirit lute with a spirit stick.

Qin Shi Huang: THAT CONSTRUCT WILL SCATTER THE MOMENT HE LETS GO OF IT.

Qin Shi Huang: PRY HIS FINGERS OPEN WITH THE WATER.

Zack swung his hand up and flashed it open, willing the water to surge up and do the same to Gao Jianli's grip. Then he made it go higher and jut into Gao Jianli's nostrils.

The melody stopped. The singing ended in a cry of pain. Other sounds flooded into Zack's ears again, not unlike when he'd blown his eardrums back to normal after the plane ride. Alarms blared from the museum. Police sirens wailed closer. But over the top of it all—

"Bear your sword, my king!" Wu Zetian and Tang Taizong yelled in sync.

The same cold length of sensation from before pressed across Zack's back. Except this time when he reached for it, his hand closed around a solid handle.

The blinded Jing Ke pinpointed his location at the same moment. As he fired a more concentrated torrent of daggers at Zack, Zack swung the sword over his shoulder.

It knocked the daggers aside. It was cold as ice, black as night, and long as his whole arm. He shivered at the power that radiated from it.

"This is a spirit construct of the Tai'e sword, heirloom sword of Qin," Qin Shi Huang explained out loud, tone holding a reverence Zack didn't think he was capable of. "It has passed through the hands of every king of Qin. Our ancestors."

Zack shivered again. It was surreal, being reminded that Qin Shi Huang wasn't just the start of his lineage, but *part* of it. That they were both part of something greater than themselves. Zack swore he could hear hundreds of voices whispering from the sword.

Then Qin Shi Huang's command cut through them all, telling him to repeat a certain phrase in Chinese. Without need of a subtitle, Zack understood it as "the king of Qin runs around the pillar." It was a weird thing to shout, given that he was no longer running around the pillar, but he'd learned not to question things. When he went to repeat it, the Chinese flowed out of him like water. Like *magic.*

Another wave of coldness flushed through him, icier than ever. His *qi* meter dropped a massive amount. His meridians turned black, visible across his bare arms. The coldness pooled particularly in his eyes, and he suspected they'd turned pure black as well. The warm night air shimmered and warped. The incoming daggers dragged to a crawl. The alarms and sirens dropped as low as beast noises.

Time itself had slowed down.

Just like it had during the Aiden fight.

"Run, Zack, run!" Qin Shi Huang urged.

Veering out of the way of the slowly inching spirit daggers, Zack hurtled down the last of the stairs. More phantom memories coursed through his head. Memories of being chased around a bronze pillar, wishing time would slow down like this as Jing Ke's original dagger gleamed in his wobbling view. A fear that wasn't his own exploded through him like a shot of poison.

A fear laced with rage.

How dare you try to stop me? Zack thought.

With a harsh swing of his elbow, he thrust his sword deep into Jing Ke's chest.

Zack had never, ever stabbed anyone before. The shock of doing it jarred his mind out of its haze of fury. Terror welled up in its place, terror that he had actually killed someone.

Time crashed back to normal. The alarms and sirens returned to their original shrill screeching. Jing Ke and Gao Jianli convulsed against the spirit blade together, grunting. The sword was so long that it'd gotten them both. To Zack's huge relief, no blood came out. He hadn't made any physical wounds. The emperors had told him that you could vanquish a spirit in two ways: with a spirit weapon, or by bringing the host body so close to death that the spirit had to escape it, like what Qin Shi Huang had tried to do to Aiden with the stormwater.

Zack liked the first option waaaay more.

Suddenly Jing Ke snatched Zack's wrist. His grip was cold as death. Behind his helmet visor, the white glow of his eyes sputtered like failing lights.

"Stop . . . helping . . . this . . . *tyrant*," he strained to get out in ancient Chinese beneath the sirens. His nails dug into Zack's arm.

Yet another flood of memories bombarded Zack's mind, but they were much different from before. These were memories of people screaming as soldiers charged into their villages. Men being dragged in chains to work on massive construction projects. Court officials being buried alive in pits. Scrolls of writing being burned in heaps.

Before Zack could react, the lights in Jing Ke's helmet faded. He and Gao Jianli—or, really, the normal people possessed by them—slumped against the sword. Zack's hand bounced away from the spirit hilt. It dissolved, letting the pair collapse to the pavement in a tangled heap.

Zack stared at them, breathing heavily. The alarms and sirens wailed ever louder, gripping his skull with their intensity.

"Good job, kid." Tang Taizong hopped down the stairs. He sprayed the pair in their faces with Meng Po broth, prying up formerly-Jing Ke's helmet visor to get him. "Now let's get out of here."

"Wait, are we just going to leave them?" Zack spun as Tang Taizong rushed back up the stairs.

Tang Taizong eyed the unconscious pair, then Zack. "We can't take them *with* us."

"But won't the police think they were the ones who broke into the museum?"

"Please." Wu Zetian joined Tang Taizong up the stairs, sounding exhausted. "They probably made sure to possess scumbags. Mobsters. People who belong in prison anyway." She snorted. "*Heroes* and their rules. So predictable."

Tang Taizong laughed. "I know, right?"

Zack stiffened, the sirens echoing between his ears. He'd had plenty of *Um, what?* moments with the emperors and highly suspected they weren't great people, but this . . .

This was the kind of conversation that only full-blown *supervillains* would have.

9

How to Cope with Being a Supervillain's Henchboy

ZACK LAY AWAKE IN HIS BED, STARING AT THE CEILING. IT WAS three a.m., yet Shanghai dazzled on beyond his windows. They'd taken the metro back to the condo. Yaling had gotten tangled in the police investigation about the motorcycle chase and serial car accidents. Thankfully, no one had gotten seriously hurt from those. And the police had released Yaling after they'd arrested the two men Jing Ke and Gao Jianli had possessed and connected their motorcycle to the incidents. The "attempted museum robbery" was now all over the Chinese news.

Wu Zetian had guessed right; the men were ex-felons with nasty criminal records. Nobody would believe the stories they were surely telling about "not remembering anything."

Zack's squad had officially gotten away with a *museum heist*, and he now had stronger powers and resistance against low-level demon spirits. Yet he couldn't find it in himself to celebrate. The horrible images from Jing Ke kept replaying in his mind, and so did his words, looping like an annoyingly catchy song with a very unfortunate subject.

Stop . . . helping . . . this . . . tyrant.

Yaling had gotten her memory erased too, and even though she didn't seem to mind before *or* after getting sprayed in the face with Meng Po broth, Zack couldn't help but see it as another disturbing, questionable move by the emperors.

He pawed his phone from his nightstand and tried to search up "qin shi huang tyrant." When the page didn't load, he remembered that Western sites like Google didn't work in China. The Great Firewall of China, Simon had called it, when Zack had first realized he couldn't open his messenger app to talk to Jess, his mom's friend who'd promised to send him updates about her condition. Apparently the Chinese internet was like a parallel dimension from everything else, with a whole different set of popular sites. Baidu instead of Google, Weibo instead of Twitter, and so on. Simon had had to install a VPN app on Zack's phone so Zack could reroute his IP address and contact Jess. Of course, there'd been no real updates on his mom beyond "she's still sleeping, honey."

A new message bubble popped onto Zack's screen, right over the failed search tab.

Qin Shi Huang: Curious about me?

A spasm racked through Zack's hands. He dropped his phone. It smacked down on his nose.

"Ow!" He held his aching nose for several seconds, eyes watering, before scrambling to unpair his phone's Bluetooth connection to his portal-lens.

It didn't stop Qin Shi Huang from speaking through the portal-lens, propped on the nightstand. "If you wanted to know more about me, I'm right here, you know."

Zack stared at the portal-lens for a long time, then put it on. He wasn't going to get any sleep like this anyway. He was pretty jet-lagged.

Qin Shi Huang appeared in his virtual form. "So?"

"Jing Ke called you a . . . tyrant," Zack said, tongue-tied.

"Many people do. Some even list me among history's worst tyrants. If you check the Wikipedia page for 'tyrant,' it lists me as an example. And it's true that much of what I did would be considered tyrannical by you modern people. But it was all to further my goals. I had a clear agenda, and I worked my entire life at achieving it. I wasn't one of those knuckleheaded tyrants who wasted their power on self-destructive indulgence. Like . . . fine, Nero, to give you a Eurocentric example. Sometimes I get called the Nero of China because we both had issues with our mothers. I resent that. I was far more productive than he ever was."

Zack felt like this speech should've come with a #NotAll-Tyrants hashtag. He gulped. "But you killed a ton of innocent people, didn't you?"

Qin Shi Huang rolled his eyes behind his headdress beads. "I was a conqueror. Of course I did. Do you think there's a single conqueror in history—or even a single ruler of a major country—who doesn't have innocent blood on their hands? What do you say about the masses of innocent Persians killed by your precious Alexander the Great? What about the innocent Black and Indigenous people who suffered under George Washington? If I recall correctly, almost all of your American founding fathers owned slaves, despite claiming to be advocates for liberty for all. At least *I* never spewed such a blatant lie."

"Then what are you really trying to do? Here, in the modern world?"

"We must reinforce the spirit portal plug before the Ghost Month, remember?" Qin Shi Huang blinked blankly. "I thought we filled you in on this."

Zack was starting to doubt that that was their true plan. Sweat beaded along his hairline. "But you're admitting you're a tyrant. You guys—you guys act like supervillains! You have a *henchwoman*! So how can you be up to anything good?"

"How many times must I—" Annoyance twitched across Qin Shi Huang's face. "Do you think that just because I don't cower or hold back when it comes to getting what I want, it must automatically be bad for the world? This black-and-white view is going to mean real trouble for you growing up, boy."

Zack twisted his covers in his hands. "But is reinforcing the portal plug the only thing you want to do? What happens after?"

"I help you achieve your greatest desire to honor your efforts in this mission, of course. Make you stronger. Like I promised."

Embarrassment flamed in Zack's face. "Th-that's not my biggest wish! You caught me at a bad time. What I really want is for my mom to be safe, healthy, and to stop having to work so hard."

Qin Shi Huang shrugged. "Very well. I could easily make that happen too. I have to say, though . . ." He gave Zack a look that Zack didn't like. "Instincts don't lie. You have an ambition for strength and power inside you, just like me when I was your age. I can see it."

"There is *no way* we are anything alike!"

"Oh? Let me tell you a story, boy. A story about how you and I are not so different." Qin Shi Huang closed his eyes. In a wave of polygons, his form shifted into a boy even younger than Zack, a boy with messy, matted hair and torn peasant clothes. But he opened the same intense black eyes, ringed by deep, dark, "haven't slept in a thousand years" under-eye circles. When he spoke again, his voice had become a kid's.

"See, what most summaries of my life leave out is that I may be known as Qin Shi Huang, but I didn't grow up a Qin boy. I was actually born in the capital of the Zhao state, Qin's greatest enemy at the time. A major war had broken out between Qin and Zhao a couple of years before I was born. It had ended with Qin burying four hundred thousand Zhao soldiers alive and then besieging its capital. My father, a minor Qin prince serving as a political hostage in that same city, fled while my mother was pregnant with me, leaving us there. So, yes, I was born a prisoner in an enemy city besieged by my own great-grandfather, after he had killed almost their entire adult male population."

"Wow, yeah, sounds exactly like my life," Zack mumbled.

"Let me finish," Qin Shi Huang snapped. "For the first nine years of my life, I was ruthlessly hated because of a connection to a kingdom and father I had never seen. Who had *abandoned* me and my mother." He clutched the torn, stained collar of his ratty kid clothes. Cuts and bruises appeared on his face. "Only by a miracle did we make it out alive and to the Qin palace. Well, if you count money as a miracle. A very rich merchant had schemed to make my father the new king of Qin. Overnight, my mother became queen, and I became crown prince of a kingdom I knew nothing about. I hadn't grown up around any Qin folk, and it wasn't as if the Zhao had let me learn anything about Qin."

Qin Shi Huang's form shifted again, this time on par with Cinderella. His face full of cuts and bruises vanished. His long hair untangled and became half tied up into a neat style. His ratty clothes turned to black silk robes. But his eyes remained the same, haunted and hateful, jarring on such a young form.

"So I was a living paradox," he continued. "I didn't belong anywhere. In Zhao, they hated me for being Qin. In Qin, even among all the riches of the royal palace, they would whisper about me. I didn't speak like them. I couldn't read their writing. I wasn't nearly as well-mannered or charismatic as my younger half brother, who my father had had with a proper princess of another state. Unlike my mother, who was a mere dancer. Maybe I would've been deposed in favor of my brother, but . . ."

His form morphed to about Zack's age. His black robes became way fancier, gaining layers and embroidery of gold dragons. The tall headdress with the bead curtains appeared over his head.

"Just three years later, our father suddenly passed away. At thirteen, I became the new king of Qin. Traditionally, Chinese people set our birth age at one year old, so I was biologically twelve when I took the throne. The same age as you. Imagine that."

Zack struggled to do so. Running an entire country at his age? He couldn't.

"So there I was, twelve years old, ruling a kingdom with the tongue of a foreigner." Qin Shi Huang lifted his arms. His sleeves were so wide they fell near the floor. "If you think becoming king made me safe, you're dead wrong. It made me the most intensely watched person in the Warring States. Qin was by far the most powerful kingdom then, so everyone in the six enemy states wanted me dead. Quite a few Qin folk did as well—like my dozens of uncles. My father had over twenty brothers.

"So, with everyone either trying to kill me or control me, I had to stay on guard every second of my life. I slept with a dagger under my pillow. I spooked at every shadow, at every off-seeming piece of food. I fought off an invasion by a coalition of the six other states. I quelled a rebellion by my brother and grandmother. I crushed a coup by my mother's lover, which my own mother sponsored because she'd become so afraid of me that she thought I was better off dead. Finally, I defeated the merchant chancellor who had put me on the throne as his puppet, and I seized absolute control over Qin." Qin Shi Huang paused to catch his virtual breath. "And then I turned twenty-two."

Zack's jaw fell. After a few seconds of silence, he stammered, "Okay—and where's the part where we're similar in any way?"

"Really? You don't see it?" Qin Shi Huang changed back to his original teen form. His voice dropped low again. "Being raised by single mothers, being ostracized for an association with a country you didn't even grow up in, being forever caught between two worlds?"

"That is a *massive* reach!"

"Is it? It makes me understand you. You cling so hard to morality out of a desperation for others to like you. You think they'd stop treating you like an outsider if you were a good boy who did everything they wanted. This is your greatest weakness. If you want any true power over your life, you must stop caring so much about what others think."

"I—I—I—" Zack couldn't make proper words fall out of his mouth.

Qin Shi Huang drifted closer. "Listen, kid, you are always going to be different. Accept that. Accept that right now. No matter how you try to fit in, the people around you will never truly see you as one of them. Because you are not. You have your own background, own heritage, own story. You cannot earn true respect by pretending to be someone else. Deep down you know this, or you wouldn't be hungering for the power to stand up for yourself and not pretend anymore."

"This—this is totally not what I was talking about!" Zack finally found a coherent train of thought. "I'm not worried about what others will think of me; I'm worried you're a tyrant supervillain who thinks doing terrible things is okay because you have a tragic backstory! So I have no idea what you're really dragging me into!"

"I am dragging you into the business of keeping China from shattering into another Warring States period, or worse," Qin Shi Huang said. "The madness I went through in my life made me realize the wars *had* to stop. There were so many wild spirits running around messing with people's heads that everyone was fighting each other, drawing lines between *us* versus *them*, for the smallest reasons. Finally, I decided the only way my life would make sense was if I erased those lines. No more borders. No more individual states to start wars with each other. I could no longer be torn between Qin and Zhao if I ruled both of them. *And* Han. And Chu. And everything else. I know you and your modern mind won't agree with my reasoning, but it doesn't change what I've done, and how China was born from it. Now I must defend China, my greatest creation. Think of me as a father protecting my child. Do my motives make sense now?"

"Oh my God." Zack grimaced. "You're like one of those comic book villains who yells about destroying the world so you can rebuild it in your own image."

"That is precisely what I did." Qin Shi Huang cocked a brow. "And no one else in history can say they did it as well as me."

"Now you're just humblebragging!"

"Kid," Qin Shi Huang scoffed. "There's nothing humble about me."

Zack groaned, massaging his cheeks beneath his portal-lens.

"All right," Qin Shi Huang went on, "I've given you my life story and motivations. Frankly, I don't care if you approve of them, and I see no point in you struggling with them. Working with us is the only way to get your mother's spirit back. So get some sleep. You'll need your *qi* at full charge to handle what comes next."

Qin Shi Huang vanished with a snap of his fingers, which Zack was certain wasn't necessary in any way whatsoever.

With a heavy sigh, Zack slumped back onto his pillow. He scrolled through some pictures of him and his mom on his phone, taken during their picnics and rare trips out of town. But looking at her bright smile only made him think of how it wasn't there anymore. How her body was lying halfway across the planet, an empty husk sustained by a bunch of whirring hospital machines.

And how, in twelve days, the demon who had her spirit would grow strong enough to rip it apart and consume it.

Dread throbbed in Zack's chest. He imagined his mom trapped in the demon's claws, scared and confused, seeing nothing but darkness all around and feeling the claws squeeze tighter day by day.

Tears pricked Zack's eyes and fell on his pillow, dampening it. He clenched his fists.

Fine. If working with a tyrant was what it took to get her back, then that was exactly what he'd do.

How a Leaf Can Return to Its Tree

ZACK DIDN'T SLEEP WELL. HE DREAMED OF ALL KINDS OF TER-
rible things. Swords clashing, fields burning, people screaming
and running. Him huddling in a sullen palace chamber of dark
wood and cold bronze, oil lamps flickering at the edges of his
vision. His mom shrieking as she got torn apart piece by piece.

He was beyond relieved when Simon woke him in the morning, and the nightmares fell away to reality, even though reality was pretty stressful too.

But as Zack rolled out of bed, he couldn't shake the feeling
that he'd forgotten something. Something important among
the mess of war and suffering. Someone . . . telling him a
secret?

He kept trying to remember as he washed up and then
stuffed his few belongings into a backpack Simon had given
him, made of thick, waterproof material, but had no luck. He
just hauled the backpack out of his room.

"Hey!" Simon beckoned to Zack from a couch in the fancy
living room. He gestured to something on the coffee table that

looked like huge skiing goggles. "Here's something you'll need for the next part of the mission. You should keep it on top of the rest of your things for easy access."

"Um—" Upon picking the goggles up, their black rubber straps flopping against his hands, Zack recognized them as XY Technologies' diving extension, made so you could see clearly underwater while using a portal-lens. "Are we going swimming or something?"

"Mmm." Simon rocked his head side to side. "Eventually. Hopefully."

"What do you mean? Where are we going today?"

"A city up north, Qinhuangdao. Which literally means 'Qin Emperor Island.' It was the place where Qin Shi Huang sent out a fleet of ships into the Pacific in search for Penglai."

"Penglai?"

Simon blinked. Clearly this was yet another thing that was common knowledge to every Chinese person except Zack. "Right, uh . . . It's this famous mythical island where Daoist sages cultivate magical pills that can grant immortality. We're gonna go there and hopefully get some. Because otherwise, there's no way we can survive the trip to where we actually need to go, which is the Dragon Palace of the East Sea."

Just when Zack thought he was getting used to this whole supernatural mission, Simon had to go ahead and bring in mythical islands and immortality pills and dragon palaces. Zack just stared blankly at Simon so he'd keep explaining.

"Okay, so the ultimate thing we need to find is something

called the Heirloom Seal of the Realm." Simon went into history professor mode. "It's the only artifact that'd be powerful enough to reinforce the portal plug. It was an imperial stamp that Qin Shi Huang had carved out of the *Héshìbì*, an already legendary piece of jade. For over a thousand years after that, it was the symbol of ultimate authority over China, and passed through the hands of hundreds of emperors, including Wu Zetian and Tang Taizong. That makes it connected to all their magic, so it'd be unimaginably powerful in the hands of a legendary emperor. It was lost to war around seven hundred years ago, but the emperors have reliable intel that it ended up in the Pacific Ocean, where the Dragon King of the East Sea plucked it into his treasure chamber. So we'll have to take a deep dive to heist it."

Zack decided to just accept the fact that there was apparently a dragon king that ruled a part of the Pacific. "But we'll have to be . . . immortal for it?"

"Duh." Melissa's door banged open. "None of our emperors have any magic that could keep us alive at the bottom of the ocean. I'm pretty sure you can't even take a submarine that deep."

Zack gaped at her messy bed head and unwashed face. He didn't think she was capable of looking so casual. The intricate silver bracelets on her arms were the only indication that she was the same girl he had met yesterday. She slogged to the kitchen in an oversized T-shirt, pajama pants, and fuzzy bunny slippers.

"Ugh. It's too early for this." She opened the fridge and pulled out a glass bottle of yogurt.

"Mel," Simon chided. "It's already nine a.m."

"*Already*—" She balked at him, then shook her head. "This is why our marriage never worked out."

"*Marriage?*" Zack's voice shot way too high.

"Ignore her," Simon spluttered, waving his hands. "Sometimes she likes to pretend we're actually Tang Taizong and Wu Zetian."

"This is why you didn't get custody of the kids," Melissa deadpanned while stabbing a thin straw into the foil lid of her yogurt.

"Tang Taizong and Wu Zetian didn't even have kids together!"

Zack let out an awkward laugh, but something sank in his heart when he noticed the color blooming across Simon's cheeks.

Did Simon *like* Melissa? Zack wouldn't be surprised. Melissa was very pretty, even without any makeup and with hair like a chicken's nest. And she was fearless. And confident. And a girl.

Boys liked girls. That was how most of the world went.

As Melissa went back to her room, Zack cleared his throat. "So how are the immortality pills supposed to work? We're not actually going to end up living forever, are we?"

"No, no." Simon shook his head. "It's immortality as in 'will not die because of mortal reasons.' The emperors plan on asking for pills that'll take effect for one day, and during that day, we won't need to breathe and won't be affected by the cold or the water pressure. But if one of the Dragon King's soldiers stabbed a spirit spear into us, we could still get hurt or die, so we'll have to be careful. It's good that XY Technologies makes these diving extensions, so you'll still have access to Qin Shi Huang."

"Ah, I bet they'd regret making these if they found out we were using them for our mission." Zack stuffed the goggles into his backpack, remembering the whole reason Jason Xuan started his company was to power up spirits so they could bust the portal open. "Wait—XY Technologies isn't going to come after us, are they?"

"Oh, Jason Xuan is definitely watching our every move," Simon said. "But he can't do too much about us. It's not like his whole company knows or would believe he's connected to the Yellow Emperor, especially when he can't use any magic to prove it. He would just look weird and petty, going after a bunch of kids. He couldn't even stop me from winning his championship, remember? So it'll just be the Yellow Emperor influencing more spirits to attack us. And we'll just have to deal with them as they come."

"Great," Zack muttered.

There was still a part of him that was sad to have Jason Xuan as an enemy, but at least he wouldn't have to fight his former idol directly.

After Melissa reemerged looking like a pop star again, hair smoothed into her signature ponytail and all skin blemishes erased, she knocked on Yaling's room to call her out as well, then their whole group went out for breakfast. It made Zack instinctively anxious, since he and his mom could never afford to go out for food, but Simon assured him that he didn't need to worry. Zack was touched to discover that Simon had picked a halal restaurant. They meandered through a small street to get there. Traffic moved slowly through the hot, stuffy air. Cars rasped down the middle of the narrow road, while bikes and motorcycles nudged past pedestrians on the sides by beeping and honking. Chinese people were certainly not shy with their horns. Sweat collected under Zack's backpack straps. He had to wear it over one shoulder, like he was trying too hard to look cool. He saw, heard, and smelled many things for the first time, including real cicadas chirping. A street vendor was selling them in stacks of tiny woven cages. The prices for them hovered in the Common AR Field. When the vendor caught Zack staring, she beckoned and called at him. Zack hurried onward, awkward.

With every step he took, he imagined his parents walking the same path years and years ago. Had the sights and sounds and smells filled them with love or hate? Zack hadn't expected to like much about China, but as they passed a street vendor plopping batter onto a sizzling grill behind the greasy glass of her cart, his stomach grumbled with a certainty that whatever it was would be delicious to try. And the general atmosphere of the street . . . it was undeniably chaotic, yet there was something comforting about the hustle and bustle, like it was proof of how vibrant life can be.

Once they got to the restaurant, which had the Arabic for "halal" in surprisingly large green type on its overhead sign, they sat down around a table with a sticky linoleum top. A greasy air conditioner unit blasted tirelessly above them, a ribbon flapping from its vent. Two other tables were taken, one by a grandma feeding her granddaughter and the other by a stylishly dressed young couple laughing as they arranged their food and snapped photos of it.

Simon beamed while passing along a stack of laminated menus tucked between the grimy wall and several sauce containers on the table. "In Asia, if you want good food, you don't go to the fancy five-star restaurants. You go to tiny places like this or get street food."

He translated the menu for Zack, then Yaling went to the counter to order for everyone. It was clearly a family-run restaurant, and Zack was startled to see how visibly Muslim they were. The dad, wearing a white *taqiyah* cap, pulling and stretching noodles behind a glass screen. The *hijabi* mom ladling a clear broth into wide bowls. The teenage son taking Yaling's order.

Zack knew the degree of oppression that Muslims faced in China varied widely by region, with it being much worse in the west than here in the very east, but he had still somehow grown up with the mental image that the Chinese government jailed every single Muslim they spotted. That clearly wasn't the case.

Now Zack couldn't help but imagine his family running a little shop like this, in some alternate universe where his dad had never spoken up against the government. Unlike in most other countries, his mom would've even had the freedom to become an imam—or *āhōng*, as they were called in Mandarin. Hui Muslims were unique in maintaining a tradition of female-led mosques, which Zack's mom, being a Muslim feminist who followed a more liberal view of the Quran, often boasted about. If Zack's family had simply stayed in the east and kept out of trouble's way, they could've lived in peace.

Zack knew it was never wrong to speak out against tyranny. Someone always had to. But sometimes he wondered why it had to be *his* family.

Why did *they* have to be the ones to have taken the risk and lost everything for it?

"Zack?" Simon touched his shoulder.

"Huh?" Zack whipped to attention.

"You okay?"

"Ah. Was just thinking about my mom," Zack tossed out a half lie. Wishing his parents had kept silent in the face of oppression was too selfish a thought to admit out loud.

Simon and Melissa went stiff. They suddenly looked very guilty, which made *Zack* guilty for making the mood awkward again.

Thankfully, Yaling started ferrying their order over right

then, plastic-wrapped plates of spice-drenched kebabs and four bowls of Lanzhou beef noodles, the signature dish of Hui people. Zack's mom made it all the time. And just like when she'd make it, the broth that bathed the heap of thin noodles was clear yet full of flavor and fragrance. A first real taste of home in this country that was supposed to be Zack's homeland. Though his mom would use thicker slices of beef, and more of them. Now he really *was* thinking about her, and he pretended to concentrate on slurping to hide the tears budding in his eyes.

Per her habit of not joining their conversations, Yaling popped her earbuds in and listened to her music at a concerning volume. Meanwhile, Simon traced the intricate blue patterns on his noodle bowl and launched into a story of how the cobalt-blue pigment had been brought to China by Islamic traders, and how the blue-and-white look iconic to Chinese porcelain was actually created for the Middle Eastern market before it got popular in China itself. Melissa chimed in with explanations of how trade between East and West had flourished during the Yuan dynasty, when the Mongols had taken over everything and basically forced everyone to intermingle.

"Your Hui ancestors probably came to China then, Zack." She quirked a neatly penciled brow. "Or maybe earlier . . . A lot of traders came in the Tang dynasty too. Fun fact: the first mosque in China was built during the reign of Wu Zetian's second husband."

"Do you have to make everything about Wu Zetian?" Simon

snapped his chopsticks playfully near Melissa's face.

"Hey! Can I help it if she was involved in so much important stuff?" Melissa retaliated with a slight shove.

Zack cracked a smile, but an unexpected pit twisted open in his gut. Teasing was a natural part of friendships, so he'd laughed along when his friends had done it to him, but it wasn't until now that he realized how strange it was that he never felt comfortable doing the same to them. He'd always been too afraid of upsetting them or losing them. It was never equal, like Simon and Melissa were. They were both unreserved with each other instead of enduring jabs so the other would stick around.

Melissa turned back to Zack. "Anyway, I think it's great that you're carrying on your traditions. We gotta let the world know there's more to being Chinese than being Han. I'm Miao, actually."

She showed Zack a picture on her phone. It was her standing in a rural village, wearing a colorfully embroidered tunic and pleated skirt, along with a gorgeous silver headdress as elaborate as a chandelier.

"Whoa," Zack said unconsciously. He had truly never seen a headdress that impressive.

"We Miao people pride ourselves on our silver work." Melissa flashed her bracelets, which had patterns of flowers and butterflies hammered into the silver. "And we dance and sing really well too. Part of the reason I wanna be a pop star is to bring our traditional music and dances to the world stage, you know? On my own terms, with my own look, not what the government decides I should do or act like. We shouldn't let this stuff die out."

"Yeah, of course not." Zack grinned, a lightness rising through him like helium. Melissa was the first other Chinese minority his age that he had met. At least, the first to specifically tell him she wasn't Han. Finally, here was someone who *got* him, got how he could be both Chinese and yet not the typical Han Chinese, sharing some traditions with the Han yet diverging on others in their unique, major ways.

Somehow, sitting here in this tiny restaurant while eating Lanzhou noodles from his blue-patterned porcelain bowl, it was the most connected to his Muslim heritage that Zack had ever felt. Usually he kept it to himself, never mentioning or talking about it. It was yet another thing different about him, different from even other Muslims he saw in the media or met in real life. He didn't fit most people's idea of one. But of course, with over a billion Muslims in the world, there were bound to be big differences. In second grade, when a teacher had asked if he was going to partake in Ramadan, he hadn't even known what she was talking about, because his mom just called it the *Zhāiyuè*—literally "fasting month" in Mandarin.

Zack's identity had always been a chore to explain to people, but Simon and Melissa understood him without needing him to elaborate. It was as if he'd been drifting as a lone leaf for his whole life, only to have found the tree he'd come from. It made him comfortable enough to finally ask something potentially sensitive that'd been hovering at the back of his mind.

"So, guys." Zack leaned in over the table. "I'm sorry if this is a weird question, but if the Chinese underworld exists, and so do Chinese gods, then does that mean other religions are . . . ?"

Simon and Melissa threw each other an alarmed look, then both seemed to descend into deep thought.

"Hmm . . ." Simon drummed his fingers on the table. "I wouldn't say it disproves other religions? Like, even if you just go by the standards of Chinese myth, there's nothing in it that makes you deny everything else. It's got stuff from Daoism, Buddhism, Hinduism, and local gods from all over the place. Nothing stops everything from existing at once."

"King Yanluo, the current ruler of our underworld, was originally the Hindu god King Yama," Melissa added.

"How does that work?" Zack tilted his head. "So did gods create everything, or are they just . . . human imagination come to life?"

Simon chewed his lip, then said, "Well, personally, I believe the gods are real forces in the universe, but human belief is what gathers them into forms that make sense to us. So the gods are like water, but our minds are different shapes of cups." He tapped the glass of water beside his noodles, then suddenly threw his hands up in defense. "We don't know anything for sure, though. Not even the emperors do."

"Yeah, 'cause spirit stuff works in very weird ways," Melissa said. "Spirits are kept strong and whole because of legends, but legends can get muddled. There's this pretty popular rumor that Wu Zetian killed her baby daughter to frame the empress before her and take her place. I don't believe she did it—it only popped up in history books long after she died—but when I asked her if she did, she said she honestly didn't know. She has phantom memories of doing it, but they're a mix of different scenes from TV shows. She doesn't even remember what she looked like, really. She sees herself as a blend of different actresses. She was definitely stunning, though." Melissa fanned her fingers beside her own face. She really did fall too deep into the Wu Zetian stuff sometimes.

"But the things spirits do can also influence human stories," Simon said. "Like, Tang Taizong says King Yanluo actually barged into the Chinese underworld and vanquished Houtu, the previous native Chinese ruler. There aren't any explicit legends about this, but it did make Houtu fade from popular belief, and only afterward did Chinese people start telling stories about King Yanluo. And that's how his power was cemented."

Zack considered this. "So spirits can be affected by the stories that humans come up with, but the spirits can also influence the stories humans tell?"

"Exactly." Simon nodded. "It goes both ways. And it's not always clear which came first."

"Wait, so what happened when I vanquished Jing Ke and Gao Jianli? What happened to their spirits?"

"They scattered. Their legends are strong, so they'll gather again, but they'll only have what lasted in their legends. No memories of anything that didn't make it into the cultural consciousness. So they won't even remember attacking us."

"Jing Ke will probably respawn in the underworld pretty soon," Melissa added. "He's way too famous. Gao Jianli is less popular, so he might take longer, but he's not so obscure that he'll disappear forever. Hopefully they won't get sent our way again before we finish the mission."

"Ohhhh maaaan." Zack rubbed his temples. "This is so *much.*"

"I know, dude." Simon patted him on the back. "We stopped trying to decide what's real or not real a long time ago. So believe what you want! It just might be true, or *become* true."

"I want to say one thing, though," Melissa said, uncharacteristically serious and quiet. "You're not wrong for believing whatever you believe in, and what the government is doing to Muslims is something Wu Zetian and Tang Taizong would totally not have stood for. The Tang dynasty under them was one of the most diverse and tolerant empires in the world, and they were proud of it. They celebrated every race and religion. Wu Zetian literally has sixty-one statues at her mausoleum to honor foreign ambassadors. They're still there. This, right now . . ." She looked beyond the restaurant's glass doors. "It's not Chinese culture."

Another wave of tears surged in Zack's eyes. He swallowed through a lump in his throat, trying his best to look nonchalant. "And what about Qin Shi Huang?"

"He knew who your parents were, and he still chose you. What do you think?"

Something quivered deep inside Zack.

Let me tell you a story, boy. A story about how you and I are not so different.

"He probably had no other choice." Zack laughed it off while pretending to scratch his eyes so he could dry them. But he smiled at Melissa. He was so glad she'd stopped being mad at him after the successful museum heist. "Thanks, though."

She shrugged but smiled back. "Just telling it how it is."

How Your Ancestor Can Be a Bird

IT WAS A TWO-HOUR FLIGHT FROM SHANGHAI TO Qinhuangdao, from central China to northern China. Zack stared out the window for most of it, watching cities and landscape pass beneath the clouds, trying to picture how they looked from ground level.

Once they landed, they had a few hours to kill before boarding a cruise for the night. This area apparently had a lot of spirits, and they'd be dangerously exposed during the trip out to sea if they rented a boat for themselves. But on a ship full of people, the spirits would have a harder time sensing them. Then "all they had to do" was steal a lifeboat and take off at the farthest point in the cruise's journey.

It said something about Zack's life now that he only resisted this idea for about two seconds.

They used their pre-cruise time to visit a bunch of historical attractions to strengthen their connection to legend magic. This included the Old Dragon's Head, where the Great Wall's eastern end stretched into the sea over a beach crowded with tourists. Zack's portal-lens gave a brief history of it. From a distance, it really did look like a pixel rendition of a Chinese dragon, with its horns being formed by a square watchtower. It wasn't the original Great Wall built by Qin Shi Huang, but one built five hundred years ago in the Ming dynasty. When Zack squeezed through the crowd of tourists on top of it—it was peak travel season—the brick sides loomed taller than him. It was cool to look out at the sea at the very end through a gap meant for archers, imagining himself as a soldier in charge of defending the wall, but he only got a few seconds. So many people pressed up behind him that he felt bad hogging the spot for any longer.

The beach itself was more relaxing. Their squad walked along it as the sun set in the west, cutting slits of shadow into the whooshing ocean waves. To Zack's relief, the weather was way cooler than in Shanghai. Cawing seagulls flapped against the reddening sky and dusk-scorched clouds. There was a commotion as a tour group of middle-aged women started digging up clams. Melissa excitedly joined them, Simon went to stop her because "that's probably against the beach rules!" while Yaling took selfies of herself flexing her biceps in front of the sunset. Zack wandered to the shifting tide line by himself. He poked a sandaled foot into the frothy water when it rolled close, then immediately jerked it back. It was freezing cold. Too bad. Something about the ocean called for him to dive in, as if every rolling wave had a magnetic pull. He had felt this way all his life, before he ever got water powers. Though back in America, that ocean had been the Atlantic. He visualized the globe in his head. He was now at almost the opposite side of the earth. A memory flew back to him—of one time, when he and his mom had gone to the beach, and a man had passed by him while he was digging in the sand and teased him about whether he was trying to "dig back to China." Zack didn't remember the man's face, only the flush of self-consciousness he'd felt and how quickly it had made him stop digging.

Funny that he'd ended up in China anyway.

"This was the edge of the world for the longest time, you know," Qin Shi Huang suddenly said, virtually appearing beside Zack. "Your precious Alexander dreamed of making it here and seeing it for himself. I did as well. Our people, the House of Ying, were once people of the East Sea. We originated on these shores. Our ancestor was Lady Xiu, great-granddaughter of the Yellow Emperor, who gave birth to our lineage after swallowing an egg from a black bird." He raised his hand before himself. Virtual polygons glimmered above his palm, stitching out a black bird that looked like it'd been blown out of smoke.

Zack opened his mouth to question how a lady could get pregnant from a bird but decided he'd heard weirder origin stories in myths. They never seemed willing to talk about how babies were actually made.

"Her grandson Boyi became the minister of animal husbandry for the mythical King Shun. Our people have a tradition of being good with animals, particularly horses and birds.

Not only that, but Boyi helped the famous Yu the Great tame China's own Great Flood by digging canals and creating irrigation pathways."

The black bird morphed into a shadowy figure digging with a shovel. Then the shovel shifted into a billowing flag that the figure lifted above his head.

"For his achievements, King Shun granted Boyi a black flag and the family name of Ying, which means 'to win.'"

The figure swirled into that character, written in Qin dynasty Chinese, which Zack had been able to understand ever since he'd touched Shang Yang's measuring vessel. Chills raced over his arms. These were the kinds of stories he wished he'd been told as a kid. His mom was more interested in the future than the past, but would his dad have been different? If they'd raised him together, how much more of his heritage would he have known about and understood? The existence of legend magic proved that there was power in passing down tales, in being remembered. Zack wondered how many more generations of his ancestors were watching over him. Had they been proud when he'd carried their bloodline to the shore of a whole other ocean? Had they been grieving over how he had no idea who they were until now? Zack peered at the construct in Qin Shi Huang's hand, pretending it was his dad who was continuing to tell him this legend.

"Since the throne was passed on by capability back then, Yu the Great became the next king, and Boyi was meant to be his successor. However, Yu's son defeated Boyi and took the throne for himself, thus creating China's first dynasty, Xia, and starting a tradition of passing the throne by bloodline instead. Our people were robbed of the chance to rule, but we persevered. Eventually, we became nobles of the second dynasty, Shang."

The individual parts of the complicated Ying character shifted into a line of shadowy people wearing heavy robes and tall hats, bowing with their hands clasped in front of themselves.

"But our fortunes hit a new low when the Zhou dynasty overthrew the Shang. The Zhou exiled us to the farthest wilds in the west for the entire dynasty, the longest in Chinese history."

The line of people turned sideways, becoming hunchbacked peasants lumbering with heavy loads of belongings on their backs.

"Eight hundred years. It took us almost eight hundred years to see this ocean again."

The people swirled together into a black bird that cawed silently at the crashing waves.

Qin Shi Huang lifted his chin higher. "I still remember my first view of it like it was yesterday."

A salty-smelling wind ruffled through Zack's hair and brought a shiver over him. He wondered what it was like to achieve something like that. To take over your whole known world. To know you had no enemies left.

Well, except death.

"Is it true that you shipped off a court sorcerer and three thousand girls and boys to find the Elixir of Immortality?" Zack asked. That was what a tour guide had said at a previous place, literally called Site Where Qin Shi Huang Sent Off His Search Fleet for Immortality. Though that had just been a tourist trap with a bunch of modern-made buildings.

"It wasn't really *kids* on those ships, and not nearly that many. But it was indeed a large search party." Qin Shi Huang laughed with surprising softness, eyelids drooping. "And it was true that they never came back. Xu Fu, the sorcerer, believed that someone like me should never have access to immortality. The joke is on him. I achieved immortality anyway. Just not in a way either of us expected." He looked down at his virtual hands, then back up at the distant horizon, gaze sharpening. "So long as China lives, I will never be forgotten."

For a few moments, Zack forgot to breathe. A tide of surreality hit him, like his senses were being carried on a wave.

What he understood of Qin Shi Huang so far was that he was a weird kind of founding father. He was definitely an impressive person who did a lot of impressive things, and everyone gave him credit for creating China as they knew it, yet they also agreed that he was, to quote Tang Taizong once, "the worst." It was like he'd shattered his world so completely that people had no choice but to accept the new reality. Zack was looking at history's most successful villain.

"So is this your real selfish reason for saving China?" Zack quipped. "So you can stay an immortal legend?"

"It's a bonus perk." Qin Shi Huang stared off across the expanse of orange-tinged waves, his black robes billowing in the ocean wind.

No, wait—

Qin Shi Huang was virtual. The wind shouldn't have been affecting him.

"Are . . . are you making your robes do that on purpose?"

Qin Shi Huang screwed up his face, then shot Zack a dirty look. "Must you ruin my moment?"

"Can you even see the ocean if my portal-lens isn't pointing at it?" Zack swiveled his focus between the waves and Qin Shi Huang. "How does this work? 'Cause you're just a projection, right?"

"I'm leaving it a digital mystery," Qin Shi Huang dead-panned.

After they boarded the cruise ship and stuffed themselves at the buffet—Zack had a lot of veggie dumplings and cold-served noodles—Yaling went to an adults-only cruise event while Zack, Simon, and Melissa strolled aimlessly through the ship. There were mostly couples laughing and mingling with drinks in their hands. Zack wasn't sure their group would've even been allowed on if it weren't for Melissa's charm magic.

Simon definitely got the short end of the stick when it came to superpowers. Fire magic, especially one that didn't let him make the fire on his own, wasn't that practical in real life when he didn't want to hurt anybody. He'd probably be really helpful during a barbecue, though.

"So what exactly does this mythical island look like?" Zack peered over the moonlit ocean after they ended up on the top deck. Since the wind was so shrill up here, there were a lot less people than on the ship's bow, bathed in brighter lights below. Disco lights streamed through the windows and glass doors of a karaoke lounge behind them, accompanied by someone singing off-key to a loud R&B backing track.

"The emperors said they're not sure. They've never been there either." Simon gazed out at the sea through a pair of binoculars. The ship sliced through the water, which rippled like a silky black sheet slashed with a million cuts of moonlight. A foghorn blew in the distance, low and long.

"They *haven't*?" Zack raised his voice over the terrible karaoke and the nonstop squawking of seagulls in the fluttering wind. This area sure had a lot of seagulls.

"The immortals on that island don't tend to like emperors very much." Melissa drew her jacket tighter around herself. "They're Daoists. Their whole deal is that life shouldn't be taken seriously, and you should go along with the flow of the universe without caring too much, because not caring is the only way to be free. That's what *dao* means. 'The way.'"

"But that's definitely not how emperors work." Simon lowered his binoculars. "Especially strong-willed emperors who are all about trying to take control of the universe. So, naturally, the immortals hide their island and secrets from them. A lot of big-name emperors have tried and failed to find Penglai."

Zack gawked at Simon and Melissa. "So there's no actual guarantee that we can find it?"

"Well, things are different this time." Melissa leaned against the deck's railing, ponytail whipping in the wind. "They're doing it to save China, not because they selfishly want to live forever. Hence why they'll only ask for one day of immortality for us. *And* they've got someone from the inside who's gonna be our spiritual GPS."

"Li Bai." Simon beamed while zipping his binoculars back in his waterproof backpack. "The greatest poet in Chinese history."

"Have you heard of his poems?" Melissa asked Zack as if demanding to know if he'd heard of a certain band.

"No?"

"Ugh, every kid in China knows his poems! *Chuáng qián míng yuè guāng—*"

To Zack's amazement, Simon began to recite with her. A translation appeared as subtitles.

> *Moonlight spills before my bed,*
> *As if frost across the ground.*
> *I lift my head to gaze upon the moon,*
> *I lower my head and yearn for home.*

They finished in laughter.

"Man, that is a *banger*!" Melissa high-fived Simon.

Simon turned his grin to Zack. "Yeah, anyway, he was pretty into Daoism, so his spirit drifted off to Penglai after he died. Legend says he drowned after trying to hug the moon's reflection in a river while drunk on a boat."

"But if he's a Daoist, and Daoists don't like emperors, why would he help us?" Zack asked.

"Because he lived during the golden age of China, yet watched it fall apart into war in just a few years. He really doesn't want something like that to happen again. And he's from the Tang dynasty, so Tang Taizong can summon him once we get on the lifeboat."

"Lifeboat?" a sudden female voice spoke behind them. "I wouldn't play on those, children."

They jumped. They were too used to not being understood when they chatted in English.

"We were talking about a video game, auntie," Melissa reacted the fastest, pointing to her portal-lens.

"Really? What kind of video game? Can auntie see?" The woman reached for Zack's portal-lens.

"Get back!" Qin Shi Huang suddenly yelled from the speakers. "She's being possessed by *Lady Meng Jiang!*"

A tag appeared. Zack read it while darting out of her way.

LADY MENG JIANG

Lived: ?–? BCE

Protagonist of one of China's Four Great Folktales. Husband was conscripted to build a defense wall but died during the process. She found out when delivering winter clothes to him, then cried so hard that part of the wall collapsed, revealing his bones. Story originated as a tale from Qi, one of the Seven Warring

States, but is now associated with Qin Shi Huang and the Great Wall due to two thousand years of RUTH-LESS SLANDER.

"You will never have me as a concubine, you vile, wicked tyrant!" Her expression warped in fury as she made another grab at Zack. Her eyes shone red. He bolted toward the karaoke lounge's glass door.

"I swear, I've never met this woman in my life! She's entirely fictional!" Qin Shi Huang insisted over the sounds of Simon and Melissa calling their spirit weapons.

Just when they raised them, Lady Meng Jiang screamed.

Forceful sound waves struck Zack, rippling like water in the air, not unlike Gao Jianli's music powers. But instead of preventing him from hearing other sounds, her voice made all strength leave his body. He tripped and tumbled across the deck until he landed over his backpack, stuffed full of clothes and chargers. The telltale coldness of Qin Shi Huang's power retreated from his limbs. The door was a single reach away, yet Zack's hand lay lifeless in the dithering light cast through the doorway, refusing to respond to him. His head lolled, just in time for him to catch Simon's and Melissa's weapons vanishing from their hands. They balked in confusion.

The door opened, spilling a louder flood of karaoke music. People poked their heads out of the lounge, murmuring. The person on the mic stopped singing. A crewman pushed his way out and rushed to the still-screaming Lady Meng Jiang while questioning her in modern Mandarin, which Zack still couldn't understand. The crewman held his hands up as if approaching a rabid animal. A crewwoman crouched next to Zack, shaking his shoulder while also speaking Mandarin worriedly. The only answer he could manage was a long wheeze.

Lady Meng Jiang's scream hitched. She coughed hoarsely. "Kids, you have to break free of the tyrants!" she rasped in ancient Chinese, so Zack understood. "They're deceiving you! They're going after the Heirloom Seal so they can resurrect Qin Shi Huang's Terra-Cotta Army and rule the world again!"

Memories rushed back to Zack. A cold, dark palace chamber. A long platform over a pool of blood and bones. A distressed voice, calling for him.

Don't fall for his lies, my child . . .

If Zack hadn't already been paralyzed by Lady Meng Jiang's magic, he would've fallen stunned all the same. He became only faintly aware of being nudged and shaken by the crewwoman. As Lady Meng Jiang started screaming again, more crewmembers ran around Zack to charge at her. She must've looked very unhinged to regular people. The first crewman kept his hands up while pleading with her.

Eyeing the incoming backup, she snatched the crewman's wrist. A second later, her eyes rolled back, and she collapsed.

Then the *crewman* whirled toward the onlookers and screamed with tunneling sound waves, as if bellowing a war cry. His rushing colleagues jarred to a halt. His eyes shone yellow—Simon had told Zack that the colors depended on the type of *qi* in the host's body. There was a whole elemental system of wood, fire, earth, metal, and water, but apparently he didn't need to know it.

Everyone else shrieked in terror, scrambling back into the lounge. To the immense credit of the crewwoman at Zack's side, she tried to take him with her, hoisting him under the arms like a cat.

"Zack, our magic's being dampened, and we can't contact the emperors! We need to get to the lifeboats!" Simon shouted over the mass hysteria as he and Melissa dashed to him around Lady Meng Jiang's hosts. "Zack?"

"It's like he can't move at all!" Melissa's breaths shortened with dread. She dropped down to drag Zack by his legs. The crewwoman exclaimed something in protest as Zack slipped from her grasp.

Melissa clutched the woman's face, glared into her eyes, and demanded something in Mandarin. She waved an arm at the metal stairs leading to the decks below.

With a dazed look, the woman clumsily scooped Zack up as if he were a bride and lumbered toward the stairs.

"Oh thank God, I still have enough magic to charm!" Melissa gasped, panting, racing ahead of the woman.

The crew was still trying to handle their screaming, possessed colleague. When his voice grew hoarse, he grabbed one of their arms. Like passing on a virus, he slumped to the deck while the new host wailed a fresh wave of magic at Zack's group. Simon had to help the crewwoman from dropping Zack as they clanked down the spiral stairs. Zack wasn't heavy, but she was a small woman.

"Why . . . can't I . . . move . . . ?" Zack slurred.

"If I were to guess—!" Simon yelled over the wailing. "Lady Meng Jiang's legend magic weakens emperors. Since she's most associated with Qin Shi Huang, it's hitting you especially hard!"

"Doesn't seem like she has any actual damage-doing attacks, though." Melissa glanced over her shoulder. Lady Meng Jiang's screaming kept in earshot, but she didn't actively chase them down the stairs.

Zack asked his next question with a nervous flutter in his belly. "Are the emperors . . . really trying to . . . rule the world again?"

"Oh, don't listen to her," Simon said. "Legends like her are formed around hating emperors, so of course she believes the worst of them."

"Besides," Melissa added, "if they were really trying to rule again, they wouldn't be working as a team. China can't have three emperors at once."

That reasoning actually made Zack feel a little better. Not enough to entirely wave away the unease in his gut, but better. He could always count on the emperors to be selfish.

On the deck below, onlookers shuffled out of lounges in hordes, peering in bafflement toward the screaming above the stairs. They crowded against Zack's descending group, spewing questions.

"How do we get rid of these people?" Melissa yelped. "There are too many to charm!"

"Tell them there's a murderer on the loose, and we're taking Zack to the sick bay!" Simon suggested.

"Then they'll definitely want off the ship! We can't have them rushing to the lifeboats too. I'm just going to—" Melissa swung her backpack in front of herself and dug out her spray bottle of Meng Po broth. Echoing Lady Meng Jiang's wail, she sprayed the front of the crowd as if peppering them with bullets.

They reacted with a level of bewilderment that could only come with losing the past hour of their memories and having no idea why they were suddenly here. Their panic infected the rest of the crowd, which collectively ran away from Melissa, footsteps thundering across the deck.

"Stealing Lady Meng Jiang's strategy of freaking people out," Simon remarked. "Nice!"

"You're welcome." Melissa spun to rip Simon's spray bottle out of his backpack as well.

The crewwoman carrying Zack blurted something in wakening confusion. Melissa said what must've been a Mandarin bad word under her breath, then looked her in the eye to charm her again.

It worked. The woman hauled Zack down the next level of stairs, with Simon helping.

"This should be the deck with the lifeboats!" Simon said.

There was less of a crowd. Restarting her war cry, Melissa charged down the long promenade deck, dual-wielding the bottles like Lara Croft and her double pistols. She sprayed every person along the way. They stumbled and spun as if drunk.

The lifeboats were suspended above the deck. Once they got under the closest one, Melissa charmed the crewwoman into handing Zack to Simon and operating the lifeboat. Simon supported Zack like Zack was an anime body pillow.

Melissa kept spraying everyone who came near them as the woman cranked the lifeboat's rigging so it descended on two metal cranes. Simon dragged Zack aboard the boat. Melissa hopped in afterward, yanking out a bunch of thick metal pins from the boat's cranes. They'd clearly researched how the boats worked beforehand.

The boat plunged toward the sea on thick wires. Just before they dropped out of range, Melissa reached up and sprayed the crewwoman in the face. The woman staggered out of view.

Zack lay limp in a neon-orange seat, thoughts racing. "What . . . about . . . Yaling?" he managed.

"She wasn't supposed to come with us to Penglai anyway." Simon settled into the lifeboat's control seat, studying the panels and switches around the steering wheel like trying to figure out an alien spaceship.

Lady Meng Jiang's newest host leaned over the edge of the deck, wailing into the night. The incessantly cawing seagulls crowded in the air above.

"Is she supposed to have power over animals?" Melissa craned her head in alarm.

"No?" Simon frowned. "Nothing about her legend involves that."

"Then—"

The birds flocked together in a pale mass and came at them.

Simon and Melissa shrieked. They grabbed life jackets from beneath the seats to defend themselves. Some seagulls went for Zack's head. He couldn't move his arms to protect it, so he could only wheeze out a scream as pricks of pain exploded across his scalp in a storm of feathers, beaks, and claws. Melissa smacked the birds away by slapping a third life jacket over his face.

"Come on, come on, come on!" she chanted. "Come back, emperors!"

After a few more seconds of chaos in which the seagulls kept attacking the life jacket over Zack's face and Melissa had to keep moving it back in place, red and white lights beamed at the edges of Zack's blocked view.

"Finally!" cried Wu Zetian. Zack could hear the subtle difference between her tone and Melissa's by now. "Cover your eyes!"

Zack squeezed his eyes shut as hard as he could. Even from behind the life jacket, a hint of light reached his eyelids as she set off her flash bomb power.

The seagulls squawked louder, wings fluttering hectically. Some of their pecking eased off, but not all. The white light of Wu Zetian's spirit whip and the red light of Tang Taizong's arrows wavered as they kept fighting them off.

The boat finally hit the water. There was the slithering noise of wires retracting, then a whirring rumbled to life— Tang Taizong must've activated the motor.

But Wu Zetian grabbed Zack's wrist. "There are too many; we need your water magic to go faster! Can you move yet?"

"No," Zack croaked.

She let out a frustrated growl.

Then she shoved her arms under him and flipped him over the side of the boat.

The shock of cold water was so intense, he could've been thrown into fire. It paralyzed his senses, his mind, his reality. His whole body charged up with a scream that escaped as a muted gush of bubbles. The taste of salt stabbed through his nose and mouth.

Limbs useless and rigid, he sank like a stone. Water pressed against his eardrums like heavy bass from a speaker. Only the dimmest blue light seeped through the churning ocean surface, cut through by the shadows of the lifeboat and cruise ship, the distance between them widening rapidly. Vaguely he saw a smattering of splashes as seagulls tried to dive after him, but they quickly flapped back out.

Is this how I'm gonna die? he thought.

The worst part was knowing that wherever his spirit would go, his mom wouldn't be there to welcome him with a hug. In twelve days, she'd never *exist* again, even though everyone else could eventually reunite with their moms.

He would be the only boy without a mother in the afterlife.

No.

No, no, no!

Zack couldn't let that happen.

He became aware that his portal-lens had ripped away, spiraling above him in a blur. Thank Jason Xuan it was waterproof. He prayed for the strength to reach it again.

His fingers twitched. His portal-lens kindled with a ghostly light. Hope blazed through him. Summoning all his strength, he kicked and flexed upward. It was like wading through concrete, but he could not fail.

He could not let this be the end.

Zack swung his arm up, fingers cutting through the currents. His hand closed around his portal-lens.

Qin Shi Huang's face appeared in his mind. His eyes flashed open, more intense than ever.

Cold magic crashed through Zack, but it was nothing compared to the entire ocean already chilling him to the bone. He put the portal-lens on. Water cycled around him, frothing up, picking up speed. Around and around, it built into a twister that pushed him toward the surface.

The moment he broke through to the air, the biggest breath he'd ever taken poured to the bottom of his lungs. It strained his chest to its limits.

Then he released a cry like a dragon's roar. It cut through the squawking of seagulls and the water whirling around him with the force of a hurricane. Howling winds whipped along the water, wet like a rainstorm. Black *qi* meridians branded his arms, and he knew his eyes had gone deathly black as well. He must've looked terrifying.

Good.

The water soaking his clothes shivered away, leaving him dry in the eye of the storm. He felt a connection to the entire ocean, how it was ready to heed his command.

Our people, the House of Ying, were once people of the East Sea. We originated on these shores.

Wu Zetian and Tang Taizong gawked up at him from the lifeboat, forgetting to fend off the attacking seagulls.

"You threw me overboard!" Zack roared at Wu Zetian, the twister continuing to churn around his legs.

She lurched to her senses, swinging her spirit whip at the seagulls again. "There was a bigger flock coming, kid! They would've torn you apart!"

"This isn't the time to bicker! We need to get away!" Tang Taizong loosed three spirit arrows in a row, hitting three different birds. They plummeted into the ocean. He winced at the recoil of pain that his arrows punished him with.

Zack abruptly saw that their bodies—Simon's and Melissa's bodies—were covered in bleeding scratches and peck marks. Their clothes were torn. His heart softened, and so did the water storm he commanded. He propelled himself into a landing that rocked the boat. The emperors yelped from the salty splash that hit them, then Zack swept the excess water away with a motion like parting curtains.

The cruise ship had sailed ahead, leaving a foamy V trail through the dark water. Zack didn't want to raise questions by catching up to it. The last thing he needed was to become a viral video. Facing the stern, he willed the sea itself to carry the boat away on an angle, throwing his hands back and pushing them forward over and over. It took a few seconds to get the hang of it; then the boat lurched forth on a speeding bulge of water. The night winds raced through his hair. He kept one hand splayed in front of himself while repeating a pedaling motion with the other.

Soon they sped on too fast for the seagulls to catch up. Tang Taizong and Wu Zetian slumped down in the seats in front of Zack, groaning.

"Ugh . . ." Qin Shi Huang appeared beside them, clutching his virtual head. "I swear Meng Jiang keeps getting stronger every century. How is it that she can control birds, now?"

"It's not her who's controlling them," Tang Taizong said. "Can't you feel it? They're being possessed by the spirits of the laborers who died building the Great Wall."

Qin Shi Huang perked his head up as if to listen for something; then his expression fell. "Oh, not the plot of *The Mummy: Tomb of the Dragon Emperor*, but with birds instead of their resurrected corpses!"

"You actually watched that movie?" Wu Zetian gave him a dirty look.

"I watch every movie about me." Qin Shi Huang threw a hand up, as if stating the obvious.

"Typical." Tang Taizong rolled his eyes at Wu Zetian.

"*Typical.*" She rolled them right back.

Qin Shi Huang flashed his palm at them. "Speak to me when *you've* had major big-budget Hollywood movies inspired by you."

"Didn't you lose in that movie?" Wu Zetian remarked.

"I was played by Jet Li. It was worth it."

"Anyway, I don't want to speak to you!" She spun away, hugging her chest. "You're the only reason those spirits attacked us! Taizong and I weren't tyrants, and we didn't bother with the Great Wall. The common people were happy under my rule. I worked hard to ensure that—even the most sexist of historians can't deny it!"

"At least they can't chase us much further than this." Tang Taizong gazed back at the waters they passed. "Their spirits shouldn't be able to stray too far from the Great Wall."

"Um—" Zack spoke up. "Which general direction should I be going?"

His arms were getting tired, so he sat down and experimented with keeping up the speed while making smaller movements.

"Right." Tang Taizong scrolled to a card in his subordinate roster. "By the command of your emperor—arise, poet of legend, Li Bai!"

The wind whooshed harder. Light streamed out of Tang Taizong's chest. In whimsical blooms like red watercolor, a man spun out of it. He wore a flowing robe with many drooping folds and came out stroking his long beard. A sword hung on a loose belt around his waist.

LI BAI
"The Sage of Poetry"
Lived: 701–762 CE
The most distinguished poet in Chinese history. Traveled all over China during the height of the Tang dynasty, left thousands of poems that could "make ghosts and gods weep" (as attested by fellow poet Du Fu). Famous for almost always being drunk and loving the moon a little too much.

"Your Majesties," Li Bai slurred, putting one fist to an open palm in some kind of traditional Chinese salute.

"It's time to show us the way, *Xiānsheng*," Tang Taizong said with a grateful nod.

Xiānsheng: respectful title equivalent to "mister," Zack's portal-lens explained.

"That . . ." Li Bai swiveled his finger before pointing firmly. "That way."

Zack was a little concerned that Li Bai was giving directions while somehow spiritually drunk, but he had no choice but to adjust the boat's trajectory. Mythical island, here they come.

Hopefully.

12

How Legendary Poets Duke It Out

ZACK DIDN'T KNOW HOW LONG HE SAILED FOR, BUT HE PERfected propelling the boat with only small waves of his hand. He tried doing it entirely with his mind, but something about that dizzied him really fast.

His *qi* meter burned lower and lower. When it dipped down to its last third, he went to ask Li Bai how much farther they had to go.

But then a glimmer showed in the distance, like the water was glowing.

The emperors lurched to alertness.

"Is that it?" Zack looked for an island.

"No, but we must be getting close." Qin Shi Huang's eyes went wild, almost manic. "This area is so rife with legend magic that certain spirits can gather the ambient *qi* in the environment and take form without a mortal host."

"Which means we'll have to fight our way through." Wu Zetian unzipped Zack's backpack. She fitted the diving goggles extension over his head and portal-lens. "You can't afford to lose these."

That was true, so Zack swallowed his complaint about how heavy and uncomfortable the extension was over his face. She also tugged his backpack off and buckled a life jacket on him before putting it back on, "just in case." It was an awkward fit, but his backpack had a waist strap that buckled at the front, so it stayed on tight. He felt like a turtle. She did the same to herself and Tang Taizong.

The distance closed speedily between their boat and the radiance. Black clouds hung over it, blotting out the moon and stars, making it look like the sea and sky had switched places. Once they came to the verge of meeting it, it became clear that it wasn't the water that was glowing, but a parade of creatures under the ocean surface.

No, not mere creatures. They looked humanoid, like—

"Are those *mermaids*?" Zack unconsciously slowed the boat down while approaching them. They turned to stare back, their hair flowing like ink in the water, their glowing faces distorted by the waves. Though, instead of a single tail swathed in scales, they had two soft limbs covered in short iridescent hairs.

JIAOREN

The Chinese equivalent of mermaids. Can be found weaving waterproof dragon silk if the moon and stars are out, the night is quiet, and the sea is calm.

Their tears can turn into pearls, and their fat can
burn in lamps for thousands of years, most famously
used by Qin Shi Huang to light up his mausoleum.

A horrible feeling plunged through Zack. Too late he noticed
the fury in the mermaids' glares.

"Uhhhh, you *made lamps out of them*?" he accused Qin Shi
Huang.

"Just go faster!" Qin Shi Huang waved his arms. "Go, go, go!"

Zack pumped the boat to full speed again. But the moment
they sped over the mermaids, their glowing arms splashed out
of the water. Their fingers clawed, scratched, and grabbed for
the boat's sides, rocking it. Zack bit back a scream.

Wu Zetian summoned her spirit whip and lashed at the
mermaids' hands. Tang Taizong also tried to push them back,
but the strain of sustaining Li Bai clearly prevented him from
doing much.

"*Xiānsheng*, can you help?" he yelled, meridians seething red
beneath his skin.

"I shall try, Your Majesty!" Li Bai smacked the knuckles of
one mermaid climbing up the boat.

"With your *sword*!" Tang Taizong pointed to the scabbard at
Li Bai's waist.

"Oh!" Li Bai looked startled to find it there. He drew it in
a flash of red, which would've looked very cool if he hadn't
immediately wobbled afterward.

"Please don't tell me you forgot you were one of the greatest swordsmen of our dynasty!" Panic edged into Tang Taizong's voice.

"Apologies, Your Majesty." Li Bai slashed drunkenly at the mermaids. "Penglai is not a place of conflict. I have not wielded a weapon in over a thousand years."

Wu Zetian threw a glare at Qin Shi Huang while swinging her whip. Her ponytail flew over her shoulder, rustling against her bright neon life jacket. "Why did you even want good lighting in your tomb? It's a tomb!"

"Yes, shouldn't the priority have been to *prevent* tomb robbers from finding their way?" Tang Taizong shuffled left and right to offset how the boat was swaying.

Qin Shi Huang threw his hands up. "All right, I'll admit, the mermaid lamps were pure vanity! A terrible and unnecessary decision in hindsight!"

"Half your life decisions were terrible and unnecessary!" Wu Zetian chided, face lit from below by the mermaids' iridescent glow.

"I know, and this isn't even close to the worst thing I've ever done! I don't know why we're being punished for it!"

"Ugh, just shut up!" Sweat glistened on Wu Zetian's forehead as she struggled to beat the mermaids down like a horror movie version of whack-a-mole. They crowded around the boat like giant writhing sardines, so densely packed that goose bumps rattled out of Zack's skin. Whenever one scattered to spiritual dust under Wu Zetian's whip strikes, another took its place.

"Kid, sink them!" Qin Shi Huang commanded.

"Uh—" Zack threw his arms out and then swirled them back in, willing the seawater to flood over the mermaids. It pushed them down, but the boat dropped as well, plummeting between two rising tides. Everyone yelped as water poured over its sides. Zack rushed to hurl it out, but that let the mermaids return, emerging from the abyss like a hundred comets.

"Never mind!" Qin Shi Huang said. "No more of that!"

"*Xiānsheng*, can you switch your *qi* source to the islands yet?" Tang Taizong shouted.

"Almost, Your Majesty!" Li Bai said between sloppy sweeps and jabs of his sword. He shut his eyes. "I can feel it. . . . We are nearly close enough. . . . It's here!"

Like CGI being rendered fully, his construct turned from spirit red to lifelike, though it still glowed like the mermaids. Tang Taizong breathed a huge sigh of relief, his lava-like meridians dimming. But his expression quickly tensed up again. He summoned his bow and shot several mermaids in succession.

Just then, another wave of light raced in from the side.

"More mermaids?" Zack shrieked.

"No . . ." Wu Zetian squinted while wrestling a mermaid who'd climbed over the boat's side. The mermaid splashed back into the sea. "They're . . . they're dragon boats!"

As she said it, Zack realized the new glowing things were above the water, not below. A fleet of radiant boats with dragon heads at the front sped toward them, rowed by long lines of spirits. Flags fluttered above them.

"Faster, faster!" Qin Shi Huang whirled toward Zack. "If there are dragon boats, Qu Yuan must be leading them!"

QU YUAN

"The Patriotic Poet"

Lived: 339–278 BCE

The most famous poet of the Warring States. Renowned for his patriotic love for his homeland of Chu. Threw himself into the Miluo River when the Qin armies broke through the Chu capital and took half its land. Legend has it that the villagers nearby then raced on dragon boats to try to find his body. When they couldn't, they threw *zòngzi* into the river to prevent the fishes from eating it. Said to be a possible origin of the Dragon Boat Festival every year on the fifth day of the fifth lunar month.

"Oh, him! *That* festival!" Zack actually recognized it. Every time it came around, his mom would buy or make *zòngzi*, rice dumplings wrapped in long, fragrant leaves. She'd taken him to the big annual dragon boat race in New York a few times too. That was a major festival, and the possible originator was one of Qin Shi Huang's personal haters? "How many famous enemies do you have?" Zack cried as the fleet chased them on an angle.

"This one is not on me, actually! He lived during my great-grandfather's time!"

"Except you took out his beloved Chu for good, so he's probably even more pissed at you than your great-grandfather!" Wu Zetian said.

"I grieve at ending up on opposing sides from him." Li Bai got a whimsical look in his eyes despite stabbing mermaid after mermaid. "I do admire his poetry. I relate very much to his sentiments of having his talents smothered by political intrigue."

"Wrote a few poems and jumped into a river and he gets his own holiday," Qin Shi Huang scoffed. "I created this country. Where's *my* holiday?"

"You might've had one if you weren't a megalomaniac who terrorized everyone you met and made oil lamps out of innocent mermaids!" Tang Taizong hollered. Then his blazing red eyes whipped toward Zack, making Zack flinch. Chill as he normally was, Tang Taizong was really scary when angry. "You know what people did when *he* died? His closest confidants immediately betrayed his last will by hiding his death and faking an execution order for his oldest son, so they could make his youngest son a puppet emperor! Then they carried his body back to the capital beside a barrel of dead fish to mask its rotting smell!"

Qin Shi Huang made an offended noise. "Must you bring that up right now? *Right now?*"

"Sorry, but I'm more than a little peeved at you!"

"Yes, why do all your enemies have to be so legendary and famous?" Wu Zetian yelled.

"Meng Jiang is fictional!" Qin Shi Huang said. "Qu Yuan didn't even live during my time!"

"But their legends wouldn't be so powerful if you weren't such a huge a—" Tang Taizong eyed Zack. "Such a huge *jerk*!"

"Can you all just focus on getting through this?" Qin Shi Huang spluttered. "They're gaining on us!"

The Chinese character on the fleet's fluttering flags became visible as *Chu*. Wu Zetian and Tang Taizong readied their weapons.

Identified by his tag, Qu Yuan stood at the front of the middle boat, gaze piercing, robes billowing in the wind. He looked kind of like Li Bai, except his robe had a crossover collar instead of a round collar, and his topknot was less messy, adorned by a tall headpiece like a wide antenna.

"The world is muddied, and I am the only one pure!" Qu Yuan called out in ancient Chinese, his voice carrying over the roaring waves. "Everyone is drunk, and I am the only one sober!"

Before Zack could ask if the poem was really as overdramatic as he was understanding it, a bout of dizziness slammed into him, so intense that he crumpled down and lost control of the seawater. The lifeboat bobbled to a stop.

"No!" Wu Zetian stumbled as well but dropped into the control seat to restart the boat's regular motor.

"Kid, get a hold of yourself!" Qin Shi Huang drifted next to Zack.

"Sorry, I . . ." Zack's stomach churned and lurched like the roiling waves. He clamped a hand over his mouth. This must have been what it was like to be drunk. If he wasn't already supposed to stay away from alcohol because it wasn't halal, this would've made him avoid it for life anyway.

Tang Taizong, swaying on his feet, took a shot at Qu Yuan. The red arrow flew straight through Qu Yuan's chest, yet Qu Yuan kept reciting his dramatic poem without flinching.

With Wu Zetian busy at the helm, mermaids crawled aboard, their weight sinking the boat lower and lower. Li Bai took them on with his sword. He seemed to be the only one who still had his wits. Laughing, he recited what must've been his own poetry, though it sounded so different from Qin dynasty Chinese that Zack needed subtitles.

A banquet of great food and music is nothing too precious. I only wish to stay drunk and never sober up!

Zack's nausea lifted.

"That's it!" Tang Taizong planted his feet steadier and shot arrows with better accuracy. "Keep going; your poems make us the enjoyable kind of drunk instead of the sick kind!"

Bizarrely, Zack wondered if this spell was haram. He still didn't get what was supposed to be so enjoyable about this drunken sensation, but the upgrade gave him the focus to command the sea again. He bobbed the boat harshly to shake the mermaids out and then regained his top speed.

If only it weren't too late.

The fleet was catching up. Zack tried to hurl a huge wave

to drown them, but they charged straight through the wall of water while the lifeboat ended up getting dragged slower.

It was totally unfair that the laws of physics applied differently to spirits.

Without easing off on his poem reciting, Qu Yuan fetched something out of his wide sleeves and chucked it at the lifeboat like a baseball. It sailed over the ocean and struck a seat on the lifeboat with a thump, denting it. The glowing thing then fell near Zack's sandals, looking like a small, triangular bundle wrapped in long leaves.

Tang Taizong gasped in offense. "He's throwing *zòngzi* at us!"

"Rude!" Wu Zetian left the helm to lash the mermaids again.

Another *zòngzi* hit the bottom of the boat like a meteorite, leaving a similar crater.

"And they're actually super damaging!" Tang Taizong looked about to lose his mind. "If he breaks this boat, we're finished! Zetian, you have to pray to Mazu!"

"What?" Wu Zetian balked mid-lashing.

"You know, the goddess of the sea!"

"I know who that is! I'm aghast that you would suggest I *pray* to her!"

"You're the only female emperor in our history; every goddess would be inclined to answer your prayers! We *are* being wrongfully attacked—we were never tyrants!"

"You think that just because I'm a woman, she would listen?"

"You're not just any woman!"

There happened to be a beat of silence in the poetry slam.

Wu Zetian stared at Tang Taizong, stunned. But then she shook her head. "We didn't become legends in our own right just to bow to others. We are getting through this by our own might!"

Flustered, Tang Taizong looked to Zack. "Kid, can you make us go any faster?"

"I'm trying!" Zack said. "You think I'm not trying?"

"You need a power boost." Tang Taizong's brows creased in thought while his arms loosed arrows automatically. Then his attention jumped to Li Bai. "*Xiānsheng*, do an experiment for me! Touch the boy and recite that poem you wrote about Qin Shi Huang!"

"Which one?" Li Bai broke off his reciting, sword swaying.

"You know, the one everybody quotes! 'The king of Qin sweeps away the six states!'"

"Ah! Right." Li Bai blundered behind Zack and slapped a hand on his back. "The king of Qin sweeps away the six states; how mighty is his tiger's stare! One swing of his sword cleaves the drifting clouds; all lords and nobles come west to bow!"

Heat surged through Zack. He gasped. His *qi* meter rose from its critically low level, though the refill was white instead of black.

"It's working!" Tang Taizong said, but slurred his words as Qu Yuan's poem magic took over again. "Don't stop!"

Li Bai kept reciting. "His decisiveness is as if granted by the heavens; his grand ambition rules all heroes and talents! He collected the world's weapons to craft his Giants of Bronze; he opened the Hangu Pass to the East. Upon Mount Kuaiji he carved his deeds; upon the Langya Pavilion he gazed out at the sea."

Zack couldn't believe the subtitles he was reading. He was so used to everyone hating Qin Shi Huang that he was shocked Li Bai had written this epic poem about him. Zack's black meridians got paler and paler. The flood of magic grew almost uncomfortably warm in his body.

"Seven hundred thousand laborers he did conscript, to craft Mount Li into a mausoleum as he saw fit. Long did he wait for the Elixir of Immortality; so lost he was that his heart befell to melancholy."

Never mind. There it was.

"With a crossbow he shot the creatures of the ocean, the whales as large as mountains. Their heads like the Five Sagely Peaks, their blow-holes spewing clouds and thunder. With their fins as wide as the sky, how could he see Penglai?"

Zack yelped as the magic turned *searing*.

"Stop!" he cried. "Stop it! It hurts! Something's not right!"

"No, this is exactly how it has to be." Qin Shi Huang winced as well. "You can't discuss me without also discussing the bad parts. They're as integral to my legend as my accomplishments."

"No, I mean the magic! It's burning me!"

"That's not surprising. You have a piece of my spirit. You're fundamentally incompatible with *qi* charged with Daoist magic."

"*What?* Then how could you—" Zack's words deformed into a scream as the pain got too much to bear.

"Xu Fu has taken off with the girls of Qin; when will the ship ever be returning? Watch how under the three springs of Mount Li, a coffin of gold buries only a cold body."

Zack's *qi* meter maxed out. His meridians turned entirely white, singeing him like molten silver in his veins.

His scream seemed to echo across the entire churning ocean. Lightning flashed upon the black clouds, illuminating every cresting wave. His awareness of the seawater expanded and sharpened, like he could feel every individual molecule of water.

But the price for this power was too high. Way too high. Zack just wanted this magic out of his body. Shrieking like he was burning alive, he charged to the back of the lifeboat, facing the fleet directly.

Qu Yuan pointed at him. "You won't get away with this, ty—!"

"Tyrant? Is that all you got?" Zack howled, raising his arms as if to lift two huge boulders. This time when the waves rose to his command, they glowed white. "Better than being a *failure* only remembered out of *pity!*"

Two tsunamis swelled up on either side of the fleet. The spirits on the boats glanced around in dread.

Zack clapped his hands together. Thunder boomed between the sea and sky. The radiant waves smashed over the fleet. Phantom screams cut off under the roaring water, which simultaneously shoved the lifeboat forward.

The momentum also carried the mermaids along, but their hands sprang free from the lifeboat. Another flash of lightning reflected off their wide, terrified eyes.

Zack was burning with too much pain to care. "Stop getting in our way, or I'll make you all into oil lamps!"

Thunder shook the air again. The mermaids took one last frightened look at him before flipping away into the depths, their radiance vanishing.

Just when the waves went pitch-black, and Zack thought he could let go of the scorching magic, something thumped against the bottom of the lifeboat.

Everyone turned. It thumped again, this time rupturing through the bottom. A *zòngzi* bounced from the hole. Another broke through its edge, making it even bigger. Qu Yuan's glowing face poked through the hole.

"Glory to the state of Chu," he said, eyes wide.

Then his face submerged. His laughter echoed. Water welled through the hole, flooding the boat. Zack thrust his hands down to push it out, but it was like trying to hold back the whole ocean.

Wu Zetian threw a spare life jacket on the hole and pressed down. "Kid, don't let go!"

"I—I'm—" Stars popped into Zack's eyes from the effort. His body blazed in agony.

"You're doing great!" Tang Taizong helped press on the life jacket. "Don't let go! We can make it there!"

Lightning flashed again. The waves surged up with a new

ferocity—and not by Zack's will. A huge patch of light grew in the water near the boat, which rolled as high as a hill.

"What—" Tang Taizong looked aside.

A gigantic spirit whale breached the surface. Its shining fins flung out against the black clouds, almost blocking the sky. Seawater showered down like heavy rain.

Wu Zetian sat back on her knees, opening her arms to the heavens. "O, Mazu, goddess of the sea, please heed the cries of your humble servant! Grant us safe passage to Peng—"

The whale crashed back into the ocean. A gigantic wave swept out in all directions. Zack rushed to brace against it but lost control of the lifeboat in the process.

The others screamed as the wall of water crashed over them. Zack lost solid footing. Ice-cold water slammed into him and dragged him down, even though he had a life jacket on.

"Fight!" Qin Shi Huang yelled against his skull. "Fight, kid, fight!"

But it was too much. Everything. Too much. Zack couldn't take it any longer.

And so he let go, and darkness swallowed him.

13

How to Pull Off a Good Boy, Bad Emperor Routine By Yourself

ZACK WAS IN THE COLD, DIM PALACE CHAMBER AGAIN, STANDing on the long platform over the pool.

"See him for who he really is, my child . . . ," a familiar ghost of a voice whispered near his ear. *"Don't forget again. . . . Remember this. . . . Please remember this. . . ."*

Zack gazed up at the shadow-shrouded figure on the bronze throne ahead, shivering with sudden fright. Yet his mouth opened by itself.

"Father." Words that weren't his own stammered out. "All lands under the heavens have only just been pacified, and the people of the distant frontiers have yet to fully bow down. The scholars only wish to study and follow the teachings of Confucius, yet Your Majesty punishes them with severe laws. I fear that the empire might become unsettled because of this."

"Insolence!" shouted the figure on the throne, his low voice booming through the chamber. "How dare you tell me how to run my empire? I shall have you sent to the Northern Wilds!"

Zack felt his body drop to its knees on the platform. "Father, I am only trying to look out for—"

The figure stood up, the bead curtains of his headdress rattling. Step by echoing step, he came down the dais and across the platform until he was so close that the chilly air itself choked with fear. His intense black gaze pierced from behind his headdress curtains like a beast in a cage.

"You disappoint me, Fusu," he hissed, his voice as dark as smoke.

Zack woke up to a low voice singing near his ear, gentle as a lullaby.

"There are *fúsū* trees on the mountains; there are lotuses in the pond. . . ."

Fusu?

That was important. He had to remember it, ask about it. It was . . .

His train of thought derailed as his eyes blinked open to a sloped ceiling of glittering, coarsely chiseled white stone. He was in a cave. The salty smell of the sea tickled his nose. He found himself on a white bed with white sheets so fine they could've been spun from clouds. But it didn't feel good, because he'd slept in his clothes and with his backpack and life jacket on. His unnaturally arched back seethed with discomfort. And worse—his portal-lens and diving goggles extension hadn't been taken off either. When he turned his head, he winced from how they dug into his face and scalp.

"There are pines on the mountain; there are lilies in the pond . . ."

To Zack's surprise, Qin Shi Huang was the one singing. Though that should've been a given, since the voice came from his portal-lens speakers. It was just softer than Zack had ever heard it. Qin Shi Huang's virtual form sat cross-legged in front of a set of bars, facing the bright light outside.

Wait, bars?

Were they in a *cell*?

Zack lurched up in the bed, then immediately cringed from a sharp pain that sliced through his body.

Qin Shi Huang's song cut off. He spun to face Zack, the bottom of his virtual form smearing like smoke over the cave's glittering white ground. "Finally, you're awake!"

"Where are we?" Zack rasped, voice weak. His skull felt filled with groggy water. He fumbled off his goggles extension. Instant relief throbbed in a circle around his head, though he made a noise of horror as he touched the dents left on his forehead and cheeks.

"We washed ashore at Penglai. The immortals were quite peeved when they found us, but the others convinced them to let you recover before deciding what to do with us. You were in no condition to be thrown out. Using the island's magic severely damaged your meridians. You've been unconscious for three days."

"*Three*—" Zack shot up again but gasped in anguish and fell back. "Does that mean we only have *nine days left*?"

"Indeed. We'll have to hurry through our remaining plans."

Terror crackled through Zack at the thought that the demon had gotten so much closer to consuming his mom while he was passed out. "What do we do next? Where are Simon and Melissa?"

"I'm not sure where the immortals took them, and I couldn't ask with you unconscious. Though there was talk of us facing a trial with the Eight Immortals, the unofficial leaders of Penglai. Hopefully, that's where we can plead our case for their immortality pills."

"When is that gonna happen?" Zack wheezed from the assorted pains in his body. With much effort, he shifted off his backpack and life jacket and dumped them beside the bed. He hoped Simon and Melissa were okay. At least none of them had drowned.

"Whenever our jailers come deliver medicine to you again and find you awake. They've come on a daily basis, when the sun reaches here." Qin Shi Huang tapped a spot on the ground.

The whole ground was laid in shadow, so Zack had no idea how long that was going to take. He collapsed again in anxiety, head thumping on his pillow. It seemed to be filled with rice, making him realize how hungry he was. His stomach felt hollowed out.

A fresh ache throbbed through him. He couldn't believe what he'd gone through. What he had *done*, controlling the ocean like that.

"Should I be concerned that using light magic burns me?"

Zack turned his head to Qin Shi Huang. "Is it anything like a demon being burned by holy water?"

Qin Shi Huang made a tsk noise. "You're still thinking of matters in terms of black or white, good or evil. Such clear distinctions don't exist in real life. The magic burned you simply because Penglai is famous for repelling my efforts to find it. Now I'm here at last." He gazed beyond the bars again. "After two thousand years."

Zack strained to see outside. A silvery sea glimmered far below, stretching almost to the horizon, then abruptly transitioned into a black sea under heavy black clouds.

"Would they really help us when you have such a history with them?" he asked.

"That depends on how convincing you are during the trial."

"*Me?*" Zack seized up.

"Yes." Qin Shi Huang nodded. "You must impersonate me and speak in my place. I can channel my magic so you'll have no communication issues."

"But—but—but *why*?"

"Because the only reason they're willing to listen is because they believe my spirit is irreversibly bound to yours, that of an innocent boy. If they discovered my spirit is bound to a mere device, they would simply sink it to the bottom of the ocean to rid the world of me for good."

"But I can't—I can't be *you*! No one's going to buy it!" Tears tumbled from Zack's eyes, worsened by how badly everything hurt. He hit his fist against the bed. "I . . . can't do this.

I don't wanna do this anymore. I wanna go home."

"Go home to *what*?" Qin Shi Huang snapped. "Your mother dying in nine days?"

Zack's mouth hung open. Another swell of tears blurred his vision.

Qin Shi Huang sighed. His tone softened. "Kid, you underestimate yourself. The mere fact that you rejected my attempt to bind to you proves you have an innate willpower that rivals mine. And, indeed, you've overcome every obstacle that has come our way. Why stop now?"

"I just . . . can't . . . anymore. . . ." Zack squeezed his eyes shut, sniffling. His throat swelled closed, and his bottom lip wobbled with a sob.

"Listen, during my unification wars, there were many moments where I doubted myself as well. Such as when I first tried to conquer Chu. It was the biggest of the Warring States, and the one that gave me the hardest time. Every spirit on those dragon boats was from Chu. They never stopped hating me for what I did."

Zack closed his raw, stinging eyes, pretending again that it was his dad telling him a bedtime story. That the danger of becoming an orphan wasn't creeping closer and closer.

Qin Shi Huang's husky voice continued in the portal-lens speakers behind Zack's ears. "When I set my sights on them, I had already defeated or worn out the five other states. I thought the world was mine for the taking. So I sent a young general to conquer it with just twenty thousand troops. But

I underestimated the willingness of the Chu folk to fight for their homeland, and the connection people have to their heritages. See, Qin and Chu were like a pair of lovers. We had a tradition of intermarriage. My invasion was sabotaged by an uncle of mine with Chu blood, who raised a secret resistance against me. They ambushed my troops from behind, cutting off their supply line. They were annihilated.

"It was the first battle I lost in my life, and it came close to destroying me. It showed the six other states I was not the invincible menace I had built myself up to be. The day I heard the news, I prayed all night to our ancestors. I wondered if I had gone too far, trying to devour the state that had been like a wife to Qin. I wondered if I should've cut my losses. But at the center of all that terror and doubt, I knew more than anything that if I gave up, I would always wonder what would've happened if I'd persisted. So I didn't let myself wonder. I took the gamble. Even though I was so terrified I couldn't eat or sleep, I personally apologized to an old general I had wronged and gave him sixty thousand troops, essentially all that was left in Qin. I wagered everything I had for a chance to end the Warring States for good.

"Throughout the year-long siege it took for the old general to wear down the Chu armies, I kept my patience and trusted him. I let my risk play out instead of sabotaging myself through second guesses. And so he won. *We* won. And that is the story of how I overcame my fears and conquered China."

Um.

Zack made a face. He opened his eyes to the sight of Qin Shi Huang sweeping his arms to the side, as if he'd just told a touching fable about the value of teamwork.

God. If Zack's dad had lived to tell him stories, Zack hoped they wouldn't have been like this.

But Qin Shi Huang was trying, he supposed. Like a supervillain dad awkwardly motivating his kid.

"Uh . . . ," Zack croaked between fading sniffles. "Thanks, but I feel like all your problems could've been avoided if you had just . . . not gone on a conquering spree."

"Could they?" Qin Shi Huang quirked a brow and raised a finger at Zack.

Zack looked left and right. "Yes?"

Qin Shi Huang laughed as if Zack were joking, which Zack wasn't. "Oh, you amuse me sometimes, kid. The point of my story is that even legends like me become afraid and overwhelmed by anxiety. Fear is a normal sensation that cannot be avoided. But what you do have power over is whether you let it hold you back. There will come risks in your life that demand to be taken. You'll feel the allure of them calling to you, but also endless voices telling you that you are not enough, or that it can't be done, or that *you* can't possibly be the one to do it. And you know what?" His eyes cut into slashes. "History doesn't remember those who listen to such voices."

"But I don't wanna be some famous historical figure. I just want . . . I just want my mom back. I just want things to be normal again."

"And there were times after I became a teen king besieged on all sides that I would've rather stayed a peasant boy on the streets of Zhao. But the universe doesn't grant empty wishes, kid. Your life has changed forever. You can either let this journey crush you, or let it transform you into someone stronger, as you wished. The trial is happening whether you like it or not. And you should get ready, because you must begin impersonating me right as our jailers come."

"Why?" Zack balled up his silk sheets. "Can't I pretend like you're hibernating inside me?"

"No. Because I would most definitely have a violent reaction if I found out the immortal jailer who's been taking care of my unconscious body for three days was Xu Fu, the man I sent to look for Penglai—the sorcerer who betrayed me."

On Qin Shi Huang's advice, Zack pretended to be asleep as soon as they heard strong winds whooshing down the mountain. Immortals could fly on clouds, he was told.

There came the sound of a gate in the cell bars squeaking open, then two pairs of footsteps touched down inside. Fear still trembled through Zack, but between languishing here and doing nothing or making an effort to get out sooner and save his mom and the rest of China, the choice was obvious.

"You sure you wanna keep healing him?" said a gruff male voice.

"His host has done no wrong," said a prim and proper one, slightly exhausted. "We can't doom an innocent mortal boy because of *his* wicked deeds."

"What a shame."

Footsteps scuffed toward Zack. Liquid sloshed in some kind of vessel. Once someone reached for him, Zack was supposed to dramatically snatch their wrist and slowly sit up.

Just as he peeled open an eye to gauge the timing, something hard got shoved between his lips.

"Mmm!" He lurched up. A bitter, tingly liquid spilled all over his mouth, jaw, and neck.

Whoops.

So much for waking up with the drama of an A-list conqueror.

Can I start over? he resisted the urge to say. He was not supposed to talk to Qin Shi Huang, and Qin Shi Huang would only send him hints through text. Coughing, Zack eyed the two immortals, who glowed in the dimness of the cave. One was a hunchbacked man with ratty clothes and disheveled hair, leaning against a metal crutch. The thing he had shoved into Zack's mouth was a gourd, like a giant smooth peanut with a wooden mouthpiece at the top. The other immortal, wearing fine robes, had a more scholarly look. A moment later, tags popped up beside them.

IRON CRUTCH LI

One of the Eight Immortals, a group of iconic Daoist immortals in Chinese myth. Was once a handsome hero who could astral-project his spirit, then didn't make it back in time before some fool burned his body. Had to take the body of a limping beggar who'd recently died of starvation. Swears he's not bitter about it. Carries a special talisman of a gourd filled with healing medicine.

XU FU
Lived: 255 BCE–?
Qin dynasty imperial physician and court sorcerer who Qin Shi Huang should NOT have hired. Took off twice with a massive fleet in search of Penglai. Claimed to have been blocked by a giant whale the first time, then never returned the second time. Rumored to have settled in Japan with the fleet.

Tilting his head, Xu Fu sized Zack up and down. "Would you look at that? His Imperial Majesty is finally awake."

And Zack knew he couldn't put off his act any longer.

"*Xu Fu!*" he roared with all the rage he imagined a tyrant would have after reuniting with a con artist who'd swindled him. Qin Shi Huang probably had this reaction a few days ago when he'd first seen Xu Fu but had had to fume in silence.

"A long, *long* time no see, Your Majesty," Xu Fu said in that polite voice of his with an eerily pleasant smile. "So glad you made it to Penglai after all. Isn't it wonderful?"

Qin Shi Huang: ASK HIM WHY HE'S EVEN ON THIS ISLAND

Qin Shi Huang: HE WAS SUPPOSED TO HAVE SETTLED IN JAPAN!!

"*Why are you here?*" Zack shouted in his best tyrannical villain voice. By a low, cold stream of Qin Shi Huang's magic, the words slipped out of his mouth in the specific dialect the immortals were speaking. The syllables felt foreign on his tongue. He hoped he didn't have a noticeable accent.

Qin Shi Huang: All right, that's a tad too much, tone it down.

Qin Shi Huang: I don't sound THAT melodramatic.

"My spirit drifted here after transcending its mortal vessel, of course." Xu Fu clasped his hands behind his back and gave a small bow. "I suppose I was simply too associated with the legend of Penglai."

"I see," Zack said. Fearing he didn't sound arrogant enough, he added, "You're welcome. It was your association with me that's allowed your legend to survive this long."

Xu Fu shook his head with a helpless grin. "You haven't changed, Your Majesty."

Zack almost breathed a sigh of relief.

Xu Fu went on, "But I hope you harbor no ill will toward me after all this time."

Qin Shi Huang: Just get on the topic of the trial.

Iron Crutch Li squinted and spoke before Zack could open his mouth. "Hey, what's that thing over your eyes?"

Zack tensed every muscle in his face to keep himself from looking panicked. "A device this boy uses to aid eyesight," he said as nonchalantly as possible. "Mortal bodies are so weak nowadays. They spend too much time staring at tiny screens." He turned his glower back to Xu Fu. "Now, take me to your leader, and all will be forgiven. It's an emergency. China is in danger of being flooded with spirits, and I only have nine days to stop it."

Xu Fu angled his head toward Iron Crutch Li. "Doctor, is His Majesty well enough to leave this prison?"

Iron Crutch Li stepped backward with the help of his metal crutch and made a beckoning gesture at Zack. "Try walking."

Zack did his best to shift out of bed.

Qin Shi Huang: HEY, DON'T LET THEM COMMAND YOU.

Too late. Zack took one wobbling step, then was so faint from hunger and pain that he collapsed to the ground beside his backpack.

A smirk crawled up Xu Fu's face. "Well, well. Never thought I'd see this sight. The great Qin Shi Huang, on his knees before me."

Despite not being involved in the original drama, a flare of fury swelled through Zack. He shot a genuine glare at Xu Fu.

Xu Fu's smug expression twitched.

Then Zack realized it wasn't the best idea to unnerve him when asking for the immortals' help, so he redirected the disgusted look at his own body. "This mortal vessel is a true nuisance."

"Well, you burned yourself pretty bad trying to use our magic." Iron Crutch Li held his gourd toward Zack. "Drink this."

Qin Shi Huang: Get up.

Qin Shi Huang: Don't drink that on your knees.

Zack's head spun with the nuances he had to balance. Straining back a grimace, he pushed himself to his feet. He took the gourd with a firm snatch and swigged it. The medicine was so bitter, it made his skin shrivel, and it tingled like the peppercorns his mom sometimes cooked with, but he gulped it all in one go so he wouldn't look weak. On the flip side, it instantly made him feel less hungry.

"All right, we'll be back tomorrow." Iron Crutch Li took the gourd back.

Zack stiffened. "Wait, there's no time to—"

"Your Majesty." Xu Fu flashed his palm. "We can't take you anywhere if you can't even walk."

They headed for the cave exit. Panicking, Zack went to call them back, but more messages bombarded his portal view.

Qin Shi Huang: Don't bother.

Qin Shi Huang: I must admit, they're right.

Qin Shi Huang: If your body can hardly stand, it's in no condition to face a trial.

"Could we finish the mission with only eight days?" Zack whispered urgently as the cell gate closed after the immortals.

"We just have to heist the Heirloom Seal from the Dragon Palace, and then we can head directly to my mausoleum in Xi'an," Qin Shi Huang answered out loud. "Eight days should be enough."

Will it?

Zack slumped back down on the bed, fraying on the inside with stress but unable to do more. He wanted to chase after the immortals but could feel that he wouldn't even make it to the cell bars unless he crawled. And Qin Shi Huang would never do that, so it'd blow his cover.

Wherever Simon and Melissa were, Zack hoped they were having a better time than him.

The next day, Zack got to be himself during Xu Fu and Iron Crutch Li's visit. Qin Shi Huang thought it'd be good to remind them that there was the life of an "innocent little boy" at stake.

Zack was glad. It felt wrong that he hadn't thanked the immortals for healing him, even though they'd stuck him in a cave cell. His mom would definitely scold him for not saying it. He wished he could rouse further sympathy by telling the immortals about the looming countdown to his mom's spirit getting ripped apart, but Qin Shi Huang told him not to. Demons taking her spirit was not something that would've happened if Qin Shi Huang had possessed him properly—a reminder that pierced Zack with guilt and regret all over again.

The immortals were a lot more willing to talk to Zack, though. He realized he had a Good Boy, Bad Emperor routine going when Iron Crutch Li readily told him that Simon and Melissa were fine and staying in a palace on top of the mountain. It flooded Zack with relief. He'd been up most of the night worried sick about them.

"Sorry that we gotta keep you here, lad," Iron Crutch Li said after Zack finished his medicine for the day. "Never know when that tyrant in you is gonna pop out and do something terrible.

This place was supposed to be the one place he couldn't sully."

"That's okay." Zack passed the gourd back, sitting on his bed. "I totally understand."

"What's it like, being his host? You scared?" Iron Crutch Li squinted, then his eyes jumped wide under his absurdly long eyebrows. "Oh, wait, he can hear everything you say, can't he? Never mind."

"Nah, don't worry. He needs me, so it's not like he can hurt me. There's just been a lot of scary battles."

"But he can hurt your family." Xu Fu frowned. "Has he threatened them yet?"

"He doesn't need to. I'm here because I want to save China, that's all. And we have less than eight days to do it," Zack casually slipped in another reminder.

"Well, you just wait until you refuse to do or give him something he wants," Xu Fu said with a dark look. "Then you'll see his true colors. If they weren't obvious enough."

Zack couldn't disagree, but he had to say something against that to get the immortals to soften their attitude. "You know, he may have selfish reasons, but he really is just trying to prevent China from getting flooded with bad spirits when the Ghost Month comes. He won't be remembered for another two thousand years if China falls apart, and neither will you guys."

Xu Fu and Iron Crutch Li shared a long look.

"I still wouldn't trust him, kid," Xu Fu mumbled.

"But we'll hear him argue his case tomorrow." Iron Crutch Li checked Zack's pulse with gnarly hands, tucking his crutch in the crook of his elbow. "You should be fine to move then. I'll speak with the others to set a trial."

Zack released a relieved breath. He didn't like that the trial couldn't happen today instead, leaving them with only seven days, but at least they were moving along.

Then he gulped, because now he had to deliver an Oscar-worthy performance as Qin Shi Huang in front of eight legendary judges, or their whole plan would fall apart....

And so would his world as he knew it.

How to Scam the Ancient Chinese Justice League

WHEN IT CAME TIME FOR THE TRIAL THE DAY AFTER, LEAVING the cave cell came at a price: Zack had to wear wooden cuffs over his hands.

"Sorry, lad." Iron Crutch Li clamped them over Zack's wrists with Xu Fu's help. It looked like they'd trapped his arms inside a faintly glowing wooden board. "We can't risk it."

Zack hissed as the luminous wood burned his skin. He tried not to compare it to a cross sizzling against a demon in horror movies.

With a fresh change of clothes and his backpack on, he let Xu Fu carry him out of the cave. His thoughts were an anxiety-riddled mess, but they untangled and slackened in awe as Xu Fu soared up the mountain on a cloud. The fluffy canopies of pine trees passed beneath them. The silvery ocean lapped at the rocks below, foam curling like lily petals. A blend of primal fear and wondrous excitement pulled at Zack's hollow belly at being so high up. Iron Crutch Li explained that the island of Penglai was really a mountain in the sea, with two lesser-known companions nearby, Fanghu and Yingzhou.

Buildings were scattered across Penglai's peak. Their white walls gleamed like the moon, and their Chinese-style flared roofs shone gold like the sun. Immortals in ancient garb flew between the buildings on clouds. Their laughter carried on the wind.

Zack wondered where the palace Simon and Melissa were staying in was, then found out the whole area was considered the palace, because Chinese palaces were more like cities than single fancy buildings. With pride, Iron Crutch Li told Zack the islands had no official ruler. Everyone was free to do what they wanted. In the rare cases of complaints, the Eight Immortals would host a trial in which every resident would have a say in what the resolution would be. It was basically democracy, though the word didn't exist in their dialect. When Zack tried to say it, his mouth just hung open, as if he'd forgotten what he was thinking about.

As they flew over the gleaming buildings, more and more immortals joined their side. Their clouds converged around a pavilion in the middle of a lake. Radiant koi swam in the clear waters, and lotuses drifted on the surface.

"Zack!" called a familiar voice.

Simon and Melissa were in the pavilion, waving their arms while jumping up and down. Zack's heart leapt like it was doing Olympic somersaults. He'd missed them so much.

"Hey! How have you guys—" It hit Zack that, unlike his,

their hands weren't cuffed. That was expected, yet it stung a little. While the other immortals scattered above the lake on their clouds, Xu Fu and Iron Crutch Li brought him down on a yin-yang symbol carved into the pavilion's stone base.

"We've been great!" Melissa said. "Isn't this place amazing? The cups never empty, and the food never runs out!"

"Food?" Zack thought the immortals didn't have any mortal food, because they hadn't brought him anything but medicine for five days.

Qin Shi Huang: Obviously, since you're my host body, they didn't feed you to keep you weak.

Zack swayed on his feet in disbelief, stomach rumbling.

Simon's excitement faded to concern. "Where exactly did they take you? They never told us." He eyed Zack's cuffed wrists. "And why are you wearing that?"

"They've . . . they've locked me in a cave for five days."

Simon and Melissa froze for a moment, then burst into different reactions. Simon swore to Zack that they thought the immortals had just been keeping him in another palace building, while Melissa yelled at Iron Crutch Li like an Asian auntie at someone trying to pick her pocket.

"Precautions against the tyrant must be made!" Xu Fu deliberately raised his voice so everyone could hear.

"Aye!" came a chorus of agreement from the other immortals.

"Down with the tyrant!" someone said.

"Banish him!" said another.

"Banish him!" more joined in, and soon the entire audience

over the lake was chanting "Banish him! Banish him! Banish him!"

Wu Zetian emerged from Melissa and yelled, "Hey! How about you knuckle-brained fools listen to what we have to say first?"

Tang Taizong took over Simon as well. "Yes, we beg of you! This is of vital importance!"

"Very well!" boomed a voice from afar. Zack looked for its source. He spotted a man casually gliding across the lake. He had a neat topknot and beard and placed his hands on his hips, though they were obscured by his wide gray robe sleeves. The water whispered and parted behind him. "Everyone deserves the chance to plead their case. Let us hear these emperors out!"

Once he glided closer, Zack saw that he was standing on a long, floating sword. A tag promptly appeared.

LÜ DONGBIN

Tang dynasty scholar and poet who ascended as an immortal after passing ten trials meant to test his harmony with the natural world. Now considered leader of the Eight Immortals. Talisman is a sword that can vanquish evil. Looks prim and proper but is actually a womanizer. Keep away from Wu Zetian.

Lü Dongbin introduced himself as he leapt into the pavilion. His sword flew from the water and into his grip, flinging out droplets. "Now, welcome my peers . . . !"

Splashing noises came from multiple directions across the

lake. Several immortals blitzed across it in all kinds of ways. There was a woman sailing on a giant lotus, an old man riding backward on a white mule, a child drifting in a flower basket, a bare-chested, potbellied man surfing on a huge fan, and more. The commotion stirred the lake like a whirlpool to the cheers and applause of those watching on clouds.

It was "The Eight Immortals Cross the Sea; Each Shows Their Mystical Talent." Qin Shi Huang had filled Zack in about this legend while they'd been counting down the hours in the cave. The Eight Immortals represented how every kind of person—whether young, old, male, female, rich, poor, noble, or humble—could live in harmony under Daoism. They were basically the ancient Chinese Justice League, fighting mortal injustices and malevolent spirits. This one time, they were invited to a banquet off Penglai. When they had to cross the East Sea, one of them suggested that instead of flying on clouds, they have some fun by getting across with their unique talismans. The scene was such a spectacle that Chinese artists loved to draw it on everything. But the Eight Immortals' fun disturbed the Dragon King of the East, who sent his legions of prawn soldiers and crab generals to fight them, kidnapping the child immortal Lan Caihe in the process. Outraged, the immortals retaliated against the Dragon King with their powers, even killing two of the Dragon King's princes. The Dragon King called his three brothers for backup, but they were evenly matched with the immortals. It took the interference of Guanyin, the goddess of mercy, to break up the battle.

As it turned out, the Dragon King of the East, Ao Guang, was the one who had the Heirloom Seal. The Eight Immortals' old beef against him was what the emperors were partially counting on to get their help.

One by one, they hopped from their vessels and into the pavilion. The vessels shrank and flew into their hands as their original talismans. The old man's white mule in particular shriveled so small he could tuck it into his robes. Iron Crutch Li left Zack's side to join them, while Xu Fu drifted away on a cloud. The Eight spread out until they formed a semicircle around Zack and the emperors.

"Now, let the trial begin!" Lü Dongbin glared down at Zack. "Why don't you show yourself, Qin Shi Huang?"

Zack's heart skipped a beat. Why didn't they assume he'd transformed when Simon and Melissa had? Was it something about the way he stood? Did he look too surprised and impressed by the Eight?

Qin Shi Huang: Come on, kid.

Qin Shi Huang: EMBODY ME.

With a deep breath, Zack made a show of lowering his head with closed eyes. He clenched his fists, then straightened himself while opening his eyes like a wakening vampire. Qin Shi Huang channeled a higher pulse of magic into him, so Zack's hair briefly stood up on its ends.

The immortals noticeably seized up. Some of them gulped. The lake went quiet except for the breeze stirring through the willows and a trickling of water somewhere.

Zack almost laughed from the absurdity. They truly had no idea he was an impostor.

"Must you be paranoid to this degree?" he spoke in a low drawl, lifting his cuffed wrists. "I swear, I mean you no harm."

"We don't believe you!" someone yelled.

Zack almost jumped but caught himself in time. He just arched a brow in that direction like a true villain. "I see that I don't have many fans here. What a shame."

Wu Zetian growled. She opened her arms and spun to address the entire cloud-borne audience. "Listen, the spirit portal that Qin Shi Huang plugged up has been critically loosened, and we have to heist the Heirloom Seal from Ao Guang to seal it tight again! We wouldn't be here if it weren't urgent. We wouldn't be working willingly with *him!*" She pointed at Zack.

"The world has changed beyond your understanding," Tang Taizong added. "The mortals have developed weapons that can kill millions in an instant. If malevolent spirits are allowed to roam the surface and cause chaos again, the consequences could be catastrophic."

"We are not asking for your precious perfect-caliber immortality pills," Wu Zetian snapped. "Imperfect products that could let our hosts survive a trip to the Dragon Palace for a day would be enough."

"But . . . giving anything of our creation to *him* . . ." Lü Dongbin narrowed his eyes at Zack, and so did the other immortals. "It would allow him to access Daoist magic without drawbacks. Those consequences are also unthinkable."

Tang Taizong sighed. "We promise to vanquish him if he tries anything."

"You wouldn't be powerful enough! Even under the extreme pain of burning his own meridians, merely channeling Li Bai's magic allowed him to sail here, the one place meant to be safe from him!"

"Actually, it was more likely that Mazu the sea goddess saved us," Wu Zetian admitted out of the side of her mouth.

Zack didn't say anything because the less he said, the better, but he was kind of glad for the confirmation that his pain was supposed to have been "extreme." He wished the emperors had warned him about it.

Lady He, the only woman among the Eight Immortals, spoke up. "Qin Shi Huang, you've been uncharacteristically silent. Have you nothing to say?"

It took Zack a second to realize he was the one being addressed.

Now everybody was staring at him.

With some speech hints from the real Qin Shi Huang, Zack drew a calming breath before saying, "It sounds like you've all made up your mind about me long ago. And I couldn't care less. However, I have one question: Do you care about *China*? Would you let it plunge into chaos solely because of your fear of me? Would you truly choose the safety of your island over the future of billions?"

The immortals mumbled among themselves.

"Give us some time to discuss this." Lü Dongbin waved his wide sleeve, turning around. He and the rest of the Eight threw their talismans into the water again, letting them transform into things they could mount, and stepped out of the pavilion.

"Lan Caihe, don't you want revenge against Ao Guang for kidnapping you?" Wu Zetian called after them as they sailed off. The regular immortals drifted to them on their clouds.

The child among the Eight peered back at her. "We immortals don't believe in revenge. We're not like *you*."

"Oh, good going," Tang Taizong muttered to Wu Zetian.

She snorted. "They're just saying that. I refuse to believe they're really as pure as they act."

"They're *Daoist immortals*."

"But their legends have been corrupted by mortal retellings." Wu Zetian grinned, jutting her chin. "How else do you explain Lü Dongbin's womanizing or Iron Crutch Li's temper? Perfect idols don't make good stories."

Tang Taizong grunted. "Let's hope you're right."

After the Eight stopped halfway across the lake, they spoke with the other immortals for what must've been hours. Zack and the emperors went from standing rigidly in place to leaning against the pavilion's pillars to sitting on the ground, not even watching them anymore. The emperors changed back to Simon and Melissa, choosing to hibernate through the wait.

Without Wi-Fi, there wasn't much else to do except improve Zack's knowledge of Chinese legends. Simon started telling him about the other times the Dragon King Ao Guang got beat up. He was supposedly infamous for it.

"The most famous time was by Sun Wukong, the Monkey King. You know who that is from *Mythrealm*, right?"

"Oh yeah," Zack said. "I caught a few special events featuring him. He wrecked heaven or something? Then went on a trip with a monk to India to get Buddhist scriptures? And he can upgrade Fire-type creatures."

"Okay, that last part is game only." Simon laughed. "But basically, Sun Wukong was born from a mystical stone, was super powerful, and caused trouble everywhere he went. The Dragon Palace of the East Sea was an early casualty of his when he went there to find himself a weapon. He trounced the Dragon King and all his soldiers, then the Dragon King's three brothers when they came to help. Wukong forced them all to hand over their best treasures before going off to wreak havoc on the heavenly court and the underworld. A lot of his story comes from a five-hundred-year-old book called the *Journey to the West*, though that itself was compiled from folk legends."

"He's an icon." Melissa shook her head with an amused expression. "I swear they make a new show or movie about him every day."

"Yeah, endless versions." Simon waved his hand. "Even *Dragon Ball Z* started as an adaptation of *Journey to the West*. Goku is just the Japanese way of saying Wukong."

Zack's brows perked up. "Is that why Goku had that monkey tail?"

"Yup! I can send you a list of the best adaptations to watch after you go back to America."

Zack nodded yet felt a sudden sense of plunging loss, like a rug had been pulled out from under him. Of course he wanted to go home—he couldn't wait to get his mom back— yet he hadn't considered that it would mean saying goodbye to Simon and Melissa. Very soon, and probably for good. The thought hurt more than expected.

"Anyway, that wasn't the first time the Dragon King got wrecked," Simon continued. "The first was way, way back in the Shang dynasty, like three thousand years ago. There was a small military town on the edge of the East Sea. The wife of its commander had a weird pregnancy that lasted for over three years. When she finally gave birth, it turned out to be—"

Zack's portal-lens suddenly threw out a flash of light, making him wince.

"Ow!" His hands instinctively went to his eyes but were stopped by his cumbersome cuffs. He blinked spots from his eyes. "Qin Shi Huang?" he said in his smallest whisper, unease crawling in his stomach.

No answer.

"All right, enough stories!" Tang Taizong took over Simon, leaping to his feet. "Let's get ready to hear this verdict."

"Are they done?" Zack asked in bewilderment. The immortals still looked locked in heated discussion.

"It's about time they are!" Wu Zetian took over Melissa. She cupped her hands around her mouth and shouted, "Hey! How much longer are you people going to take?"

Lü Dongbin looked up from at least a dozen immortals speaking to him at once. He sighed, neat beard stirring. A few moments later, he said something that made nods travel through the crowd. Then he glided back to the pavilion on his sword.

Tang Taizong helped Zack up from the ground. Zack still stumbled from a bout of nerves.

He did well, right? The immortals shouldn't deny his and the emperors' request. They had perfectly good, altruistic reasoning.

"We have reached an agreement." Lü Dongbin and the rest of the Eight disembarked from their vessels and formed a semicircle again. "We are willing to grant Tang Taizong and Wu Zetian pills that provide their hosts with a single day of immortality. But after much debate, we have decided as a collective that we cannot risk the same for Qin Shi Huang."

"*What?*" Zack and the emperors blurted.

"However, we remain sympathetic to your cause!" Lü Dongbin spoke over them. "Thus, we the Eight Immortals are willing to join your heist of the Dragon Palace in Qin Shi Huang's place. That should make up for his absence."

"No!" Zack stumbled forth. He thought he'd be relieved to be exempt from the battle, yet in this instant, all he could think of was how terrible it'd be to wait for their results. What if they didn't win? What if they lost all because he wasn't there?

After all, *he* was the one with the water powers. "No, you don't understand. I can't sit this out—*I need to save my mom!*"

Lü Dongbin's next words failed to leave his mouth. His eyes narrowed suspiciously at Zack. The rest of the Eight made similar expressions.

Qin Shi Huang: KID.

Qin Shi Huang: NO!!!

"Your mother?" The old man among the Eight leaned forth.

"You hate your mother!" said another, a potbellied man with his hair done in twin buns and a vest that exposed his torso.

Lü Dongbin scowled. "On the day of your coming-of-age ceremony, she gave her command seal to her lover so he could summon an army against you. The rebellion swept through your capital. You barely defeated it. You personally killed the two sons she had with him, your own half brothers, and banished her from the palace."

"And you boiled twenty-seven officials alive for daring to suggest you bring her back!" yelled Xu Fu from the sidelines.

"Oh God, seriously?" Zack whispered under his breath, grimacing.

Qin Shi Huang: I WAS VERY EMOTIONAL, ALL RIGHT?

Qin Shi Huang: SHE WAS ALL I HAD FOR THE FIRST NINE YEARS OF MY LIFE, YET SHE TRIED TO KILL ME.

Qin Shi Huang: Though the twenty-eighth official did convince me it'd break the balance of power in my palace if I left her exiled

Qin Shi Huang: BUT THAT'S BEYOND THE POINT.

Qin Shi Huang: TELL THEM YOU'RE NOT ME.

"Oh, no, no. I'm not Qin Shi Huang." Zack tried his hardest to laugh this off. "I'm the host kid! Sorry, I took over because I got . . . emotional."

Lü Dongbin studied him from head to sandal.

Then he drew his sword and swung it at Zack.

Shrieking, Zack thrust his cuffed hands up to defend himself. The ache through his meridians intensified with cold magic. The blade stopped above his shoulder. It made a breeze that tickled his neck.

When he dared look up, an orb of water was spinning in front of him. The moment he noticed, it splashed to the ground. He must've drawn it from the lake on impulse.

Lü Dongbin stepped closer, eyes darkening, not taking the sword away from Zack's neck. "You say you are not him, yet you are using his magic with this intensity? What is the meaning of this?"

Zack's mouth opened and closed. He improvised. "Well, *now* I'm Qin Shi Huang. How dare you draw your blade upon my host, an innocent boy?"

Lü Dongbin pressed the flat of his sword against Zack's neck. It sizzled, but Zack bit his lip against the sting.

"My evil-vanquishing sword should hurt you much more if you were truly the tyrant." Lü Dongbin pressed harder.

Zack pushed back against the blade with his cuffs. "Maybe I'm not as evil as you think," he said through gritted teeth. Though the boiling-officials thing was making him seriously reconsider his opinion of Qin Shi Huang. Not that he had a high one to begin with.

"No . . ." Lü Dongbin shook his head slowly. "You are lying. You are . . ."

There came a huge gasp; then Iron Crutch Li said, "The device over his eyes!"

Understanding shot through Lü Dongbin's expression. He shifted his sword onto Zack's portal-lens. It sparked like a blown fuse. The interface glitched. Zack tripped backward with a cry of horror.

"It's true!" Lü Dongbin pointed with his sword. "The tyrant is possessing the device instead of the boy!"

"That means he must've messed up the possession!" Iron Crutch Li limped closer. "He can be vanquished with the device!"

"No!" Zack fought against his cuffs despite the wood searing his skin. "No—actually, okay, he didn't bind to me properly. But that's a good thing! It means he can't force me to do anything. I'm in total control, so he can't misuse your magic! Please, I just want to save my mom! Her spirit was captured by demons!"

"What sort of demons?" Lü Dongbin demanded. "Never have I heard of a demon with the ability to capture spirits. And I have bested many demons in my time."

"I—I don't know. But Tang Taizong was there." Zack turned his head. "Did you see . . . ?"

"It was a kind you wouldn't know, languishing on this island as you do!" Tang Taizong cut in. "As we said, much of the world has changed."

"Enough of this!" Xu Fu drifted in on his cloud. "They are clearly deceiving the boy. Cast the device into the Guixu so the tyrant will never haunt the earth again!"

"Here, here!" other immortals chanted.

"What's the Guixu?" Zack looked between the emperors in a panic. That was a place-name, so he couldn't understand it.

"The Return Point to Nothingness," Wu Zetian said in a rush. "The mythical abyss where ocean water drains out to keep equilibrium as rivers pour in. It's near the bottom of these islands."

Qin Shi Huang: RUN!

Zack tried, but Lü Dongbin snatched the portal-lens off his head. The potbellied immortal with the twin hair buns waved his talisman, a huge fan. A gust of wind hurled Zack and the emperors backward. Lü Dongbin stepped off the yin-yang symbol on the ground. He waved his sword in a pattern. Stone rumbled and shook as the symbol spiraled open to a black abyss.

He dropped the portal-lens into the hole.

"No!" Zack screamed.

He didn't hesitate. He didn't think. He didn't care that his hands were cuffed.

He ran and dove in after it.

The shocked cries of the emperors and immortals echoed in his mind as he plunged through windy darkness, then splashed into a tunneling vortex of black water.

15

How to Turn the Tides. Literally.

ZACK HAD ALWAYS WANTED TO GO TO A WATER PARK. BUT since his mom could never go because of modesty reasons and no friend had ever invited him to one, he'd never gotten the chance.

He didn't want to go anymore. Not after this. Ever.

He felt as if he were tumbling down the world's steepest waterslide. The air shocked out of his lungs. His chest clenched for more but couldn't find anything but cold water. His nose stung as water stabbed up his nostrils. With his hands cuffed, he couldn't brace against anything. His body smashed through aches and pains like a can going down a trash chute.

At least the darkness meant the portal-lens bobbled visibly ahead of him like an anglerfish. He made grab after grab for it before finally snatching hold.

Magic rushed back into him, relieving the pressure in his chest somewhat. But the moment he tried to control the water, pain flashed through his meridians like a wound tearing open.

He remained at the mercy of the torrent until it spat him into the ocean.

The water turned salty in his mouth, and the darkness pulled away into a dark blue. His bruised body no longer bumped into walls, but a current kept tugging at him. Faintly, he saw a widening slit of blackness in the ambient blue—a trench? Was that the Return Point of Nothingness? What would it do to him? He held his portal-lens over his eyes in hope of some guidance from Qin Shi Huang, but his vision was so blurry and gritty that he couldn't make out anything on the interface.

Zack was so tired. Everything hurt so much. Maybe it'd be better if he . . .

A hand spun him around by his shoulder. A golden light gleamed in his face, then got shoved into his mouth. It was a small, solid orb that bashed against his teeth, making him jerk back, but it gave off such a pleasant, buzzing warmth that he trusted and swallowed it.

The warmth trailed down his throat and spread through his body like a gulp of his mom's beef broth during the deep Maine winter. It melted his pain and hunger and heightened his senses. He no longer felt like he needed to breathe.

Tang Taizong's—well, Simon's—face sharpened in Zack's view. But his expression was panicked. He beckoned urgently with his hand, then pointed behind Zack.

The Return Point, the Guixu, kept sucking them closer like an underwater black hole.

Zack clenched his fists. The cuffs no longer burned his skin. With a harsh jut of his elbows, he snapped them apart, freeing his arms. Amazement swelled through him but was quickly replaced by alarm when the Guixu's pull grew stronger, almost sucking off his sandal.

Zack threw an arm around Tang Taizong and furiously kicked his legs while willing the seawater to propel them upward. The water slowly turned lighter as the ocean surface became visible, webbed with shining sunlight. Zack reached for it, the light marbling his arm. The surface loomed closer and closer until he broke through it with a mighty cough.

Water retched out of him. Swirling his hand, he flung away every droplet clogging his lungs and clinging to his head. He shook his hair, now magically dry.

"Kid," Tang Taizong exclaimed between his own bout of coughing, latching on to Zack's shoulders. "You're a genius!" He shook Zack, eyes wide with giddiness. "You forced their hand! They had no choice but to send me down with an immortality pill, or they would've been guilty of condemning a kid to death! Amazing! Marvelous! Absolutely astounding!"

"They seriously did that?" Zack gaped. "So I'm immortal now?"

"For about a day, yes! I must admit, kid: I am truly impressed with your bravery. The Guixu could've shredded your body *and* your spirit!"

"It could have?" Zack's brows shot all the way up.

Tang Taizong's mouth dangled, his expression mellowing. He pressed his lips together for a moment before saying, "Maybe it was best that you were uninformed, then."

The tunnel must've been magic that could transcend physical space, because although Zack had taken quite a long dive, it couldn't have been as far as the three immortal islands now were. Holding on to Tang Taizong, Zack swam back toward them with the propulsive help of seawater, as if he were a cyborg mermaid. The mountains appeared to expand across the horizon as they got closer.

A herd of cloud-borne immortals gathered at the mountainside Zack headed for. There wasn't a beach or anything, so Zack and Tang Taizong ended up climbing onto some rocks. Zack dried them both with a wave of his hand.

Lü Dongbin and the rest of the Eight Immortals descended on clouds, looking tense and anxious. Lady He held Wu Zetian in her grip—as a hostage? Zack hoped not.

He was about to give an awkward bow in thanks, but then Xu Fu rode in at the edge of his view, and Zack didn't feel like looking weak anymore.

"Thank you all for giving me this chance," Zack said instead, flatly. "I promise I won't use this magic for evil."

Lü Dongbin sighed through his nose. "Very well."

"Will you still accompany us on our mission?" Tang Taizong asked.

Lü Dongbin exchanged weighted looks with his peers before saying, "We shall lure away the Dragon King's army by rousing a supernatural commotion on the seas. That is all."

Qin Shi Huang: Ah.

Qin Shi Huang: They don't want to risk being double-crossed by me while being too far from the islands and at their weakest.

Exasperation crested in Zack. Sure, the immortals had good reason to be wary of Qin Shi Huang, but their extreme caution was getting really old. Thinking back on how they'd treated him—locking him in a cave for five days, starving him, cuffing him with wood that burned him, chucking his portal-lens down an abyss of doom despite his pleas—Zack got so annoyed that he swung his arms up, channeling his magic with maximum force. His meridians beamed golden with the power of the pill in his stomach. A huge tsunami whooshed up behind him. The salty, misty wind it made lifted his hair.

The Eight lunged for their talismans as if drawing weapons. The regular immortals screamed, scooting back on their clouds.

Zack gave a bitter smile, particularly at Xu Fu, then snapped his fists closed. The tsunami dropped, collapsing into the ocean with foam like a fizzing soda. "Just kidding!" He threw his palms up. "Still not evil!"

The immortals muttered among themselves.

Tang Taizong struggled to hold back a laugh. "Kid, why'd you do that?"

"Because I could," Zack muttered.

The *how* of getting to the Dragon Palace required an encore from Li Bai, who'd sat out the trial due to his collusion. In his poems, he compared himself a lot to a *kūnpéng,* a mythological creature that could change between a whale and a huge bird. Zack actually knew that one from *Mythrealm.* A boy on his team, Blake, had caught one near a waterfall when he'd gone on vacation. It could change between Water type and Wind type.

How surreal, the difference between Zack's life then and his life now.

Thinking back, Zack realized his teammates weren't much of friends at all. Especially Aiden. Zack couldn't believe he used to live under Aiden's thumb, walking on eggshells just to be part of the group. What had been the point? Not like they ever accepted him for real. Everything he'd worried about at school seemed so laughable compared to what he had to deal with now.

Simon had said he'd wiped everyone's memories of the possession incident, but what Zack really wanted to do was go back, flash his powers in front of Aiden, then walk away, knowing nobody would believe Aiden when he screamed about it. Maybe that was petty, but Zack didn't care anymore.

Zack, the emperors, and Li Bai hitched a ride on the Eight Immortals' talismans to where the peaceful silver sea met the gloomy black one, which seemed to act like a magical barrier to protect the islands. Standing on Lady He's lotus, Wu Zetian and Tang Taizong each pressed a hand to Li Bai's back. With their new access to the islands' magic through the pills they'd swallowed, they helped manifest his poem into existence.

"One day the great péng *bird will rise with the wind, ninety thousand leagues straight up like a twister,"* the three of them recited together. *"Even if the wind takes a rest, one flap of its wings can still dry the ocean!"*

The emperors' meridians lit up golden, while Li Bai's spirit form glowed brighter. He gasped, eyes beaming brilliant white. The trio chanted the lines over and over. Just when Zack was wondering where this was going, the black sea stirred with increasing ferocity. A blue glimmer swept in beneath its waves.

With a hurl of water that would've thrown them all off the talismans if Zack hadn't kept the waves in check, a blue whale lurched out of the black sea. Beautiful white lines patterned its colossal body.

"Wait, is that the whale that knocked our lifeboat over?" Zack exclaimed in offense.

"It's no whale," Li Bai breathed. "This is the *kūnpéng.*"

He was right. No whale had flippers that long and vast. When the *kūnpéng* flapped them, blue feathers appeared wherever a patch dried off. Salty moisture swirled through the air like mist and showered down like rain. Buoying above the churning surface, the *kūnpéng* leaned toward Li Bai. Li Bai touched his hand and forehead to its huge snout. Reciting his poem one more time, his form scattered into tresses of white light and merged into the *kūnpéng's* shining patterns. The *kūnpéng* opened its gigantic mouth, making a songlike sound that echoed across the sea.

"That's our entrance," Tang Taizong said.

"We're riding inside?" Zack said. "Like Pinocchio?"

"There's no better covert magical submarine," Wu Zetian quipped.

"Indeed." Tang Taizong patted Zack on the back. "You ready to heist a Dragon King's treasure stash, kid?"

"No," Zack mumbled. "But when has that ever mattered?"

16

How It Feels to Have an Easy Fight for Once

ZACK, SIMON, AND MELISSA RODE IN THE *KŪNPÉNG*'S LUMI-
nous mouth, sitting on its soft tongue. A strong hint of salt
lingered in the damp air. Thankfully, it didn't smell too bad.
Zack reckoned that a mythical creature didn't need to eat, so
there were no rotting food particles lodged anywhere.

"Hey, so . . ." Melissa peered at Zack with her head low. The
blue light painted them like they were in a game of laser tag.
"Sorry for ever acting like you were an annoying burden to the
team. You're actually surprisingly hard-core."

"You thought I was an annoying burden?" Zack recoiled.

"Not anymore! It was just that you didn't know anything in
the beginning and kept messing things up and we had to go
on a whole detour for the Shang Yang vessel, so . . . But you're
definitely not a burden anymore." She waved her arms. "Far
from it."

"Yeah, thanks for getting us away from those birds and mermaids and angry Chu people." Simon scratched his own head,
eyelids fluttering. "It looked really intense. I watched the

whole thing from inside my mind and could hear you scream-ing. I felt so bad. So, really, thank you."

"It was nothing." Zack blushed, looking down. "Well, actu-ally, it hurt a lot—like, a *lot*—and cost us several days, but we're here now." He gestured around the *kūnpéng*'s mouth. "Though it's true that I still don't know what's going on half the time. I'm just rolling with it. Speaking of, you never fin-ished that second story—what was that about a fortress com-mander's wife being pregnant for three years?"

"Uh—" Simon and Melissa looked at each other.

Did Zack remember the detail wrong?

"The second Dragon King story?" he tried again.

"Right." Simon blinked but seemed distracted.

"Do you really wanna hear the story?" Melissa said. "It's kind of long-winded and confusing."

Simon tilted his head. "Yeah, and you know what? It's not really that important."

Zack frowned. "You *never* think history stories aren't import-ant."

"Well . . . I just feel bad about boring you all the time."

"Boring me? Simon, I don't think your stories are boring. What do you take me for?" A sharp pain struck Zack's heart. He had jumped from school to school enough times to know that friendships were hard to maintain after moving apart, but this adventure was truly something special. He didn't know if he'd somehow given off the impression that he was eager to be rid of Simon and Melissa, but that couldn't be further from the truth. Even after going back to America, Zack wanted to keep in touch and hear more of Simon's stories. "C'mon," he insisted. "Try me."

"Okay, um," Simon said. "The fortress commander's wife ended up giving birth to this super-powerful child who could walk and talk right away. He was so powerful that by the time he was seven, him just taking a bath in the East Sea was enough to rock the waves and startle the Dragon King. The Dragon King sent up a scout to investigate what was happening, who saw the child and scolded him. The child got so pissed, he killed the scout, then killed the Dragon King's son when he came as backup. He even tore out that dragon prince's tendons. The Dragon King was understandably furious at what Nezha did—"

"*The child,*" Melissa corrected, eyes flying wide in alarm. "What *the child* did."

"Oh, yeah, the child!" Simon smacked himself in the forehead. "You don't have to remember his name. It's a weird one."

"What, Nezha?" Zack said. "That's fine. I can remember that. *Nuh-zha.*"

"You really don't have to!" Melissa flashed an overly bright smile.

A sour mix of irritation and sadness churned in Zack like the ocean currents outside. "Listen, guys, you don't have to simplify things for me. I'm not *that* bad at understanding these stories. I'm following along fine so far. The Dragon King was pissed off at Nezha for killing his son. And then?"

"And theeeeen he went to report . . . Nezha . . . to the Heavenly Emperor," Simon said, looking nervous for some reason. "But Nezha caught him at the gates of the Heavenly Palace and beat him up so badly that he had to slither away as a small snake instead of a dragon."

"Wait, so this Nezha is a real spirit, right?" Zack looked around, though he couldn't see outside the *kūnpéng*. "Is that why you guys are acting so weird? Are you scared he might show up? 'Cause he sounds pretty mean."

"Yeah . . . yeah!" Melissa blew out a huge sigh, shaking her head. "You can never predict who might attack us, you know?"

"Then why didn't you just say so?"

Simon burst out laughing, though it sounded weirdly stiff and wooden. "Getting Melissa to admit she's scared? I mean, come on!"

Zack held back his own laugh. Simon must've been freaked out as well. "All right, you don't have to use his name. Just call him 'the child.'"

"Okay." Simon made a calming motion with his hands. "So the Heavenly Emperor got wind of what the child did, and condemned the entire town he was born in because of it. Not wanting to let his family and neighbors suffer, the child took his own life to make up for the stuff he did. A Daoist sage later gave him a new immortal body made out of a lotus, but that's another story."

"And it's not important," Melissa said.

"Yeah. Not important. The Dragon King's not in it anymore."

Zack stroked his lips. "So an angry kid born with too much power killed a scout and a prince and beat up the Dragon King and then killed himself so other people wouldn't be punished 'cause of him. Okay. That wasn't so hard to get."

"Well, we're leaving out a lot of details," Simon said.

"That don't matter either!" Melissa insisted.

"Nothing that could help us defeat the Dragon King?" Zack asked. "He doesn't have a special weakness in these legends or something?"

"Nah, we can just unleash our powers on him until he begs for mercy," she said.

"It should be easy," Simon said. "All the Dragon King does in the legends is get beat up."

"Yeah, we got this." Melissa clapped her hands together, grinning.

"Awesome." Zack sighed in relief.

It was about time they had an easy fight.

The farther they cruised from the islands, the dimmer the *kūn-péng* shone. By the time it slowed to a stop, Zack could barely see Simon's and Melissa's faces. The three of them stripped down to the Olympic-style swimsuits they'd packed in Shanghai and then put on under their clothes before embarking from Penglai. The immortality pills would keep them from freezing to death or needing oxygen. Supposedly.

"Are we sure the pills still work out here?" Zack checked his hands after stuffing his regular clothes into his backpack. His fingers were almost silhouettes in the dimness. Simon had mentioned that the pills, like the *kūnpéng*, were dependent on Penglai's magic.

Simon put a finger to his temple in concentration, then said, "Tang Taizong's telling me the islands' magic does have a smaller range than expected, but we should hold out fine. Worst-case scenario, the pills will wear off sooner. But we've got plenty of leeway. There's no way we'll take *that* long to get the seal."

"Especially with the Eight Immortals distracting most of the Dragon King's army." Melissa also looked deep in thought while putting her backpack on again, probably talking to Wu Zetian in her head. "We won't have to sneak around anymore. We can just swim straight for the treasure chamber and heist the seal. Though Wu Zetian says she and Tang Taizong should still take a back seat so their spirit signatures don't attract every remaining soldier in the palace at once. You ready?" she asked Simon.

"Oh boy." Simon peered at Zack, tightening the straps of his own backpack so it fit snugly against himself. "Guess I'll also have to take some pain for the sake of magic."

Since the pills didn't give them the ability to talk under water, and neither did their emperors' magic, Simon and Melissa summoned their weapons right then. The constructs both beamed golden. Simon grimaced at his bow and its self-punishing arrows. Melissa upgraded her spirit whip to her spirit hammer. Unfortunately, sustaining the chant for

Zack's sword was gonna be impossible, so he just strapped on his goggles extension and prepared to use his water powers to help.

"Remember to keep your lips zipped if you don't want a mouthful of salt!" Simon put his free hand to the roof of the *kūnpéng*'s mouth. The mouth gaped open. Water coursed inside. Zack instinctively tried to hold it back or at least save the air bubble around them, but the effort was as impossible as when he'd tried to keep the lifeboat from sinking. They became submerged in milliseconds. To Zack's amazement, it really didn't affect his body. He didn't feel cold, and no urge to breathe seized his lungs.

But the spectacle far across the dark waters stunned him even more. It was another palace city, except the Chinese-style buildings looked to be made of radiant blue crystal.

After saying goodbye to Li Bai and the *kūnpéng*—they planned on regrouping with the Eight Immortals for their way back to land, a safer option than risking an underwater chase—Zack, Simon, and Melissa swam toward the city. Zack surged the water around them so even the weight of their backpacks didn't slow them down. The closer they got, the more details transfixed Zack. Intricate motifs were carved into every surface of the crystal buildings, like murals of corals, crustaceans, fish, and other sea creatures, as beautiful as ice sculptures. Searchlights swept up from the city, their long blue beams scattering into the abyss. Only when a burst of salt attacked Zack's tongue did he realize his jaw had slipped open. He spewed out as much of the taste as he could and commanded himself to stay more vigilant. They were entering enemy territory, after all.

Just when Zack wondered if Simon and Melissa had any idea where the seal was, he sensed it. Unimaginable power, concentrated at a single point at a specific building near the center of the expansive palace complex. They really could just swim right over.

If it weren't for the soldiers.

Of course the Dragon King wouldn't leave his palace totally unguarded. The first soldiers rushed up as soon as the glow of the city grazed Zack and his friends. He'd heard the term "prawn soldiers and crab generals" being used to describe the Dragon King's army, and now he knew why. They literally looked like giant prawns, lobsters, and crabs, though they were patterned with shining blue and humanoid enough to hold what looked like sci-fi laser guns. Spirit beams spewed out of the guns, coming straight for Zack's squad. He felt like he'd intruded into an Aquaman movie. It was almost weird that the guns didn't go *pew pew pew* as they fired.

Simon loosed several quick spirit arrows. Each stricken soldier seized up and shattered into blue specks like stardust, but Simon also winced from the recoil of pain. The ones he didn't get, Melissa smashed into glitter with her spirit hammer. Since Zack couldn't vanquish anything without a spirit weapon, he focused on propelling his squad toward their target. Simon and Melissa defended him from the streams of incoming soldiers while racing above the palace complex. As intense as things got, it was eerily quiet, nothing but the whooshing of water.

The double doors of each building were built into their sloped, tiled roofs. Zack brought his squad down to the right building in a vortex of bubbles. With several swings of her hammer, Melissa bashed its doors open.

The hole gaped into an astonishing treasure chamber bigger than a gym and piled full of glimmering bronzes, jeweled ornaments, and patterned porcelain, all distorted by shimmering currents. Pale lines like the water reflections in a cave undulated on the chamber's crystal walls. And in the middle of it all, in a glass box, on a pearly pedestal, there it was: the lost Heirloom Seal of the Realm. The most significant artifact in Chinese history, carved by Qin Shi Huang and passed down through the dynasties from emperor to emperor.

Anticipation pounded through Zack's every vein. The seal was no bigger than someone's palm, yet he could feel that the moment he touched it, he would be unstoppable. This battle would be over.

He lunged down.

Just before his fingers met the glass box, the water around him suddenly squeezed against him. He couldn't move anymore.

Qin Shi Huang: What are you doing?

Qin Shi Huang: Free yourself!

Zack couldn't. No matter how hard he mentally screamed at the water, it wouldn't respond to his command. Instead, it pried him upright and brought Simon and Melissa down next to him. An invisible force wrenched their hands open. Their spirit weapons smeared out like dissolved candy.

"Arrogant mortals!" a gravelly voice hummed right against Zack's skull, not unlike how his portal-lens speakers conducted sound through bone. "Did you really think I'd allow my home to be devastated *yet again*?"

A figure floated in from a crystal hallway in front of the chamber. It had a human-sized body dressed in fancy green robes, yet its head was that of a Chinese dragon, with antlers, blue skin, and a long, whiskered snout. A headdress like Qin Shi Huang's sat between his antlers.

"I have spent the past millennium doing nothing but cultivating my powers over my kingdom!" It must've been the Dragon King talking, yet his snout/mouth didn't move. The sound of his voice came out of the water itself. "I have gained utter control of every molecule of water that surrounds my home. I can sense everything down to the tiniest drifting krill. But you didn't realize that, did you? No, you three . . ." The Dragon King glided in front of Zack's squad. "The great and mighty Wu Zetian, Tang Taizong, and Qin Shi Huang . . ." He looked each of them in the eye. "You were arrogant enough to think you could break into the heart of my palace, where my power is at its strongest. Well, now you shall never escape my control. You shall serve as fine trophies, effective warnings to all who dare think of invading my home in the future."

Zack might've been immune from the cold, yet an icy fear

soaked through him, a fear that the Dragon King was right. The power of the Heirloom Seal pulled at him, inches from his back, yet he couldn't channel it. He couldn't do anything. The water's grip on him was as strong as solid concrete. The only things he could move were his eyes, dry in his goggles.

The water spun him and the others so they faced the seal directly.

"It pains you, doesn't it?" The Dragon King drifted behind the display case and placed a blue hand on it. His skin was tough as leather, and his nails were long as claws. "To be so close to what you schemed for, bled for, killed for in your mortal life, yet powerless from reaching it?"

Zack prayed for the Dragon King's hand to accidentally crush the case or something, but of course that didn't happen. Frustration built in him like lava without a volcano to rupture through. He wanted the seal so badly that he would've happily broken his own arm to lay his hand on it, yet nothing would go his way. He was trapped in his own body. And he was scared there really wasn't a way out. They'd be locked up at the bottom of the ocean, and the immortality pills would wear off, and then . . .

Tears surged and wobbled in his eyes. He looked at the Dragon King pleadingly, silently begging him to let them go.

The Dragon King's expression shifted. He looked closer at Zack, his long snout almost touching Zack's chin. "You're . . . not Qin Shi Huang! You can't be. I have never known Qin Shi Huang to show fear like this."

The Dragon King pulled back and swept an accusing glare across the three of them, though Tang Taizong and Wu Zetian had taken over for Simon and Melissa, as indicated by their virtual tags. Their glares seethed with hatred.

Zack wished he could also retreat into his body and let a legendary emperor face reality for him when things got too much. But no. He was on his own. He had nowhere to run.

Qin Shi Huang: Don't panic.

Qin Shi Huang: There has to be a way out.

Qin Shi Huang: There always is.

Or . . . Zack wasn't entirely on his own, he supposed. Harder than ever, he prayed for Qin Shi Huang to unleash the world-conquering maneuvers he bragged so much about.

Get us out of this! Zack wanted to yell.

The Dragon King glided around the display case and back toward the hallway he had come from, green robes drifting. The water hauled Zack and the emperors after him like three statues.

Dread pulsated harder inside Zack. What was happening? Where were they being taken? Was it good or bad that the Dragon King had realized he was an impostor?

The water held Zack so tightly he couldn't even shake in fright. At the end of the hall, the Dragon King stepped through a barrier membrane that distorted and hazed his form.

When Zack and the emperors were pulled through, the sweet, dry feeling of *air* hit his face, but the rest of their bodies were held back from crossing.

Wu Zetian composed herself first. *"Like the sun and moon—"*

Her incantation cut off with a wet gurgle. A band of water flowed around her mouth like a gag.

The Dragon King stepped onto a dais and sat down on an elaborate throne, made of the same glowing blue crystal as everything else. He then spoke with his real mouth, his rumbling voice booming through the cathedral-sized throne room. "You boys try anything like that, and you will be silenced as well. For good."

A pair of lobster-headed soldiers stood guard on either side of his throne. Chiseled crystal pillars spread through the dim blue ambiance. They soared high into a ceiling of pure wavering water, which cast down a flowing white-and-blue light.

"You—" Tang Taizong wheezed. "You aren't supposed to be this powerful! There are no records, no legends about it!"

"Oh? I suppose the mortals are simply late to catch up. I should thank them for keeping my element of surprise. But if they weren't caught up on my power before, this will surely update them. Perhaps there is someone out there right now getting the inspiration to spin a tale about how the Dragon King of the East took down three of the mightiest emperors in Chinese history."

"There won't *be* anyone to tell your legends if you don't give us the Heirloom Seal!" Tang Taizong retorted. "The spirit portal is loosening, and what comes out might—"

"Throw the mortal world into chaos and possibly cause the extinction of humanity. Yes, yes. I am also fine with that."

Tang Taizong's head recoiled against the wall of water holding them. "You *are*?"

The Dragon King's expression darkened in the throne room's watery blue light. "Think of how the mortals have dumped their trash into the ocean, polluted its waters, and fished its species to mass extinction. I would happily let them fight themselves into oblivion."

"But it would mean your legend would die out. And so would *you!*"

The Dragon King was silent for a beat. Then he said, "If that shall restore peace and life to the ocean, that is a sacrifice I am willing to make."

"You can't be seriou—"

With a wave of his hand, the Dragon King gagged Tang Taizong with water as well. "I will hear no more of this." His attention swiveled onto Zack. "Now, boy. Care to explain your situation?"

Qin Shi Huang: Kid, you're our last chance.

Qin Shi Huang: GET HIS SYMPATHY HOWEVER YOU CAN.

Are you kidding me? Zack almost screamed.

Qin Shi Huang didn't have any ideas? It was up to *Zack*?

"Okay, Lord Dragon King, sir, Your Majesty. I—I'm here because Qin Shi Huang didn't possess me properly," Zack stammered, fearing any word could be his last. "And because of that, I couldn't stop demons from stealing my mother's spirit. So I need that Heirloom Seal to save her."

The Dragon King burst into bellowing laughter, the sound

echoing off the glowing crystal walls until it sounded like a whole army of him was mocking Zack. "Oh, that is rich! Qin Shi Huang, failing to get what he wants because of a little boy. But this cheap attempt at earning my sympathy will not work. Goodbye." The Dragon King raised his clawed hand.

"*What would you do with the Heirloom Seal if you could use it?*" Zack blurted.

"I beg your pardon?" The Dragon King's hand lowered somewhat.

"You can feel its power, right? Or you wouldn't have hoarded it. But I was told you have to have the spirit of a legendary emperor to use that power, or else it's just a pretty rock. Doesn't that make you mad? If that restriction wasn't there, what would you do?"

"Why are you asking?" the Dragon King snapped, yet put his hand down entirely.

"*We're* legendary emperors." Zack panted in desperation. "So we could use the seal to do something for you. Something you otherwise can't make happen. As long as it's not as extreme as killing all humans, I mean."

Qin Shi Huang: Oh, this is a good angle!

Qin Shi Huang: Keep going!

The Dragon King stamped a fist on his throne's wide armrest. "Of course I don't wish to kill all humans! I simply would not stop them from slaughtering themselves. But are you seriously suggesting a bargain with me? Why would I ever trust a bargain with *you*?"

"Because I'm not Qin Shi Huang! He can't control what I do, or he'd be taking me over to yell at you right now. The reason he couldn't bond to me was because I wasn't raised with a big spiritual connection to Chinese legends. I don't know your story by heart. So as long as you want something reasonable, I have no reason to betray you."

The Dragon King's slit-pupil eyes fell shut. He drew his claws over his lap. "The only thing I have ever wanted is to protect my home and ensure it can never be invaded or sullied again. You could never stay down here as a soldier in my army, so what help could you be to me?"

"We could help in other ways! We'll become environmentalists! We'll campaign against SeaWorld! Oh—why do people even keep attacking you? I don't actually have a clear sense of who you are. Are you some kind of cruel sea tyrant who terrorizes the shores or something?"

"Of course not! At least, not for the past three thousand years! Ever since that menace Nezha killed my son and almost destroyed my palace, I have done nothing but mind my own business. Yet those like you keep charging in or wreaking havoc in my waters, with no regard to the well-being of my citizens!"

Zack furrowed his brow, puzzled. "Would you have lent us the Heirloom Seal if we had asked nicely?"

"If you had treated me with respect, perhaps!"

Zack angled his head as much as he could to glare at the emperors. "So none of you thought to just *ask* him for the seal?"

Their eyes darted away in guilt.

"Of course they did not," the Dragon King said bitterly. "Wrecking my palace is practically a cultural tradition. Even now, the Eight Immortals are trying to do it for the second time. But no more!" His gaze sharpened. "Not after word gets out that I bested the three of you."

"What if . . . what if we defeated the Eight Immortals in your name?" Zack suggested, heart beating faster against his trapped chest. "If you still haven't taken them down, that must mean you're evenly matched, right? You would get weaker if you went out to meet them in battle, but *we* wouldn't. We can fight them. Get revenge for you."

"Please, don't think I didn't realize they're in cahoots with you! You must've taken their pills to survive down here in your mortal bodies."

"But we can double-cross them."

In Zack's periphery, Tang Taizong's eyes widened.

Qin Shi Huang: KID, WHAT ARE YOU—

Qin Shi Huang: Never mind.

Qin Shi Huang: Never mind, this could actually work.

"You wouldn't," the Dragon King said, though his tone teetered on the edge of uncertainty.

"Why not?" Zack said with an almost mad, manic laugh. He had nothing left to lose. "I don't think there's anything inherently good about them or inherently bad about you. Actually, they didn't treat me very well, and I'm honestly a little pissed about it. They only gave me a pill 'cause I would've died if they hadn't. Long story."

The Dragon King leaned back in his throne, brows drawn tight, claws drumming against his armrest.

"Come on," Zack nudged. "I'm Qin Shi Huang's host. You think I wouldn't happily double-cross some immortals? They're even expecting me to do it. That's why they didn't come down with us. Wouldn't three emperors fighting an epic battle in your name with the Eight Immortals make a way more exciting legend than you just trapping us here with water? If legends are to be remembered, they have to be exciting!"

The Dragon King was silent for another long spell before saying, "*After.* Vanquish the Eight Immortals as part of my army, and I shall grant you the Heirloom Seal *afterward.*"

How to Slay Immortals By Becoming Underwater Darth Vader

ZACK AND THE EMPERORS RODE TOWARD THE SURFACE ON small sharks fitted with radiant blue armor. Now they really looked like they belonged in an Aquaman movie. It was a new extreme on the List of Things He Never Thought He'd Be Doing, But He Was Doing Anyway.

To keep some control over Zack's squad after they left the palace, the Dragon King had conjured armor over them as well, made of the blue crystal he could freely command. The helmets, which left only two sharp slants of peepholes for their eyes, jutted up like lobster heads, making them blend with the rest of the soldiers rushing up through the black waters. The way their armor curved over their backpacks made them look even more crustacean-like. Bubble trails streaked behind the army, reflecting their armor lights. They couldn't talk, but Wu Zetian and Tang Taizong passed Zack plenty of *Hope you know what you're doing* looks from behind their helmets.

Zack did not, in fact, know what he was doing. His head was

a big mess filled with his pounding pulse. But he saw no choice but to push onward.

It didn't take long for him to see why a surface attack by the Eight Immortals would warrant a response from the Dragon King's army. The water roiled like a storm. He had to hang on fiercely to his shark's reins with one hand while steadying the currents with his other. Using his water powers felt like being able to breathe again after being crushed between two walls.

Beams of light flashed above, shot from the guns of luminous soldiers. The immortals fought back with their talismans, starkly visible among the masses of blue armor. With the water so dark, it looked exactly like a space battle, except without the noises. Though, according to Zack's science teacher, there shouldn't be any sound during a battle in space in the first place.

Qin Shi Huang: Take out their leader Lü Dongbin and the fan-wielder Zhongli Quan first.

Qin Shi Huang: They're the most powerful.

A spasm jolted through Zack's nerves. Sure, he'd been all gung ho about betraying the Eight, but the thought of vanquishing them for real gave him pause. It was true that they would respawn eventually, but they would lose any memories that hadn't been passed on by Chinese culture. Was it okay for Zack to do that to them just to get what he wanted?

On the other hand, if they had fought with his squad down at the Dragon Palace, maybe things would've gone differently.

A tag on his portal-lens encircled and alerted him to the

presence of Zhongli Quan, the bare-chested, potbellied immortal with his hair done up in twin buns. As he gleefully swung his huge fan, soldiers were consistently pushed back to a wide berth around him.

Qin Shi Huang: Hold him in place with water so Tang Taizong can vanquish him with an arrow.

Oh no. It's really happening.

The thought of running away flashed through Zack's mind. The Dragon King had threatened to pull them back down if they "made a single move out of line," but Zack was pretty sure he was far enough from the palace that he could escape if he really tried.

But then he'd lose all hope of getting the Heirloom Seal— and with it, all hope of saving his mom and the rest of China in seven days.

Zack nudged Tang Taizong with his elbow and pointed at Zhongli Quan. Tang Taizong nodded, readying his bow. The Dragon King had let him and Wu Zetian summon their weapons again in the throne room (before immediately binding their arms with water, of course). At least Zack only had to be an accomplice, not the one taking the shot.

Sorry, Mr. Zhongli, Zack thought, then tensed his hand into a claw like Darth Vader using the Force.

Zhongli Quan froze mid-fan swing. His eyes widened. By Tang Taizong's rapid hand movements in Zack's periphery, a spirit arrow flew into Zhongli Quan's bare chest. Then another. Then another, until he shattered into glimmers.

The entire battle seemed to stop and turn toward the nebula-like cloud. Several immortals let out silent screams, their mouths forming Zhongli Quan's name. A cold boulder plummeted in Zack's chest.

I've made a huge mistake, he couldn't help but feel.

Qin Shi Huang: QUICK, GET LÜ DONGBIN BEFORE HE SEES YOU.

Qin Shi Huang: NOW.

Another tag highlighted Lü Dongbin in a nearby cluster of soldiers, raising his evil-vanquishing sword as he scanned for Zhongli Quan's attacker. Although Zack's hand shook out of control, he Darth Vader–choked him as well. Tang Taizong quickly worked his bow again.

The arrows hit, but Lü Dongbin was too far for Zack's binding to hold at full strength. He broke free and spotted Zack and the emperors. Yelling without sound, he pointed his sword at them before a final arrow smashed him into spirit glitter.

Now everyone was looking at Zack and the emperors. Iron Crutch Li's expression contorted with rage, sending a stab of guilt and fear through Zack's heart. Iron Crutch Li lunged toward Zack, but Lady He snatched his shoulder and pointed upward.

Qin Shi Huang: She means for them to abscond to the surface to evade our water powers.

Qin Shi Huang: STOP THEM.

Wu Zetian was already charging after them on her shark. Zack yanked his own shark's reins to get it to follow, then stretched out his hand to drag the immortals down with water.

Straining against his power, they gathered around Lady He as they swam. She slashed her arms upward. Her lotus grew huge and twirled shut around them. It rocketed up like a torpedo.

The ocean surface came down much sooner than expected, tumbling with pale patches and creases of moonlight. The trip from Penglai had taken so long that night had fallen.

Lady He's lotus broke out of the ocean, sending tides of foamy ripples across the surface waves.

Qin Shi Huang: Be careful.

Qin Shi Huang: They're far more powerful than you think.

Qin Shi Huang: They weren't taking this battle seriously before, but they will now.

Swallowing the anxiety of possibly charging toward his doom, Zack let his shark erupt out after Wu Zetian's.

The moment seawater splashed away from his head, angry yelling bombarded his ears, mostly colorful variations of "How could you?" But among the berating immortals on the lotus, one faced backward. The child Lan Caihe, throwing handfuls of glowing flowers out of their basket. Instead of falling into the ocean, the blossoms drifted away across the night.

Qin Shi Huang: OH NO!

Qin Shi Huang: LAN CAIHE HAS CALLED FOR BACKUP.

Qin Shi Huang: END THIS BEFORE THEY GET HERE.

Just as Zack launched a tide at them, the immortals unleashed their powers. A fancily dressed one clapped a pair of long castanets, and the tide parted around their lotus. With coaxing motions behind the petals, Lady He thrust out a dizzying scent that made Zack's head spin. An old man started singing while slapping the bottom of a long, slender drum in his arms. The sound waves swept across the ocean like storm winds, buffeting Zack and the emperors backward on their sharks. If that wasn't enough, a loose-robed immortal started playing a flute.

As if they'd caught a whiff of blood, the sharks beneath Zack and the emperors went berserk, bucking and writhing, hurling them off. Just after Zack plunged sideways into the water, his shark's huge jaws full of sharp teeth flashed open before him. Internally screaming, he shoved it away with a blast of water.

The other sharks were doing the same to the emperors. Zack had to focus on forcing the sharks into the depths instead of resisting further attacks by the immortals. He could barely keep track of who was doing what in the onslaught, just that it was like being in a vortex of nauseating agony. The immortals had a clear advantage when they were above the water, so Zack tried to sink them. Yet the fancy man with the castanets broke every wave he heaved.

Qin Shi Huang: USE MY TIME-SLOWING POWER.

Zack was about to, then noticed mists of golden light coming off him and the emperors, being sucked into Iron Crutch Li's gourd. Their *qi* meters shifted.

Zack hadn't paid attention to their meters since the immortality pills had made them solid lengths of gold, but now they were dropping. Shrinking. Depleting.

They were losing their immortality.

Zack violently remembered Qin Shi Huang's story of having to choose between giving up and repenting or gambling everything for total victory during his conquest of Chu. Zack hadn't thought he could ever relate to a story like that, but now he did. The time-slowing magic used a lot of *qi*. He could drain himself if he activated it.

Help, he almost cried into the chaos, but who'd want to help him after this?

Well. There was one dragon-person whose best interest was that they win this fight.

"Your Majesty!" Zack hollered down at his armor, using all his power to keep the tumbling water out of his mouth. "I don't know if you can hear me, but we've seriously pissed off the immortals, and it turns out they're way stronger than we can handle! And they've got backup coming! And our immortality is wearing off! If you don't give us the seal, we'll lose this battle, and your reputation will be ruined yet again!"

No response.

Qin Shi Huang: KID, JUST FIGHT.

How?

It was six immortals empowered by rage versus the three of them, who'd soon have to worry about drowning in the ice-cold water. Wu Zetian unleashed her flash bomb power, and Tang Taizong kept loosing arrows, but the immortals worked in perfect harmony, defending themselves while disrupting every attack. Zack's immortal *qi* dropped to its last stretches.

And he was getting sleepier. It must've been an effect of Lady He's lotus fragrance.

"Guys, I'm pretty sure the moment we lose our immortality, we're gonna pass out from this smell!" he said. But the emperors were too busy trying out more incantations to listen.

There was no longer any time to waste.

Zack drew a riptide to drag the three of them deep underwater. The emperors flailed and thrashed, but Zack relaxed. He closed his eyes, letting go. Maybe the only way to win was to admit there was no possibility of it.

Not unless they had help.

Your move, Dragon King.

He sank almost peacefully on the last bit of his immortality, the weight of his armor and backpack pulling him down like an anchor.

And then he felt it: a massive power surging up from the depths of the ocean.

A glowing blue box spun up beside Zack. He lunged to rip it open. The seal was inside. He snatched it into his grip.

A shock wave radiated out from him, shearing through the ocean. Countless images flashed behind his eyes. Qin Shi Huang being offered the legendary *Héshìbì* jade by a king groveling on the ground. Qin Shi Huang's most trusted minister writing the inscription to make it China's official imperial seal. Qin Shi Huang using that seal over and over to issue edicts that would define China for the next two thousand years.

And not just Qin Shi Huang. The images sped up, flurrying

through the lives of the hundreds of others who'd wielded the seal after him. Zack saw it being offered up by last rulers of dynasties, being snatched by victorious warlords. An empress dowager threw it to the ground in a fit of helpless rage, chipping its corner, as a usurper surrounded her chambers and demanded her surrender after they had deposed the child emperor. The usurper restored the corner with gold before being overthrown himself. It tumbled from bloody hand to bloody hand, gaining more inscriptions as founders of new dynasties tried to justify their rule, becoming more powerful as more people fought and killed for it as a symbol of ultimate power. Including Tang Taizong. Zack's visions stuttered when he sensed the familiar presence, then very quickly Wu Zetian's, and all the emotions she'd felt as she pulled off what no other woman had done, ruling as a legitimate emperor herself. But they passed as quickly as shooting stars, sending the seal into more war and bloodshed until, finally, a boy too young to know what being emperor meant held the seal as he plunged toward the sea.

The visions shattered. Zack took a huge, long gasp, like some unholy force had stopped pressing his head into a tub of water. Reality slammed back against his senses. He found himself literally out of the water—he hovered above the ocean in a massive, raging cyclone. Foamy seawater whipped and howled around him. His meridians shone glittering gold, so bright that their rays streamed out from between his armor pieces. After so long of channeling foreign Daoist magic, it was like he'd woken up from a deep, nightmare-plagued sleep. This was something born of Qin Shi Huang's own legend, a magic truly meant for him. As it coursed through Zack and out into the world, his arms spread wide. The ocean warped and dented around him like a meteor crater. Storm clouds gathered in the sky above. Zack had felt a faint connection to storms ever since Qin Shi Huang had come into his life, but this one was the first to be utterly under his control. As he willed it, bolts of lightning struck down around him, accompanied by booming thunder. He might've been laughing maniacally, but the storm was so loud, he couldn't hear it. He threw off his helmet. His hair blew wildly in the wet, lashing winds.

Just outside the edge of his water cyclone, the immortals' lotus tossed like a small ship on the huge, heaving waves. They desperately used their talismans to resist their doom.

By a swoop of Zack's arm, a gold-tinged water dragon morphed out of the cyclone and circled around him like a mighty serpent. It roared at the immortals, a world-quaking sound that raced visibly across the waves and blew back their hair and clothes. The immortals shrank away, arms flying up to guard one another. Some looked over their shoulders. In the distance, a glowing flock of their backup brethren closed in on clouds.

Vanquish them, screamed several hundred voices in Zack's head, Qin Shi Huang's the loudest of all. *Conquer their islands! Conquer the seas! Conquer it all!*

Unease streaked through Zack like the lightning coming down all around him.

No, that's not what we came here to do, he reminded the chaos in his head. *We got the seal. We can go.*

Yet the voices intensified. An overwhelming urge to win and conquer and rule tore through him. It took every bit of his willpower to resist it. Floating beyond another side of the cyclone, Tang Taizong and Wu Zetian stared at him, eyes beaming red and white respectively behind their helmets, and he knew they were part of the voices. The gold-tinged water dragon flew faster around him, roar echoing between the sea and sky, seeming to compel him as well. Lightning struck down so often that the night turned as bright as day. Fury and bloodthirst boiled inside Zack's very flesh, growing close to tearing him apart. He cried out, clutching his head.

"Run!" he screamed at the immortals. "Run, *unless you want to die!*"

They simply tried to attack him again with their talismans.

Zack gave another scream from the sheer effort of holding back the destructive power that wanted to burst out of him. He didn't know if he could stop if he let it loose. He didn't want this to turn into a massacre.

He was not a tyrant.

He was not Qin Shi Huang.

"I . . . said . . . *no!*" Zack's voice echoed unnaturally across the sea.

The voices were expelled from his head. Wu Zetian and

Tang Taizong jerked back, eyes dimming. The electric forest of lightning strikes faded. The last of the thunder rolled out.

But the momentum in Zack didn't die down. His every cell kept humming with power that needed somewhere to go. And he decided where that would be: to Qin Shi Huang's mausoleum to reinforce the portal plug and save his mom.

With another swing of his arm, Zack commanded the water dragon to fly directly under him. He dropped onto its head, right behind its wet antlers, then rode it like a tunnel of water toward the emperors.

"What are you doing?" they shrieked as he picked them up, securing them behind him by sinking them partway into the dragon.

"What really matters!" Zack flung his hand forward, fingers outstretched. He could sense the mainland, where the seal's legends were born. The dragon lurched in that direction, soaring away from the immortals.

"No!" Qin Shi Huang yelled from his portal-lens. "You can't run away from this battle!"

"Yes, I can! If we waste magic to win a fight we don't need to, are we really winning? We'd be letting the seal control us, not the other way around! Our priority is the portal plug!"

"The House of Ying does not back down from a war!"

"Says who?" Zack snarled, misty wind howling in his face between the dragon's antlers. "You're the one who taught me to not care about what other people think, and I'm the one who has the Heirloom Seal now! So guess what? *I* make the rules!"

18

How the Great Wall Can Be Appropriated as a Racetrack

THE BATTLE TURNED INTO A CHASE. ZACK'S WATER DRAGON whooshed and undulated across the ocean surface, the immortals hot on its tail via clouds. Clearly they weren't going to forgive what Zack and the emperors had done to Lü Dongbin and Zhongli Quan. The emperors kept yelling at him to turn around and fight, but Zack ignored them. He focused on the legend magic calling to him from the mainland—more specifically, a legend that spanned the north of China, ordered into existence by the very seal in his hand.

The Great Wall.

Zack clutched the seal tighter. Ancient maps flickered in his mind. Where they needed to go was Qin Shi Huang's mausoleum near Mount Li in the city of Xi'an. It was possible to get close by stopping in the middle of the Great Wall near Yulin, an ancient garrison city against the northern nomad tribes.

As he persisted toward his goal, the distance widened between his dragon and the immortals. The armor from the

Dragon King weakened and dissolved into water, probably reaching the limits of the Dragon Palace's magic. Soon they started passing mortal fishing boats and ocean liners. Zack hoped no one happened to be filming. Raising a hand, he summoned storm clouds overhead to block out the moon and stars so that even if someone switched their camera on, the footage would be too dark to prove anything.

Eventually the shoreline sped into view. The exact place they'd visited before this mad ocean voyage: the Old Dragon's Head, where the Great Wall leaned into the sea. It looked like another dragon bowing its head, waiting for Zack. Its Chinese name, the name to invoke its legend, floated into his mind by a cluster of whispers.

"*Wànlǐ chángchéng!*" he called out.

The Long Wall of Ten Thousand Leagues.

Gold light lit up the Old Dragon's Head along the seams of its bricks. Two patches beamed especially bright, looking like two sharp eyes.

The image of a Qin dynasty war chariot flashed in Zack's head, pulled by four horses and a charioteer standing behind them. When his dragon leapt out of the ocean, it shed most of its water and gathered into something similar to the chariot, except it was Zack pulling the chariot on a single water construct shaped like a motorcycle. Wu Zetian and Tang Taizong jarred into the chariot itself.

They slammed onto the Old Dragon's Head. Zack instinctively cringed but leaned over his watercycle and had faith in the seal's pulsing power in his hand. Instead of taking damage, more of the Great Wall lit up ahead. The golden radiance coursed through the night like a futuristic racetrack. Zack knew this wasn't hurting the wall itself. They were racing over its spirit construct, a manifestation of its legend. His watercycle and chariot threaded through radiant watchtowers, going faster and faster. The scenery soon whizzed by so quickly that everything blurred over. There was only the night wind whistling in Zack's ears and the golden path of the Great Wall beneath them.

A sea of neon shocked in from the distance and streamed beside them like the lights outside a rumbling subway. They must've been passing Qinhuangdao's city proper. The lights reached several peaks of brightness, then trailed off.

There was a distinct moment when Zack realized they were no longer within city bounds. The speeding neon buildings turned into sturdy silhouettes of mountains and forests. The stars became visible above. His blood thrummed inside his veins, charged with a restless energy. A lightness rose up inside him, as if he was becoming one with the world. They could've been warping through the cosmos on the golden path of the zodiac.

But it wasn't all amazement and awe. Zack started seeing things, hearing things. The spirits of those who'd died building the Great Wall wailed with the wind, reminding him of the terrible and bloody cost of any ancient wonder. The constructs of dirtied hands grasped at his legs, splashing through his watercycle.

"I'm sorry," Zack choked out over and over, until his voice grew too weak to make another sound.

He had no idea how long they raced for, but by the time he sensed their destination closing in, he was straining everything to his limits.

Almost there, he told himself. *Hold on.*

A map reappeared in his mind, the dot of his chariot inching toward Yulin.

Almost . . . almost . . .

His body ached like he'd been out of air for too long. But he thought of the pain and grief of the laborers. The least he could do was make their sacrifice mean something.

Almost . . .

The moment the dot on the map in his mind reached Yulin, Zack let his water constructs collapse. A sigh left him, like his very spirit was slipping away. His consciousness plummeted with it.

"You are so close, my child . . . so close . . . please don't forget this again. . . ."

Zack was in a lamplit military tent, kneeling on the dusty ground. A general in leather armor knelt beside him. Before them, an imperial messenger guarded by soldiers unrolled a scroll of silk and read out an edict.

"By the command of His Majesty, Prince Fusu and General Meng Tian—you are to take your own lives for your acts of treason!"

"*What?*" The general's head snapped up. "What treason? We have defended the Northern Wilds with nothing but our utmost loyalty!"

"It's no use, General Meng." Tired words left Zack's mouth. Though he internally screamed against it, he felt his hand draw the sword slanted at his waist. "Father has spoken."

"No! Fusu, there has to be a misunderstanding! His Majesty would never command you to take your own life!"

"Why not?" The body Zack was inhabiting raised the sword with both hands, the point directed at his own chest. "*Remember what he did to my mother?*"

No!

Zack's eyes flung open to the sight of Tang Taizong pointing his bow and arrow at him, eyes beaming red. The heat of his magic rippled in Zack's face.

"Ahh!" Zack shot up in the bed he was in, backing against the headboard.

"Hand it over," Tang Taizong growled. "It's mine."

When Zack tensed up, a hard object dug inside his fist. The seal was still in his hand.

"Um, can we talk about this?" Zack raised his free hand in surrender, his voice raspy from disuse. He must've passed out for quite a while.

Oh no, how many days did they have left?

Tang Taizong pulled his bowstring, his spirit arrow shining brighter.

"I command you to drop your bow!" Zack shouted on a burst of urgency. The seal shone inside his fist, gold light leaking between his fingers.

Tang Taizong's eyes flashed from red to gold. He jerked back as if hit with something invisible. His bow vanished like red mist.

"Hey!" Melissa barged through the door of the small bedroom. She threw her hands against her head. "Oh no, Tang Taizong, did you try to kill Zack again? I was in the bathroom for five minutes!"

"*Again?*" Zack wheezed.

"Apologies, kid." Tang Taizong massaged his temples. "That thing is . . . very hard to resist." He swiveled a guilty look between Zack and Melissa. "I should go."

He took a long breath that suddenly hitched. Simon blinked awake. He looked at his hands, then at angry Melissa in the doorway, then at Zack, shrinking against the headboard. "Oh man, did Tang Taizong shove my consciousness down and try to kill Zack again?"

"*How many times have—*" Zack's words came out more high-pitched than he wanted to sound. "Never mind. What happened? Please, please, *please* tell me we didn't miss the deadline!" He pawed at the swimsuit still on his body. It was covered in dirt. Huge bruises sank across his bare arms.

"It's okay; we still have four days," Simon said to Zack's tremendous relief.

"And, boy, you missed so much drama after you passed

out," Melissa quipped. "When the Great Wall construct disappeared, we basically tumbled down on a pile of dirt in the middle of nowhere. 'Cause, you know, most of the wall is long gone. It doesn't all look like the tourist brochures. We didn't want the mess of calling any authorities for a professional rescue, so we had no choice but to walk."

"You two *walked* all the way here?" Zack brushed whole clumps of dirt out of his hair, soreness and hunger sharpening inside him as his adrenaline waned. At least he hadn't slept with his portal-lens on this time; it sat on the nightstand beside the bed. It must've been the seal's power that let him see spirit stuff now.

"No, just toward the nearest village on our phone maps," Melissa said.

"We had to carry you while holding our emperors back from snatching the seal from you though." Simon bugged his eyes at the floor. "So, um. Sorry about all the dirt. And the bruises. We dropped you a few times."

"More than a few times," Melissa mumbled.

"Is that why I'm hurting all over?" Zack grazed the tender patches on the back of his head. He sucked in a breath as his arm ached with the motion.

"Yeah, we're really sorry about that." Simon scratched his elbow.

"You sure are heavy for how tiny you look." Melissa put her hands on her hips. "Thankfully, we ran into this group of backpackers when the sun was getting really nasty. I charmed them into carrying you for the rest of the trek without asking questions; then we sprayed them with Meng Po broth and called a rideshare."

"That's—" Zack decided not to dwell on it. "So where are we now?"

"A place we rented in Yulin," Simon answered, lifting his finger as he went into history professor mode. "It's an ancient frontier city between the Central Plains, where Han Chinese people lived by farming crops, and the Northern Wilds, where nomad tribes like the Mongols lived by hunting and gathering."

The term "Northern Wilds" tickled something deep in Zack's mind—something he should not have forgotten—but then Melissa strode to the window beside the bed and pulled back the curtains.

Zack winced from the light, then blinked at the sight of grimy buildings across a street full of slow-moving cars, honking motorcycles, and pedestrians in face masks. Trees lined the sidewalk, but a haze even worse than Shanghai's hung in the air.

"Why is it so dusty?" He shielded his eyes.

"We're basically in the desert," Simon said. "The Loess Plateau. It's all yellow dirt. They've done a lot of greenery restoration lately, but there's only so much you can do."

"We've been waiting for you to wake up so we can fly to Xi'an," Melissa said. "We thought about calling Yaling to come drive us, but it's, like, a seven-hour trip. We didn't think we could hold the emperors back for that long while being stuck in a car. Better to sit very far apart on a plane. And we couldn't exactly get you on a plane with you unconscious."

"You could've put me in a wheelchair and pretended I was sick," Zack remarked in irritation at them dawdling for this reason alone.

"Would that have worked?" Melissa tilted her head.

"Dunno." Zack rubbed his arms gingerly. "I read it in a book called *Not Even Bones.* That was how the main character's mom transported a boy she kidnapped."

"Well . . . you're awake now. Do you feel okay to move? I wanna book our flight as soon as possible."

"Yes, definitely." Zack swung his legs off the bed. Dirt showered onto the floor. A spell of dizziness swayed his head. "Oh man. I am *so* hungry."

"We'll make you something to eat while you go shower," Melissa said, whipping out her phone. "But take the seal with you! Don't let it leave your sight. The emperors don't need the extra temptation. They say the seal has gotten way more powerful than any of them expected, so it messes with their minds. We don't know what will happen if one of them snatches it."

"That bad?" Zack loosened his grip to examine it. Five entwining dragons were carved on top of a square jade base. One chipped corner was filled in with gold. A dull ache and the red dents in his palms told him he hadn't let go of the seal since getting it.

"I can't even take a bathroom break in peace! Do you know how we slept last night?" Melissa gestured harshly between her and Simon. "In the same bed, with our arms tied together, so neither of us could get possessed and sneak off without the other noticing!"

Simon lowered his head, blushing practically fluorescent red. "We've had to keep each other's emperors in check."

"Though, to be fair, Wu Zetian has only lost control, like, four times."

"Five!"

"That one time doesn't count when I talked her down myself in my head." Melissa poked her tongue out, then addressed Zack again. "She gave her throne back to her son at the age of eighty-two and announced that she wanted to be buried as empress—like, as the wife of her dead emperor husband—instead of emperor herself, so it's easier for her to resist the temptation. Unlike Tang Taizong, who killed all those brothers and nephews to get the throne."

Zack groaned. "I can't believe I used to think he was the nice one."

"Really?" Melissa choked. "Tang Taizong, the nice one? The red eyes never tipped you off?"

"Yeah, actually, I feel him trying to take over again." Simon held his stomach like he was about to throw up. "Let's get out of this room."

"Right!" Melissa shoved Simon out the door. "I just booked the flight. It's in three and a half hours!" she told Zack over her shoulder before slamming the door behind them.

Huffing through his nose, Zack went to clean himself up.

There was so much dirt on Zack, the shower water took several minutes to run clear. He lathered himself with soap and shampoo until his hair squeaked. After he got out, he dug his spare clothes out of his backpack.

His phone fell out with them.

It was dead. Of course, it'd been over a week. He plugged it in to get a bit of charge in before the flight. To keep the seal on him while making it hard for the emperors to heist it, he picked a black shirt with a breast pocket, slipped the seal in, then pulled it on inside out.

Simon had made noodles with a sweet and sour sauce and chopped cucumbers. Zack accepted a bowl of it with a blush. When he'd first gotten on the plane on this journey, he hadn't expected that he'd end up liking Simon Li, the normal boy, way more than Shuda Li, the prodigy world champion. Shuda was cool, so cool that Zack never would've had the courage to speak to him, but Simon was kind, dependable, and *real.* Zack was surprised to discover that he liked being around someone like that way more. He swore that when he got back to America, he'd drop out of his *Mythrealm* team and go befriend whomever he wanted without caring about how other people would judge him.

Since Zack couldn't be around the emperors, he ate in his room while sitting on the bed. The shady supervillain emperors who were supposed to be his teammates were now constantly fighting down the urge to kill him. Great. Just great.

After wolfing down the noodles, Zack couldn't help but turn his phone on. It was counterintuitive to the charging, but he had to check if his mom's body was still fine in the hospital. He figured out how to reroute his IP address with Simon's VPN app, then sent a message to Jess, his mom's friend. It was the middle of the night in Maine, though, so he didn't expect a response.

He went to check what was new on Reddit instead. But the moment he opened a search tab, a different curiosity hit him. He eyed his portal-lens on the nightstand, made sure his phone's Bluetooth was turned off, then typed in *Nezha*.

Why had Simon and Melissa acted so weird about that kid who'd attacked the Dragon King?

When the results appeared, the images up top were a mix of a shirtless teenager with hair like a Super Saiyan and a kid with his hair done up in twin buns, wearing a traditional Chinese tank top above baggy pants. Both had flaming wheels beneath their bare feet and a red sash flowing above their heads and around their arms.

Unease crawled into Zack. His mom had been bound and dragged with a sash like that. Was it something common in Chinese myth?

He tapped on an article about Nezha. The gist he got was that Nezha was a Daoist protection deity who'd evolved from Hindu and Persian myths. He had a bunch of titles like Third Lotus Prince, was a major character in a bunch of classic Chinese books, and wielded a bunch of fire-themed weapons like a flame-tipped spear and the flaming wheels under his feet. He seemed ridiculously overpowered.

But what caught Zack's attention was a picture of Nezha's dad, Pagoda-Bearing Heavenly King Li. He was drawn as a caped and armored man, holding a tiny pagoda in one hand.

Just like what had been used to suck away Zack's mom's spirit.

Blood shriveled away from Zack's fingertips. With a slight tremor, he tapped on the article about the dad. As he read, one factoid hit him like a blow to the stomach:

The Heaven King Li carries a pagoda that can capture spirits. He is based on famed Tang dynasty general Li Jing, who served under emperor Tang Taizong.

19

How to Get What You Want at All Costs

ALL OF ZACK'S SENSES SHRANK TO A SINGLE TREMBLING POINT in his mind, leaving his body limp. He stared blankly at the wall.

Never have I heard of a demon with the ability to capture spirits. Lü Dongbin's words echoed through his empty head like the haunting whispers of a ghost.

Of course not.

Of course not.

Of course not.

Every memory of Simon, Melissa, and the emperors acting weird about his mom's situation tore through him. All those times Simon and Melissa were randomly super nice and apologetic to him . . . all those times they tripped up when talking about Nezha . . .

They knew. This whole time, they *knew.*

Zack lurched up, stomped to the door, and wrenched it open. The handle rattled in his grip.

Simon and Melissa were sitting at the kitchen table, scrolling on their phones. Their heads flew up at the sight of him.

"Zack?" Simon frowned. "You should stay in—"

"Who really took my mom's spirit?" Zack snapped, jaw and neck quivering with tension. He was shaking all over, like his very spirit was humming out of control. Sunlight dimmed outside. Wind howled, hurling a sudden splatter of rain over the kitchen window.

"Uh . . ." Simon slowly got up from his chair, raising his hands. "Sorry, I—"

"I command you to tell me who took my mom's spirit!"

Heat swelled from the seal near Zack's thrashing heart. Simon's eyes flashed gold. Words tumbled from his mouth, "Li Jing did. Tang Taizong summoned him and Nezha into your landlord and his son."

Simon slapped his hands over his mouth, eyes widening in horror.

Zack's next breath shuddered into him. The room spun. He squeezed his eyes shut. Simon's face was now too painful to look at. "You . . . ," he choked out. He could barely get enough air. "You guys staged the attack."

"Zack . . . ," Simon started, but had nothing else to say. No other *lies* to spew.

Zack's eyes swung open. Lightning flashed outside the window. Alarmed cries spurted from the street. A hissing noise rose through the wailing wind, and so did the smell of burning wood.

"Kid, enough!" Tang Taizong emerged from Simon. "Yes, we

staged the attack—which means your mother's spirit is in no actual danger of being consumed!"

Zack was simultaneously overwhelmed with relief at his mom's safety and fury at the audacity of the lie. *How dare they have put him through all this stress and anxiety?*

"I command you to put her spirit back!" he screamed as thunder exploded from the sky. "Right now!"

Tang Taizong's eyes glinted gold, but he just winced, as if enduring a wave of pain. His hands tensed and flexed at his side. "I'm sorry; there's not enough time before the Ghost Month. I'd have to go back to America and summon Li Jing near her. But I promise, as soon as we seal the portal, I'll do that. Your mother may not be in danger, but China still is! All of China!"

"You have four days! That's more than enough for you to take the next flight out! *I command you* to take the next flight to Maine!"

Tang Taizong's eyes gleamed again. He doubled over. "I . . . can't . . ."

Guilt recoiled in Zack at seeing him—seeing Simon's body—being racked with torment, but he reminded himself that Tang Taizong didn't have to bear this pain. Not if he just did what Zack wanted!

Melissa rushed to catch Tang Taizong as his knees buckled. She whipped her glare to Zack, and he knew Wu Zetian had taken over. "Calm down, kid!" she said, features straining, probably trying to use her charm magic. But it didn't work on him anymore. He'd gotten too strong. She gave up with a gruff sigh. "Kid, it'll be cutting it way too tight if he goes. We need his power at the mausoleum in case a big attack comes!"

"I've got plenty of power now!" Zack threw his hands up. Another bolt of lightning struck outside, accompanied by an immediate thunderclap.

"Not after you seal the portal! It would take all of the seal's magic to do it, and the spirits that have leaked out won't just get sucked back in. You need both of us to handle the aftermath. Just finish the mission, and we'll restore your mom. We were always going to do that!"

"No." Zack shook his head, a muscle twitching near his nose. "Who knows what could happen during the mission? Restore my mom first! Tang Taizong, I command you to fly to Maine right now and restore her spirit!"

A cry of pain wheezed out of Tang Taizong. Wu Zetian had to use both arms to keep him upright. His eyes flickered between red and gold, as if he were a malfunctioning machine.

Zack inched toward him, unblinking. His shadow loomed over Tang Taizong. "Not obeying these commands hurts you, doesn't it? I'll keep giving them. I'm not going to stop. I—"

He caught Wu Zetian eyeing the seal's bump in his hidden breast pocket.

"I command you to stay still!" He flashed a hand at her.

Her eyes glinted. She stiffened, though managed to force out, "You . . . little . . . twerp . . ."

As the rainstorm picked up outside, pummeling the kitchen

window, non-lightning flashes came from behind Zack. He glanced over his shoulder.

It was his godforsaken portal-lens in the bedroom. It was Qin Shi Huang.

Zack marched inside and put it on.

"Stop punishing them." Qin Shi Huang appeared beside the bed, muttering. "It was my idea."

"*Why?*" Zack spun to face him fully. "*Why* would you do this?"

Qin Shi Huang didn't answer for several seconds, then his expression fell utterly sullen. "Because I knew there was no other way of getting you out of America. You clearly weren't going to cooperate without an incentive. Without a personal stake in this mission."

Zack's stomach twisted. Bile scorched up his throat. "You . . . you . . . you *fridged* my mom?"

"Fridge?" Tang Taizong rasped, coming in with Wu Zetian.

"It's a media term," she quickly said. "For when a female character gets killed solely to motivate a male character."

Tang Taizong gave her a look.

"What?" she said. "You don't think I've kept up with feminist discourse?"

"Relax, your mother isn't dead." Qin Shi Huang made a pacifying gesture at Zack. "Her spirit is safely within Li Jing's tower."

"That is so not the point!" Tears wobbled in Zack's vision. "You lied to me! You all lied to me! Just to get me to come on this . . . on this . . ."

"Yes! Yes, we did!" Qin Shi Huang raised his voice. "And for a very good reason! Who knows how many times you would've given up if you hadn't been motivated to push through? I'm sorry that I wasn't going to let China fall to ruin because of one wimpy boy who hates everything about himself!"

Thunder boomed outside like a boulder tumbling between the heaven and earth. Zack backed against the bedroom window, the words stinging like successive slaps to his face.

"The terms still stand." Qin Shi Huang pointed at Zack, eyes black and cold. "Seal the portal, and you get your precious mother back. There is nothing you can do to change this."

Zack didn't know why he was so shocked, really. Literally everyone had warned him about Qin Shi Huang, a tyrant so legendary for being a tyrant that they'd been attacked by his enemies nonstop on this journey. Yes, the Yellow Emperor may have sent those spirits, but they all had legitimate grievances against Qin Shi Huang.

How could Zack have listened to him sing and tell stories and imagined him as his dad?

How could Zack keep doing his bidding?

"No . . . ," Zack said under his breath. "I can do *this*."

He spun, ripping the window open.

Then he hurled his portal-lens out like a Frisbee.

Shouts tore out of Tang Taizong and Wu Zetian. They charged toward him.

"I command you to bow down and keep your mouths shut!" Zack said while whirling back.

They tripped onto their knees before him, then screamed frustrations through their teeth.

Zack darted around them, breath shortening, pulse throbbing down to his fingertips. "New terms: I won't do anything you guys say unless my mom is awake again."

"There's . . . no . . . time!" Tang Taizong strained out.

"I don't care." Zack stuffed his phone and charger into his bag and kept backing away. "Make it happen, because you can't force me to do anything. I'm sure you'll know how to find me."

He ran all the way out the front door, letting it slam behind him.

20

How to Handle Ultimate Power

ZACK STUMBLED THROUGH THE STREETS OF YULIN, SANDALS splashing in puddles. The rain came down in relentless sheets, beating against the ground. Pedestrians everywhere ran for cover. Street vendors scrambled to pack their stalls up.

Zack had no idea where he was going, just that he had to get as far away as possible. Nothing felt real. His mind lagged several seconds behind everything happening around him. He didn't even think to use his powers to stop himself from getting soaked. He could barely feel it anyway.

He must've looked as lost as he felt, because an older woman stopped in concern and leaned down to speak to him. Lightning flashed across her worry-wrinkled face. But he couldn't understand what she was saying. He had the artifact of ultimate power over China in his shirt pocket, yet he couldn't understand her.

So there I was, twelve years old, ruling a kingdom with the tongue of a foreigner, intruded a line from Qin Shi Huang's dramatic life story.

Zack staggered back.

"I command you to leave me alone and keep walking to where you were originally going," he whispered to the old woman through a growing lump in his throat.

Her eyes gleamed gold. She did exactly that.

He watched her go until she was out of sight.

Zack felt naked without his portal-lens. He couldn't understand anything. Though, eventually, he spotted the comforting green Arabic sign of a halal restaurant. It was funny; he could read that, yet he couldn't read the Chinese next to it. Simon's noodles hadn't really been that filling, so Zack magically whipped the rainwater off himself and stepped inside.

The restaurant only had four tables, and the aisle between them was barely wide enough for someone to get to the cashier. But he could already tell their food was amazing. Even though it was raining this hard, there were several people lined up. His mouth watered at the scent of spiced lamb kebabs roasting over a live fire in the back. An industrial-strength exhaust hood sucked away the heavy smoke. Under the rumbling was the thump, thump, thump of a chef chopping something— and then Zack noticed the chef's knife was chained to the metal counter.

Zack's blood iced over. Right. They were in western China now, where the restrictions on Muslim minorities were worse, so much that a chef couldn't even take his knife out of the kitchen. But it wasn't as if he could eat anywhere else, so he stayed in line and dug his phone out of his backpack. Back in Shanghai, Simon had transferred five thousand Chinese yuan to Zack's e-wallet and showed him how to pay people by scanning QR codes. That was supposedly how everyone paid for everything in China nowadays. Cash was practically obsolete.

The moment he clicked his phone open, messages from Simon and Melissa bombarded him. Biting his lip and barely holding back another flood of emotions, he deleted them from his every contact app.

The cashier was a girl who looked distinctly more Central Asian than typically East Asian though she didn't wear a hijab. Grimly Zack wondered if it was her personal choice, or if she legally wasn't allowed. When he got to her, he channeled what he hoped was his Chinese-speaking magic. "Excuse me, can I have ten of those kebabs?"

She just gave him a confused look.

No good. His dialect must've been ancient—it sounded way different from what everybody else spoke. Kind of like Cantonese, actually. His command powers didn't seem to have a language barrier, though, since it'd worked on the old woman. He felt bad about doing it, but he had no choice but to say, "I command you to give me ten of those kebabs."

Her eyes pulsed gold. She turned around like a robot and snatched two handfuls of kebabs off the grill.

Zack sighed. Was this the only way he could communicate with other Chinese people here? By ordering them around?

She handed the kebabs to him on a paper plate. He took it

with one hand and operated his e-wallet app with the other. He opened the money transfer option, typed in the number he'd calculated based on the picture menu above her head, then scanned the QR code on the counter to pay it.

It clearly took him longer than usually expected, because a suit-wearing man behind him cleared his throat loudly and tapped his dress shoe against the greasy floor.

Zack almost awkwardly scurried out of his way at first, but when he turned around, annoyance heaved away his guilt. So what if he'd taken a bit longer?

He peered up into the man's eyes and said, "I command you to move to the back of the line."

The guy's face twitched, but he did as told, marching stiffly. The next person in line looked up from her phone, baffled, but shrugged it off and went to order. Grinning weakly, Zack followed the man to head out while ripping a chunk of kebab with his teeth. It was exactly the comfort he wanted: juicy, tender, and seasoned just right.

But the moment the man hit the back of the line, he spun around and marched back to the front, yelling at the woman who'd taken his place. The woman startled, then yelled right back, pointing down the line. The man growled, darted a troubled glance at Zack, then continued to yell.

Uh-oh.

Zack didn't need to understand their words to know they were arguing about what counted as giving up your spot in line. Meanwhile, the cashier tried to calm them down.

Zack rushed back. "I command you to leave!" he told the man.

The man's next argument crumbled in his mouth. He dragged his feet out the glass doors like a zombie.

Everyone in the restaurant breathed a sigh of relief.

Until the man came raging back right after disappearing from sight, shouting even louder.

Zack spluttered, "I command you to go back to wherever you work and never come here again!"

The man did a U-turn into the rain yet again.

For several seconds, everyone stared out the doors, muttering to each other. Only when it was clear he wasn't coming back did they relax and go back to what they were doing.

Oh God, Zack thought, *I'm like Lelouch from Code Geass.*

He gave himself a firm reminder to word his commands very, very carefully and to never crack any terrible, ill-timed jokes about making someone massacre a whole population.

Zack devoured the first kebab and moved on to a second. He headed out the doors as well but stopped under the canopy outside. He couldn't eat kebabs in the pouring rain. Scowling in concentration at the sky, he willed the storm to calm down.

"Zack!" Melissa's sharp voice pierced his thoughts. He almost spat out his mouthful of lamb, which would've been a terrible, tragic waste.

She and Simon ran down the street toward him, clothes and hair drenched in rain.

Zack bolted away from them while refusing to let the rain hit his kebabs. The diverted drops formed something of a water shield, like when he'd accidentally put a spoon upside down under a faucet.

After the initial racing panic, he ran for a different reason: to handle this where there wasn't anyone else to ask questions.

Zack rounded the corner into an alleyway. The pungent smell of sewage and wet garbage hit him in the face.

"Zack, come on!" Simon skidded in with Melissa. He clutched his legs, frantically catching his breath, wiping his wet bangs out of his eyes. "Can you please come with us? We're really, really sorry we lied. Believe me, we feel so, so, *so* bad about it."

"Then why'd you do it?" Zack lashed an empty kebab stick like a sword, eyes burning with angry tears. "You guys could've told me the truth at any time! What were you afraid of? The emperors making you not rich and famous anymore?"

Simon flinched, lower lip wobbling. "We were scared you wouldn't come with us to seal the portal."

Zack made an indignant noise. "Did you think I was that selfish? None of you even explained the mission to me before taking my mom!"

"I—I don't know!" Simon pressed the heels of his hands against his head. "We didn't know you!"

"And after we did, this was only gonna take, like, two weeks!" Melissa stomped her foot in a dirty puddle, though her voice teetered on the edge of a sob. "What would've been the point of telling you if you would've acted like . . . well, *this*?"

Zack couldn't believe the words coming out of her mouth. "I could've stopped worrying! There would've been more time for Simon to restore her!"

"Zack, please, we're so close to the end," Simon pleaded. "Let's seal the portal first, then we can fly out together to get your mom back to normal. Please?"

Something wavered in Zack, but he shook his head harshly. "No! So close to the end? How do we even know that for sure? How do we know the emperors aren't lying about other things—about this whole mission? What if something happens to Tang Taizong during a battle? My mom comes first, then the portal!"

Melissa pointed at the sky. "This storm you summoned has grounded all flights, genius!"

Zack peered up with a pinch of guilt, but steeled himself before glaring down again. "I'll make it go away. This should barely be a problem."

"Zack! Please!" Simon choked out.

A fissure cracked across Zack's heart at the sight of Simon full-out crying in the rain, his hair and clothes plastered to his body, but Zack caught himself—how did he even know that sealing the portal was the right call? It was a mission by Qin Shi Huang, who he now knew was definitely *the worst*.

"No," Zack growled. "I command you to stay still and shut up. For the next ten minutes," he added, because it seemed that the more specifically he worded a command, the harder it was to resist.

Simon and Melissa stiffened in horror as their eyes glinted.

Slowly Zack walked up to them. A nasty, nauseating feeling pulsated through his body. "My mom comes first. That's final. Stop finding me, and stop trying to change my mind." He eyed both of them in turn. "There are worse commands I could give. Don't make me give them."

He swept away, leaving them in the rainy alley.

To Zack's surprise, a storm was a lot harder to will away than to bring down. It seemed to be tied to his emotions, which would be super cool . . . if he didn't need it gone so Simon could fly out.

He wandered all afternoon, making himself calm down. The downpour softened to a light rain. He stumbled upon an amusement park and commanded his way onto the Ferris wheel, where Simon and Melissa wouldn't be able to reach him. He commanded the attendant to let him stay on for as long as the park was open.

Huddling alone in the chilly Ferris wheel car, he leaned his head against the glass. Rain tinkled down all around him. The smell of wet plastic perfumed the air. He couldn't fall asleep, so he reached for his warmest memories of his mom. Their Central Park picnics. Them building a fort out of blankets and pillows and propping her laptop on a chair to watch horror movies together. Them making noodles and dumplings. Tears slipped down Zack's cheeks from his raw eyes. He sniffled. What he wouldn't do to taste her cooking again. He couldn't believe he used to dump the lunches she'd make for him; what had he been thinking?

If—*when*—he got her back, he would never, ever do that again.

By the time the attendant opened Zack's car, telling him they were closing, night had fallen. Only the occasional drop of rain plummeted from the sky.

Zack's stomach grumbled again. He wished he had marked down where the halal restaurant had been, but he managed to search for another one on his phone.

The way there took him through a shady-looking street. A bunch of bikers in leather jackets stood around smoking. Music thrummed from a club beside them. Dazzling, shifting neon signs reflected in the puddles at their feet.

Oops. This must've been the bad part of town. For the sake of food, Zack walked faster.

The bikers eyed him, then grinned at one another.

A bad feeling settled in Zack's gut.

They gathered around him, blocking his way, saying things he didn't understand. One man with a scruffy beard leaned into his face, tone mockingly sweet. The smell of alcohol poured from his mouth. Zack wrinkled his nose, backing away.

The bikers drew tighter around him in a circle. Some of them laughed. He got the sense that they were teasing him and trying to scare him. The scruffy man ashed his cigarette near his nose.

Zack flinched, fear quivering inside him, but after a moment, he relaxed.

What was there to be scared of? He had the power to make them do anything he wanted.

"I command you all to quit smoking!" He quirked a brow. "Permanently. It's bad for your health."

Their eyes gleamed. Stunned looks overtook them. Then, in sync, they dropped their cigarettes. Some of them looked about to cry as they pawed out more packs from their pockets and threw them into the neon-drenched puddles.

Zack made an offended noise. "Hey, don't li— I mean, I command you to not litter! Ever again!"

They picked the soggy packs back up, looking confused about what to do next.

Zack cocked his head. Come to think of it, he did need a place to sleep tonight, along with people to watch over him so Simon and Melissa couldn't sneak up on him.

Slowly he slid a pointed gaze across their faces. "I command you all to obey me as your new leader!"

Their eyes flashed again. With a collective rustling and splashing, they fell to their knees around him and pressed their foreheads to the wet ground.

Zack took a deep, long breath while standing in the circle of them, then released it. Muffled club music pumped like a heartbeat around him.

It was funny; he'd gotten his original wish after all. He was strong and powerful. And he had to admit, it felt good, having the ability to get people to do whatever he wanted. Life was so much easier. He could see the appeal.

But aside from power, he had nothing else.

How to Be a Benevolent Gang Leader

"HERE'S YOUR TAKEOUT, BIG BOSS YING!" LAWRENCE, THE only member of the biker gang who spoke English, strode into the club's back room with two handfuls of grease-stained paper bags. Music and sweeping lasers poured through the doorway, then muffled again when another gangster closed it after him.

"Oh, thanks!" Zack rose from his leather couch to take the bags, printed with green halal symbols. He spread the food out on a coffee table before him and passed some chopsticks to the two pretty girls beside him. They grabbed boxes of noodles while giggling. Apparently it was their job to sit here and praise whatever the previous gang leader did. They had salaries and everything. Zack wasn't into it—it made him feel really awkward, honestly—but he didn't want them to lose their jobs, so he let them stay.

"Lawrence, what's this?" Zack picked up something in a thin paper pouch that looked like a pastry but was stuffed with glistening chopped meat.

"Lamb *ròu jiāmó*! Basically Chinese burger. Very popular in the northwest." Lawrence nodded enthusiastically, stray hairs quivering in his gelled Mohawk.

Zack took a bite. It tasted like a juicy sandwich, except the bread was crispy and crumbly. "Mmm! That's really good. I knew I could trust you, Lawrence."

A huge smile stretched across Lawrence's black-painted lips, but his stomach growled. He clutched it with a look of horror.

"Lawrence," Zack exclaimed. "You didn't get any for yourself?"

Lawrence didn't meet Zack's eyes. "The old boss . . . would not have approved of such a thing. . . ."

"Ahh." Zack peered at the door, where the gang's old leader was standing outside with a command to protect Zack without complaint or resentment. "Well, I'm your new boss now, and I say have some!" He pushed a box of food toward Lawrence.

"Really, Boss?"

"Come on. You did the leg work."

"Thank you, Big Boss Ying! Thank you!" Lawrence sat down in a fold-up chair, grabbed a pair of chopsticks, and dug into a box of fried rice.

Halfway through the amazing food, a knock sounded at the door. Lawrence put down his chopsticks to go get it. After he opened the door, he had to yell over the pounding music to talk with the gangsters outside.

Lawrence closed the door. "Boss, there's someone here for you," he said, expression puzzled.

Zack tensed up. "Is it a girl and a boy my age?"

"No, it's a woman. Said she's from XY Technologies."

Zack's chopsticks slipped from his fingers and clattered onto the coffee table. "Is . . . is she looking for me specifically, or your old leader?"

"You, Boss." Lawrence blinked blankly. "Ying Ziyang."

Zack's heart hiccupped. Simon had been right. Jason Xuan had been watching them—there was no other reason XY Technologies would know his Chinese name, which hadn't been on any of his official documents for ten years.

XY Technologies had looked deep into him. Jason Xuan *knew* what he was.

Zack's first instinct was to run, but why? He had the power to handle whatever they threw at him, and honestly, he was curious to know what they wanted.

Zack rose from the couch. "Let her come in."

Lawrence started to turn the doorknob but looked back. "Boss, who are you?"

"I'm . . ." A wave of exhaustion came over Zack. He sighed. "I'm just a kid who got dragged into a big, big mess."

Lawrence nodded but didn't seem to know what he was nodding about. He cracked open the door again to pass on Zack's message.

About a minute later, a woman in a sleek black suit strode through the door. She wore her hair in a tight bun and had heavy, smoky makeup around her eyes, a style Zack hadn't seen very often since landing in China. She came with a tall male bodyguard who insisted on wearing sunglasses despite walking into a dark club. Zack let him in too, after the gangsters patted him down and confirmed he wasn't carrying a gun or anything. Finally, he told Lawrence to leave with the two couch girls, who headed out the door while waving their fingers at Zack.

"Keeping lovely company, Mr. Ying," the woman remarked after the door shut behind them. She spoke English with a slight British accent.

"It's not what it looks like!" Zack threw his hands up. "They had this job when I got here. I—I don't even like girls!" he blurted, then immediately flushed lava hot at what had slipped out of his mouth.

"All right." The woman flashed a smile.

Zack cleared his throat, calming himself down. This was not the time to be having an internal crisis. "Anyway—" He stared into the woman's eyes. "I command you to tell me what you really want with me."

"For you to help us thwart Qin Shi Huang's plans," she spilled out in one breath. Then she touched her lips, startled. "Oh my. What a power."

"So." Zack put his hands on his hips. It felt so weird to be discussing this madness with grown-ups for once, like it made everything so much more *real*. "You guys know."

"Indeed." She walked over with her bodyguard to extend a hand over the coffee table. "My name is Tiffany Lei. I am the personal assistant of Mr. Xuan."

"*The* Mr. Xuan?" Zack gaped while shaking her hand awkwardly. He was pretty sure he had never actually shaken anyone's hand before.

"Yes—" The bodyguard suddenly took off his sunglasses. "Me, Jason Xuan."

Zack's jaw dropped.

"It's a pleasure to finally meet you, Mr. Ying Ziyang." Jason Xuan—the man Zack wanted to be, the reason he'd learned to code—offered his hand to Zack, hair styled nothing like his usual look but face definitely matching, handsome with high cheekbones.

Oh my God, he pulled a Simon, was Zack's only coherent thought.

"It's Zachary Ying. Zack." He somehow gathered enough sense to shake Jason's hand.

"Well, Zack, apologies for the brief deception. I didn't want the paparazzi to know I was here. There would've been a lot of unwanted attention. May I . . . ?" He gestured at the fold-up chair.

"Yes, yes, of course!" Zack nodded a little too enthusiastically, then pointed out another chair for Tiffany. "You can take that one."

After they all sat down around the coffee table, Zack eyed the food. His mom would chide him for not offering any to guests of his. "You guys want any *ròu jiāmó?*" He poked an uneaten pouch.

"We ate before we came." Jason waved his hand graciously. "Truth be told, Zack, I've been tracking you for quite some time."

Zack took several deep, slow breaths, trying to get his last two functioning brain cells to stop screaming at how Jason Xuan—

the Jason Xuan!—was sitting in front of him. Jason was his enemy.

Or . . . was he?

"Did you know I ditched the emperors because they lied to me?" Zack asked, dropping all pretenses.

"That is precisely why I am here now. Because, at last, we can chat without their interference."

"So you also know they took my mom's spirit on purpose?"

"Did they?" Jason scowled. "I'm afraid I didn't know that particular detail. It sounds heinous. I'm truly sorry. I am not omniscient, you see. But I expected the emperors would show their true colors sooner than later."

"They sure did," Zack mumbled.

"What did they tell you about me?"

"That you're the chosen host of the Yellow Emperor. That he helped build your company by influencing people in their dreams. That he did it because he wants to rupture the spirit portal and gather a supernatural army to control humanity again."

Jason huffed with a small smile, eyes flicking down briefly. "That last point is a misunderstanding, but the rest is true. Though of course, only Tiffany here and a few other close confidants of mine know about my . . . condition. It's a hard thing to tell people without sounding out of my mind, unfortunately. But speaking of my company, I must tell you why I came to you, Zack. You see, video games and AR devices are only one part of what we do. We also do work in information and surveillance." Jason's expression grew much more solemn. "Ten years ago, we assisted the Chinese police in capturing a group they claimed were dangerous extremists by tracing and blocking their methods of communication. During the arrest, our filters caught a video by one certain suspect. A suspect by the name of Ying Qiaosong."

Zack's eyes widened. He forgot how to breathe.

Dad.

Jason's chair creaked as he leaned forth. His words dropped to a murmur. "I deeply apologize for my company's role in this. We were led to believe they were genuinely dangerous individuals. But there is something I can show you. It's technically illegal to reveal, but I feel you deserve a chance to see it."

He took his phone out of an inner pocket of his suit and handed it to Zack with a video playing.

It was Zack's dad, speaking urgently as harsh knocks pounded in the background. The self-recorded footage wobbled as he rushed from room to room. The microphone crackled.

Zack grabbed the phone, attention glued to the screen. His breathing shuddered and shook as badly as his dad's. His actual dad, nothing like Qin Shi Huang. Zack couldn't believe what he was seeing. All those scattered pictures and imaginings of what his dad acted like, sounded like, spoke like, now real and concrete before his eyes.

Ziyang, Zack caught him saying several times. His heart clenched. This message was meant for him.

Yet he couldn't understand it. No matter how his dad's voice wavered and broke with desperation, his words couldn't translate into meaning in Zack's head.

A loud noise sounded in the background of the video. Zack's dad cried out, the footage shaking out of control. It cut off abruptly, just under a minute long.

Through the walls, the club's music thumped into the silence that followed. Zack sniffled and gasped, sobs tripping out of his throat. His tears battered the phone screen.

"I—I can't understand him." He looked up at Jason with swollen eyes. "These are my dad's last words, and I can't understand him."

"Play it again," Jason said softly.

Zack did.

Jason translated. "He wanted you to know that everything he did, he did so your generation wouldn't have to live in fear and silence like his did. He wanted to fight for a world where you could be proud to be yourself and not afraid to believe what you want. He hoped he could see you again, but if he couldn't, he hoped you would forgive him."

Zack pressed his knuckles against his eyes, crying so hard that no sound came out of him anymore. The weight of the Heirloom Seal in his shirt pocket further tugged at his heart.

God, what was he doing? What had gotten into him that he was wielding magic to control others, the very kind of cruelty that his dad had given his life to fight against?

Jason came to sit beside him on the couch, patting his back.

"There is good news. If you work with us, you might be able to see him again."

"Huh?" Zack's sobs hitched. "He's alive?"

"No, but death didn't always mean being cut off from your loved ones for good." Jason's eyes glistened under the room's dim lights. "All our ancestors used to be able to speak to us in our dreams when the portal was freely open. Now only the strongest of spirits can do it. Qin Shi Huang cut the link between two realms that are meant to be connected. That is why they have continuously resisted his tyrannical attempts to keep them separate."

Zack wiped his eyes. "He told me it could bring war and chaos."

"That's him projecting his own fear and twisted mindset onto millions of innocent spirits. If the portal was freely open, every-one he ever wronged could attack *en masse* and tear his spirit apart."

"Of course," Zack muttered. *As if they weren't trying to do that already.*

"But the vast majority of spirits would simply want to con-nect with their loved ones. With your help, with the power you hold, we could give them the ability to do that again. Come with us, and I can tell you the details."

Zack peered at the final video still of his dad, then at Jason. He decided to use the seal's commanding power one last time. "I command you to tell me if you're telling the truth."

"I am," Jason said, eyes glowing gold, no strain in his face.

Zack stood up. "Then let's go."

22

How to Wake Qin Dynasty Romeo Back Up

"So, Zack, what do you know about Fusu, Qin Shi Huang's eldest son?" Jason swirled a square glass of brown liquor. Tiffany drove them in a very fancy car, one where the seats in the back were lit up with blue strips of light and faced each other like a limo. Maybe it technically *was* a limo, though it didn't look as long as a typical limo from the outside. There was even a built-in cooler holding all sorts of drinks.

"Fusu?" Zack's brows drew tight. That name was achingly familiar, yet he couldn't put his finger on it.

"Indeed. He was Qin Shi Huang's rightful heir. A kind, charming prince who everybody wanted to see on the throne after Qin Shi Huang. But he was banished to the Northern Wilds for speaking up against Qin Shi Huang's campaign to bury Confucian scholars alive and burn the history books of the six states he conquered."

Dreams fluttered back to Zack. He gasped and snapped his fingers as they *finally* clicked together. "And then—and then he was told to take his own life because of treason!"

"Yes, but what he didn't know was that the order was fake. In actual fact, Qin Shi Huang had suddenly died while on a tour across the country. His closest confidants hid his death and issued a command in his name to sentence Fusu to death, all so they could put Qin Shi Huang's gullible youngest son on the throne. That was Huhai, who ended up being far worse than his father. The Qin dynasty crumbled within three years. Though, honestly, it was on shaky legs to begin with. But if Fusu had become the second emperor, maybe it would've lasted longer. It's one of those big what-ifs in Chinese history. See, Fusu wasn't powerless when the suicide order arrived. He was stationed right here with the great general Meng Tian, along with three hundred thousand elite Qin troops."

"Hold on. Stationed *here*?" Zack touched the window. Dim streetlights flew past like shooting stars.

"Indeed. This *is* the Northern Wilds. And here, over two thousand years ago, Fusu could've rebelled against the order. He could've marched the three hundred thousand troops down to the capital, Xianyang, and demanded answers, which even General Meng Tian urged him to do. But Fusu was too afraid of his father. He simply gave up and took his life. It's interesting to speculate about why. There's a clue between the lines of the historical records: when the anti-Qin rebellions first broke out in the lands that used to be the Chu state, they rose up in the name of the great Chu general Xiang Yan, but also . . . Fusu. Now, why would a Chu rebellion call for justice for a Qin prince?"

Zack sipped on a bottle of Bīngfēng, an orange soda that

Jason had told him was the Shaanxi province's most iconic drink. "Chu's the state that Qin Shi Huang had the most trouble with, right? The one he had to attack twice because his uncle raised a secret rebellion against him?"

"Exactly. And the fact that the Chu people held Fusu in such high regard suggests his mother might've been a Chu princess. There's no surviving record of this, but the people back then would've remembered the lavish wedding. In ancient China, marriage was so important that you weren't considered a complete man until you married. Bachelors were laughingstocks. However, for some reason, Qin Shi Huang went down in history as a bachelor. He's the only notable emperor to be buried without an empress. Even Wu Zetian gave up her emperor title on her deathbed so she could be buried with her husband. Yet Qin Shi Huang chose to be all alone for eternity." Jason shook his head. "All alone in that mausoleum that's bigger than the whole Valley of the Kings in Egypt."

Zack bit his lip. "Serves him right."

"It goes deeper. Funny thing about Fusu's name: It was taken from the *Shījīng*, the *Book of Songs*, a collection of folk songs from across China back then. More specifically, it was taken from a teasing love song. So Qin Shi Huang basically named his first son Romeo."

Zack almost choked on his soda. "No way."

"Yes way." Jason pointed with his liquor glass. "There's legitimately an obscure historical tidbit about how Qin Shi Huang loved to listen to love songs. He must've been a romantic when he was young. I mean, just listen to the poem Fusu's name came from. 'There are *fúsū* trees on the mountain; there are lotuses in the pond. I couldn't have met a handsome lad like Zidu, but an arrogant one like you?'"

Zack flashed back to the cave on Penglai, mouth slackening. That was the exact song Qin Shi Huang had been singing when he'd woken up.

Jason made an incredulous gesture. "You can practically hear a young lady singing this to him, right? Yet there's no record of her. There's no record of any woman in Qin Shi Huang's harem. It all points to them having been systematically erased. The inkling I get is that this lost queen of Qin eventually sided with her homeland of Chu and contributed to the rebellion that destroyed Qin Shi Huang's first invading army."

Zack blinked in disbelief. "He did tell me attacking Chu was like going against a wife!"

"Maybe he meant it more literally than you thought. If things between him and this lost queen really ended in such an ugly way, it would explain a lot about him and Fusu. Like how he never named Fusu his official crown prince, which planted the seed for the succession disaster. And how Fusu was so readily willing to accept that his father had ordered him to take his own life. But if Fusu were given another chance, I bet he wouldn't be so blindly obedient anymore." Jason stared intently at Zack.

An uneasy feeling drew taut in Zack. "What do you mean, another chance?"

"You have the ability to host Fusu, Zack. He is half Qin Shi

Huang, after all. And because of the strength of his association with Qin Shi Huang, the portion of Fusu's spirit that stayed in his body at death, his *pò*, has persisted in his tomb. That's where we're going right now."

"Y-y-you want me to let him possess me?"

"He's our best chance at navigating Qin Shi Huang's mausoleum. Plus, your magic would get even stronger."

"Why would we need to go to his mausoleum? I thought we're trying to thwart his plans."

"We are." Jason's gaze darkened, catching a glint of the car's blue light. "By doing the opposite of it. He wants to seal the portal—we'll break it all the way open."

"Couldn't we just wait until the Ghost Month comes?"

"The flood of spirits might only break the portal partway open. If we weaken the plug further with the Heirloom Seal's power, we can make sure it blasts open for good."

Zack rubbed his soda bottle absently. "Is that really safe to do?"

"It makes no difference other than allowing common spirits to finally be able to get through. Like your father. Like mine." Jason leaned in, forearms crossed over his knees. "I lost him when I was very young too."

"I know," Zack murmured, two words that weren't nearly enough to capture what that fact had made Jason mean to him.

Jason nodded, continuing, "Legendary spirits can cross over at the slightest weakening of the portal plug, but ordinary people? They'll have no chance unless we give them one. This is the only way we'll see our fathers again."

Zack clutched his bottle to his chest. "But it feels . . . extreme."

"That's because you're not used to making decisions that impact the world so much. Believe me, I was scared out of my mind too, when my company started taking off. Suddenly I was responsible for so many people, and every choice I made could affect so many others. But I held on to the belief that I was meant to change the world. I may owe much of my success to the Yellow Emperor, but I believe he chose me for a reason. And Qin Shi Huang must've seen something special in you, as well. We can handle this. We were born to."

Zack relaxed his hands. Thinking of his dad, he straightened himself and said, "Okay."

Fusu's tomb was on a small mountain in the middle of a dusty, rural-looking town. Once they got to the top, they came to a tall tombstone that was clearly a modern addition, topped with a flaring, Chinese-style roof. A round mound of earth was piled behind it, surrounded by a low concrete barrier. Zack shivered from the haunting wind, rubbing his arms.

"Here, take this." Jason passed him a plastic-sealed sword that Tiffany had taken out of the car. "This is the sword that Fusu used to take his life. It was found among a bunch of tombs of Qin Shi Huang's children in an empty plot by itself. My people acquired it from the archaeological team earlier. It should help you connect to him."

Zack gulped. Carefully he took the ancient sword. "How do I do that?"

"Just lie down on the tomb mound and wait." Jason patted his shoulder. "Don't be scared. He's your ancestor, after all."

So is Qin Shi Huang, Zack mused. "Okay." He drew several deep, long breaths, calming himself down. "Okay."

With dragging steps, he crossed the low concrete barrier and climbed on top of the mound. Jason and Tiffany watched him from beside the tombstone.

Here goes nothing.

Zack lay down on the cold dirt. It was uncomfortable at first, tiny rocks digging into his back, then something about the change in perspective made everything less creepy. A sky full of stars twinkled above him. The wind sighed through the night, weirdly peaceful instead of eerie. He held the sword like a knight with one hand and placed the other hand in the dirt. Soon his nervous jitters melted into calmness.

My child . . . , a voice whispered in his head.

A soft gasp slipped through Zack's lips. "Fusu?"

A pale light kindled beneath Zack's hand. Spectral fingers slid between his own.

Suddenly, as if tugged from behind, his consciousness plunged into whooshing darkness. It swung several times through infinite nothing. His scream lagged behind his awareness as if coming from far away.

Then, just as abruptly, he found himself on solid footing in a chamber lit with blue flames. A beautiful man in ghostly robes stood before him.

"It's you," Zack breathed. "You're the one who's been calling to me this whole time."

"I am," Fusu spoke, gentle voice echoing from every direction. His eyes glimmered with gladness. "And I am so sorry I could not send clearer messages to you. *His* defenses were simply too strong. But at last you have broken free of him. You found me."

"You're also my ancestor?" Zack stepped closer, looking up at him in wonder.

"Yes. They did not get all of my sons in the massacre." Fusu raised his hand toward Zack. "Now, let us end my father's tyranny together."

Chills came over Zack. He touched his small hand to Fusu's, twice the size of his.

But a frown twitched at Fusu's fine brows. "You are hesitating about the mission."

Zack withdrew his hand. "I—well—releasing all those spirits at once . . . I mean, I want to see my dad again, but it feels . . ."

A change crawled over Fusu's demeanor. His skin shriveled, turning bluish gray like a corpse's. His eyes sank into their sockets. Out of nowhere, a sword appeared, lodged in his chest. A pool of dark red bloomed across his robe. Zack backed away, goose bumps shocking out all over his body.

Fusu shook his head while advancing on him. "If there is one lesson I have learned from my life and death, it is that weakness will only lead to failure."

He yanked the sword out of himself and plunged it into Zack's chest.

23

How to Force Your Way Through Someone Else's Daddy Issues

ZACK OPENED HIS EYES IN THE GARDEN OF AN ANCIENT PAL-ace. Everything was a little unreal, moving a little too slowly. Lines of eunuchs in tall hats and handmaidens with their hair gathered up in bundles shuffled under canopied walk-ways in the distance, but their movements left trails through the air.

"My prince, what are you looking for?" said a sweet, kind female voice behind him.

"My mama," Zack said automatically, frantic. "Where has she gone?"

"Oh . . ." The woman's voice went sullen and shaky. "My prince, I'm afraid the king has . . ."

She touched his shoulder. He looked over it.

The woman's face was nothing but blank flesh.

He screamed, but no sound came out. He shook her hand away and ran in the opposite direction. Yet no matter how hard he tried, he could only go in slow motion. The world wavered around him. Hushed voices drifted in and out of his hearing.

"... the queen betrayed Qin ..."

"... did you see His Majesty's face when the soldiers dragged her off ..."

"... scariest thing I have ever seen ..."

"... he would do anything to win ..."

"... anything ..."

"... what will he do with the eldest prince?"

"... no orders yet ..."

A sharp, ringing pain skewered through Zack's head. He crouched down, grasping it. Images of the real world flickered through his mind. Him back in the fancy car, him talking to Jason, him walking through the gleaming lobby of an expensive hotel, him getting on a plane in daylight.

"Oh no." He hyperventilated. "Fusu, what are you doing with my body?"

"My prince!" called the faceless woman. "Where are you, my prince? Come back!"

No. He had to get out of whatever this place was.

Zack did his best to run along a canopied walkway, past red-painted pillars.

"My prince, you can't go there!"

He kept running, but time moved like slush. More eunuchs and maidservants came at him, all with blank faces. The sound of his own breathing dragged between his ears.

The walkway took several twists and turns between

flareroofed structures before leading in front of one humon-gous building. Its open double doors were several times his height; he had to crane his neck to see the top. As shouts chased him, he hiked up his robe skirts and leapt over the tall wooden threshold lining the bottom of the doorway.

Darting through the shadows inside, he passed giant bronze pillars wreathed with dragons. A narrow platform stretched out before him over a long pool of water. Firelight glistened on the dark surface, from hundreds—maybe *thousands*—of oil lamps flickering through the chamber on extravagant bronze trees. Ghostly white smoke gusted from their flames, weaving into the smell of incense in the chilly air.

At the end of the platform, on a dais with a bronze throne, stood a black-robed man who, even with his back to Zack, was obviously Qin Shi Huang. His sword—the Tai'e sword, heir-loom of the kings of Qin—dangled at his waist.

Against Zack's better judgment, he charged over the plat-form, over swirling fish motifs carved into its stone. Dark water shimmered in their eyes and scales. When Zack was almost to the dais, Qin Shi Huang turned around, headdress beads swinging.

He had a face. The only face Zack had seen in here. Behind the strings of beads, firelight reflected off his sharp eyes, making them glow like a tiger's. A full beard wreathed his chin.

Zack seized up with a fear like he'd never known. So this was Qin Shi Huang's true form—or what he'd looked like at the height of his life. Zack was suddenly glad he'd usually appeared as a teenager to him.

"Father," Zack heard himself say, shuddering.

"Fusu . . ." Qin Shi Huang's voice slid out like smoke and echoed like a haunting.

Zack trembled so badly he just might crumble into pieces.

Then more images barged into his head. Him—no, Fusu in his body, struggling to figure out a computer. Fusu trying to use a pencil, then switching to a traditional ink brush to draw marks on printed satellite pictures. Fusu speaking and gesturing to a group of people dressed like the Ghostbusters, miner helmets on their heads, clearly ready to go tomb raiding. Jason and Tiffany were among them.

"Stop it—" Zack slapped the heel of his hand on his temple, doubling over. "That's my body! Mine!"

"Nothing is yours," said imaginary Qin Shi Huang. "Everything is mine."

Imaginary. That was right. Whatever this place was, it wasn't real. A real place would have more faces than just Qin Shi Huang's scary mug.

Then why was Zack so afraid to do what he had to?

"No . . ." He straightened himself, eyeing the Tai'e sword at Qin Shi Huang's waist. "No, it's not yours."

He dashed up the dais, stole the sword out of its scabbard with a *shing*, then drove it up into Qin Shi Huang's heart with both hands.

It only went in a little bit before Qin Shi Huang grabbed the hilt, clenching it in place. Black blood swelled and dribbled from his bare hands. Each droplet sizzled on the dais.

Terror consumed Zack again. When he made the mistake of looking up, Qin Shi Huang's furious black gaze paralyzed him, burning in his mind.

He could not be defeated. This was the guy who had won all of China, his whole world at the time.

But Zack had to take him down, or he'd be stuck here forever. He could feel it.

He had to conquer this.

With a rising scream, Zack dug his feet against the ground and pushed the sword farther up. It inched between Qin Shi Huang's hands and ribs, drawing more black blood.

"This is for my mom!" Zack yelled, voice not quite his own, yet fitting.

The sword broke all the way through. Everything whirled apart.

When Zack came to a higher level of consciousness, he was back to reality, walking through a dark tunnel. Or rather, *Fusu* was walking. Light from a miner helmet on his head swept before him. Several other footsteps echoed around him, accompanied by more cones of light. Yet no matter how he tried, he couldn't control his body.

"Fusu!" he screamed, though he had no idea how he was making the sound. It didn't feel like he had a mouth or anything.

"Oh. You've awoken." Fusu's voice also came disembodied.

"Give my body back!" Zack felt like he was bound in a trap, except the trap was his own body.

"I'm afraid I can't do that. I cannot let you ruin the mission."

"I—" Zack hesitated. Could he promise to not ruin their plans? What was the right thing to do? "Would I really see my dad again?" he asked, mellower.

"You will. And I'm afraid I will see mine soon as well. The Ghost Month is almost upon us."

Just when Zack was about to bombard Fusu with more questions, Fusu shushed him.

More voices spoke in his head, distant and frail.

. . . crossbows . . . be careful . . .

"Halt," Fusu said out loud, flinging his arms wide. "Another pressure trap."

The tomb-raiding crew stopped and crouched low. Fusu used a stick to press the ground ahead of them. It gave in slightly with the noise of stone scraping on stone, then the alarming swoosh of crossbow bolts whizzed over their heads. They bounced off the walls with crisp pings.

"Whoa," Zack said. "Who just warned us about those?"

"The spirits of the engineers who were killed in this mausoleum so its secrets would never get out," Fusu replied in his head. "I can hear them. They're protecting us. They want us to succeed."

Zack fell silent. Could this mission really be wrong if the one going against them was Qin Shi Huang, infamous ruthless tyrant?

"Astonishing," Jason remarked, picking up a bolt while rising to his feet. He twirled it in the light of his helmet. "Pure chromium-plated bronze. Over two thousand years, and it hasn't rusted. What a shame this technology was lost with your dynasty, so the credit went to the Germans for discovering it again in the 1920s."

"It wasn't my dynasty," Fusu snapped. "It was my father's."

For fear of distracting Fusu, Zack didn't say anything more as they moved on. Watching the crew dodge and outsmart traps was like watching a first-person horror movie. Not even a video game, since he had no input. It took a long time to tamp down his terror of having no control over his own body. He didn't know how Simon and Melissa did it on a regular basis.

Ironically, the whispering ghost voices were what prevented things from reaching another level of nerve-racking. It was like being warned of all jump scares several seconds before they happened. The crew came across hidden pits of spikes, which they crossed by putting down planks. Pressure plates that released poisonous powder, which they avoided by putting on respirators. More automatic crossbows. Many, many more of those. Every few steps, someone flicked on a fluorescent rod and threw it on the ground so they could find their way back. Whenever they came across a sealed door, an explosives expert rigged it to blow up while they stood at a safe distance.

The tunnels went on for so long that even death traps and

explosions became monotonous, but Zack's anxiety didn't die down. He wasn't worried about the crew being hurt. He was worried about what would happen once they reached their destination.

The spirits gave them plenty of hype when they got close.

"You're here! You're here! You're here!" they cheered like they were at a concert.

"The main burial chamber's behind there," Fusu said out loud as the lights of the crew's helmets converged on a wall that appeared to be a dead end.

"Finally." Jason gazed at it wistfully, then turned to Explosion Guy and said something in Mandarin while pointing at the wall.

That was everyone else's cue to back away and put on ear and eye protection. Explosion Guy pressed his ear to the wall and tapped it with a bunch of instruments, then placed a bunch of explosives at the bottom. He joined the crew at a safe distance, so far they couldn't see the wall anymore, before pressing the trigger in his hand.

Boom! The bombs went off like thunder, rattling Zack even through the dulled senses that came with having no control of his body. Debris showered from the ceiling.

After the quaking settled down, a light persisted at the end of the tunnel. An ebbing, fiery light. Murmurs of concern swept through the crew, though there wasn't any sound of a fire whooshing out of control. There were, however, strange new echoes of mechanicals things creaking and churning.

Zack would've waited for one of the adults to check it out first, but Fusu strode his body right toward it.

The sight behind the blast hole short-circuited Zack's thoughts for a solid half minute. In a humongous cavern like a hollowed-out mountain, so big he couldn't see the end, bronze mountains rose and fell several times taller than he was, sculpted with textures of snowcaps and forests. Flowing silver rivers laced through them.

No, not silver. *Mercury.*

Oh my God. Those were literal flowing rivers of mercury. Just like Simon had once mentioned.

Fusu stepped into one, the mercury splashing up to his knees.

"Oh, no, no, no, that's poisonous!" Zack mind-shrieked.

"Fret not." Fusu trudged on through the river. The mechanical noises got louder—they must've been what kept the mercury flowing. "This burial chamber is bound by legend magic to stay the same as it was built two thousand years ago. The mercury will not stray into your body."

Tiffany and the rest of the crew stayed at the blast hole, while Jason laughed and splashed in after Fusu. "Oh, we would be so dead if this made any scientific sense."

Zack looked around the best he could as Fusu moved his head. Stars made of glowing, glittering gems adorned the black ceiling high above them. The low, flickering ambient light was cast by bronze trees full of oil lamps, just like the ones in Fusu's memory world (or whatever that was).

"The mermaid oil," Zack gasped. "It really did burn for thousands of years."

"An extremely unnecessary addition," Fusu mind-muttered.

"Right, yeah. We did get mobbed by an angry pack of them because of it."

"My father has never taken an action with regard to anyone's well-being but his own."

"That's true. So true."

Zack was starting to feel better about this whole thing. As long as Fusu didn't hog his body after this, maybe it would all work out okay.

Once the river led out of the mountains, a massive army of soldier statues and horse-drawn chariots came into view, stationed over vast bronze plains laced with more mercury rivers. They were sculpted like the Terra-Cotta Army, except colorfully painted instead of uniformly clay colored. They guarded a raised dais with a huge ornamented coffin on top. Bronze trees of mermaid-oil lamps surrounded it.

"There it is," Fusu remarked out loud while stepping out of the river. As promised, no poisonous droplets clung to his— *Zack's* pants. "My father's body."

"Where's the portal?" Jason came to his side.

"Beneath him, of course. Can you see those shimmers in the air? Those are the early leaking spirits."

Zack spotted them upon the mention—a constant rippling around the base of the coffin, like summer heat.

"Ah," Jason remarked. "Just used his own coffin like a

paperweight over the very gate to the underworld, huh? Typical."

"Typical." Fusu shook his head.

"Well, then. Let's—"

Fusu yanked Jason to the side. A red spirit arrow zipped past them and smashed a hole through a warrior statue.

"My father's lackeys." Fusu spun around. "They're here."

24

How a New Emperor Is Born

"WE'RE NOT HIS LACKEYS!" MELISSA SHOUTED, HIDDEN AMONG the mountains.

"I thought my people had them locked up until this was over." Jason pulled his phone out of his tomb-raiding jumpsuit. "Ah, no signal."

"You kidnapped Simon and Melissa?" Zack exclaimed, before remembering only Fusu could hear him. "He kidnapped Simon and Melissa?"

"Clearly they've escaped," Fusu said out loud. "The emperors must've stayed dormant while letting their hosts follow us the entire way so that I couldn't sense them."

Simon and Melissa had gone through that entire death trap obstacle course by their own will? Granted, Fusu's crew had disabled most of the traps, but still . . . what made them trust the emperors so much? Money and fame couldn't be *every-thing.*

"Don't hurt them," Zack urged. "They have my mom's—"

Without waiting for Zack to finish, Fusu shouted, "Tang

Taizong and Wu Zetian, I command you to relinquish your weapons and come out to face me!"

There came the sound of one of them slipping off slick bronze and landing with an oof. Then they splashed visibly into the mercury river and waded toward Fusu, movements as awkward as puppets.

Zack mentally cursed. He'd been hoping Fusu didn't know how to use the seal.

Or . . . why? Didn't he want Fusu to succeed?

"I'm sensing hesitation in you again, my child," Fusu mindspoke. "What is it that you're unhappy with?"

Yes, what was Zack's problem? They were the enemy. They weren't his friends. They lied to him, *badly.*

Maybe them looking like fellow kids was messing with his head. Now he knew how the immortals felt when they'd believed Qin Shi Huang was stuck in his body.

While lumbering through the river, Tang Taizong made the motion of holding a bow again. *"Coup at Xuanwu—"*

"I command you two to stay silent!"

"Mmm!" They kept trying nonetheless.

"How pitiful." Jason shook his head. "Two of China's greatest emperors, making a fool of themselves because they refuse to accept that their battle has been lost."

Every oil lamp in the chamber flickered. A black wisp slithered out of Tang Taizong's backpack. Another rose from Qin Shi Huang's coffin. They wove together above the backpack, which must've held Zack's portal-lens, and gathered into the form of—

"Father," Fusu said, so charged with emotion that Zack felt it like a recoil blast.

"Fusu," Qin Shi Huang said with the slightest waver, his form inching forth with the foundering pace of the other emperors. "Fusu, don't do this. You don't know what you could be plunging China into. You have no idea of the true meaning of war and chaos—I ensured that!"

"Don't act like you ended the Warring States for my sake instead of for your own glory and vanity!" Fusu gestured around the lavish burial chamber.

Qin Shi Huang looked like he was seriously regretting his interior decorating choices. "All right, yes, I am a vain, tyrannical megalomaniac! But I am also one who cares deeply for China. I can be both! There is nothing that prevents me from being both. Now, you have to stop this! The more the portal loosens, the more powerful the spirits become, including the gods!" He pointed to Jason. "The Yellow Emperor is using you to make himself stronger!"

"So?" Fusu said coldly. "From what I have seen, humanity could use the guidance of the gods. The Yellow Emperor was a far better ruler than you ever were."

"That is not true! He simply did a cleaner job of covering up his tyranny! Didn't you hear about the rediscovered legends of what he did after defeating Chiyou, the god of war? How he stretched Chiyou's skin onto archery targets, blew his organs into balloons to kick around, and cooked his flesh into meat sauce to force-feed to anyone who defied his rule?"

Wait, what?

Zack didn't know that. Nobody had told him that.

Qin Shi Huang had been right about one thing—there was no good versus evil, heroes versus villains. Everyone in this burial chamber was horrible in different ways.

But then . . . what did that mean about this mission?

"The gods are dangerous," Qin Shi Huang went on, a black edge seething around his spirit like dark fire. "Rogue spirits are dangerous. Demons are dangerous. You have no idea of the consequences of loosening that portal!"

"Consequences?" Fusu yelled much louder, voice ringing through the burial chamber. "How dare you speak to me of consequences? You have never cared about consequences in your life! In your *existence*! If you had simply named me crown prince or let Mother become the first empress as she was supposed to, or made *any* woman empress, Qin wouldn't have fallen apart the moment you died! All my brothers and sisters— all *your children*—wouldn't have been killed. Mutilated. Erased. But no. You couldn't fathom the idea of sharing power with anyone. You were so utterly confident that you could find the key to immortality and reign forever!"

"Fusu . . ." Qin Shi Huang struggled to speak, his tone frailer than Zack had ever heard it. "I am truly, truly sorry for all the wrongs I brought down on you."

"No, you're not!" Tears poured from Fusu and Zack's shared eyes. "You're Qin Shi Huang, uniter of the Seven Warring States, the Dragon Emperor himself! You have never been sorry for anything!"

"You must realize that our dynasty was doomed from the beginning," Qin Shi Huang continued softly. "Everything I did was to destroy the old ways, destroy the old powers, and usherChina into a new era. But Qin was an old power as well. The final clinging one. There was a reason we only lasted fifteen years longer than the other Warring States. We represented something that only hindered the progress of the new world."

"Keep telling yourself that. Keep excusing your failures. Look around, Father. What's the final line of that Li Bai poem about you? 'Watch how under the three springs of Mount Li, a coffin of gold buries only a cold body.' You lost then, and you lost now. You lost because all you thought about was you. You, you, *you*. *Your* mission, *your* country, how to get what *you* wanted. Well, you are not getting that today. And there's no longer anything you can do to stop me."

Tang Taizong and Wu Zetian stumbled onto shore before Fusu.

"I command you to bow down and stay bowing in silence!" Fusu said with a sweep of his arm.

They dropped to their knees, faces warping in horror before being forced to bow low.

"No, get up!" Qin Shi Huang frantically said to them, but

they stayed pinned to their knees, and he stayed stuck above Tang Taizong's backpack.

Zack couldn't decide what to do. Maybe he didn't need to. He was trapped in his head—whatever happened next wouldn't be his fault.

"Finally," Jason said. "Is your family drama over? Because the spirits should be ready to burst out any time now."

"Yes. Let's do this." Fusu placed one hand on the seal in Zack's hidden shirt pocket and extended the other toward the ground beneath Qin Shi Huang's coffin.

Jason grabbed Zack's shoulder and intoned, "O Yellow Emperor, ancestor of the Chinese people, give your humble servants strength to weaken this blockage of the natural gate between the mortal and spirit realms!"

"No, stop!" Qin Shi Huang yelled.

A great heat flooded through Zack's body, igniting his meridians a glittering gold. Rainbow colors rose like an aurora beneath Qin Shi Huang's coffin. Spirits shimmered out with a greater intensity.

Zack's heart hovered in anticipation for his dad's.

"Stop!" Qin Shi Huang cried again, voice breaking. "Stop, *please!*"

Zack's consciousness shivered.

I have never known Qin Shi Huang to show fear like this.

If only the Dragon King could see him now.

"Kid—*Zachary!*" Qin Shi Huang suddenly shouted. "I know you're in there, and I sincerely apologize for using your mother as a pawn! But I did it because I was terrified of failing China when I realized I'd have no control over you. I did it for China, not for myself! You have to believe me!"

"Don't let him mess with your mind," Fusu mind-spoke. "He is simply terrified of the wronged spirits that will come seeking revenge against him."

But who was really messing with Zack's mind?

"Fusu, is the Yellow Emperor really gonna take over?" Zack asked.

"Not in the tyrannical way you're thinking. Once he can embody his mortal host, he will only use his power and resources to make China better. This is Qin Shi Huang, legendary tyrant, versus the Yellow Emperor, revered ancestor of us all. Why are you wavering?"

"Zachary, I know how much you hate being controlled!" Qin Shi Huang kept yelling. "Do you want to live in a world full of entities with power beyond your imagination? In a world with ten thousand *me*s all competing for dominion over the powerless? You have gone above and beyond my expectations. Not only did you acquire the Heirloom Seal, you refused to let it compel you into wreaking havoc! Do not let that all be in vain! You expelled me; you can expel him! He is only *half me*!"

"Enough!" Fusu snapped. The rainbow light roiled harsher. The force of the outpouring spirits became a wind that blew in his face and fluttered his hair onto its ends. "You've lost, Father! Accept it! Nothing you do will make things go your way this time!"

"What if . . . what if I gave up my existence?" Qin Shi Huang said, tone regaining its sternness.

"*Mmm?*" The other emperors looked up at him, alarmed.

Qin Shi Huang ignored them. "I know you think I don't deserve to exist. I can make that happen. I will give up my existence if you would stop weakening the portal plug, Fusu! Let me prove to you that I fear only for China, not vengeance from everyone I've ever wronged!"

"You would never—"

"*Wouldn't I?*" Qin Shi Huang roared. "As I am the conqueror of the Warring States, every citizen then is a subject of mine, and thus I can summon any one of them. Including—" A speeding reel of spirit images appeared before him. He swept to a particular one. "By the command of your emperor—arise, Jing Ke, assassin of legend!"

A plume of black *qi* lurched out of Qin Shi Huang's chest, spiraling up. It gathered into the shadowy form of Jing Ke, a dagger in hand.

"Mmmm—no!" Wu Zetian strained to say. "Don't . . . do this!"

"This . . . version of you . . . will never exist again!" Tang Taizong pleaded.

Qin Shi Huang breathed hard, a wild grin jerking at the corners of his mouth. "My fear of death was the one enemy I could not defeat in my lifetime. Today is the day I conquer it." He opened his arms, exposing his chest to Jing Ke. "Finish what you started all those thousands of years ago."

Without hesitation, Jing Ke thrust his dagger into Qin Shi Huang. Qin Shi Huang lurched in place, grabbing Jing Ke's shoulder. His eyes widened and trembled.

"No!" Tang Taizong and Wu Zetian screamed. Jason let out a startled laugh. An intense wave of emotion rolled out of Fusu, so complicated Zack couldn't figure out what exactly Fusu was feeling, just that it was a *lot*. Zack himself watched in a daze as Qin Shi Huang's form unraveled like black smoke. Qin Shi Huang clearly tried to bite back a scream at first, but then it tore out of him uncontrollably, the sound filled with such excruciation that Zack's own piece of his spirit resonated in singeing pain.

"China . . . ," Qin Shi Huang said with his last efforts. "Save China."

Like ink dissolving into water, he and Jing Ke scattered and vanished. An invisible force knocked the emperors over and buffeted Fusu and Jason sideways.

The severed-limb ache inside Zack told him it wasn't a trick. Wasn't manipulation. Qin Shi Huang was really gone. He had really vanquished himself.

Qin Shi Huang just vanquished his own spirit.

Shock turning to horror turning to revelation, Zack surged through the stunned lapse in Fusu's consciousness and fought for control of his body.

"What are you doing?" Fusu mind-screamed, grasping his head, mentally wrestling back. An extended growl ruptured from his real mouth.

"Fusu?" Jason said behind him, seizing both his shoulders. "Keep in control!"

"If Qin Shi Huang was willing to stop existing to close the portal, then it can't be selfish!" Zack exclaimed. "It really must be important!"

"Don't you want to see your father again?"

"I will," Zack realized. "Someday. I know he'll wait for me. He gave his life for China too. The China he thought was possible. He wouldn't want me to doom it because I'm too impatient!"

The spirit winds blew harder and louder in his face. He swore it was giving him strength. With one culminating burst of effort, Zack expelled Fusu's spirit from his body. It left his mouth in a warping shimmer.

"No, no, no!" Jason's hands bounced off his shoulders.

Zack's mind slammed fully into his senses again. Like waking from a dream, he'd almost forgotten what it was like to feel things so sharply. The metallic and sulfurous smell in the air, the mechanical noises from the rivers, the whooshing of spirit wind, the slight draping weight of his clothes—

The burning heat of the seal against his chest.

As he darted to get away from Jason, Zack dug under his shirt and snatched the seal into his bare hand. To his shock, it was much smaller than before. It was dissolving into golden mists of magic. He willed its remaining power to undo what Fusu had done.

Get thicker, he commanded the portal plug. The rainbow auroras shrank like a stove flame being turned down.

"Insolent boy!" Jason roared, clearly not himself anymore—the Yellow Emperor must be taking over. His eyes and meridians beamed bright yellow. His voice echoed a thousandfold through the burial chamber, shattering the closest soldier statues. "*The* Book of Bái Zé*!*" he chanted.

A spirit book conjured before him in yellow wisps of light, pages flipping rapidly. He raised his arms to the side with much effort. Yellow constructs of gnarly myth creatures morphed out of the spirit winds, connected to the book by thin tendrils, like a whole *Mythrealm* roster come to life.

"Vanquish him!" He pointed.

The spirit army flew at Zack.

In his spiking panic, Zack realized what to invoke: "*The king of Qin runs around the pillar!*"

Time slowed. He dashed away from the inching army and gave a firm shove to Jason—no, *the Yellow Emperor*—who stalled mid-holler. The Yellow Emperor's body tilted backward, leaving imprints through the air, the front of his shoes lifting off the ground. He'd take a hard fall the moment time loosened. His spirit book hovered in place, one of its hundreds of glowing tendrils stretching to keep attached to his chest. Zack instinctively waited for an explanation of what this *Book of Bái Zé* was, then remembered that Qin Shi Huang was gone. Biting his lips together, Zack tried to knock the book away, yet his hand passed through it.

He wished there were more he could do, but he couldn't summon a spirit weapon by himself. He settled for unzipping the Yellow Emperor's jumpsuit and twisting it as awkwardly around his limbs as possible so he'd get tangled up, as well. Jason Xuan's handsome face, which Zack used to admire so much, was caught in a laughable expression. Zack realized now that Jason's existence was laughable too. Everything he'd achieved was by the Yellow Emperor's magical influence, not his own talents, and now he was just a vessel without control of his own body.

Zack hooked his arms through Wu Zetian's and Tang Tai-zong's, thinking about carrying them away. But a sense of doom ate at him. They were too late. The Yellow Emperor had gathered into Jason. They'd never make it out before his spirit army caught up. Not when Zack couldn't sustain the time slowing forever.

In fact, he was wasting the seal on it. It kept dissolving into gold light. He was using its precious final magic to stall, when he should've been using it to heal the portal plug.

His frantically darting attention skimmed across the legions and legions of soldier statues throughout the burial chamber, then landed on Qin Shi Huang's coffin. He thought of how Qin Shi Huang had drawn on the lingering, heavyweight *pò* pieces of his spirit inside to fuel his construct.

A daring idea came to Zack.

He hauled Wu Zetian and Tang Taizong right in the direction of the army. It wasn't easy, with them being trapped in slowed time. Their bodies left a trail of afterimages. Zack's muscles soon ached with the effort. He really should've taken gym more seriously. Not that his teacher had ever taught how to drag two emperor-possessed kids through slowed time. But he pushed through the pain, as he'd done this whole journey, and kept dragging them, bumping spirits aside to go all the way up the coffin dais.

"I nullify all previous commands on you two," he said, panting, while steadying them beside the coffin. He wasn't sure if that would let them talk and move freely again, but he'd have to count on it. Wu Zetian's hammer was the only thing he could think of that could smash open this huge coffin.

Zack held up the dwindling seal, heart aching with guilt at how he hadn't been immune to being corrupted by it. He'd given so many self-righteous speeches to Qin Shi Huang, but in the end, he'd fallen into the trap of power and control himself. Grief could make people do such terrible things.

Sorry that I almost lost my way, Dad.

No one should have this kind of power. It was better off gone.

Zack willed it to simultaneously hold down time while healing the portal plug until it disintegrated into some last specks of shining gold.

Then time coursed back to normal again. The spirit creature army charged on, not realizing Zack was now behind them. The displaced creatures among them caused several hiccups. The Yellow Emperor yelped while hitting the ground, tangled in his jumpsuit. Wu Zetian and Tang Taizong gasped in surprise at their new location.

"Wu Zetian, summon your hammer and smash this coffin open!" Zack urged.

To her credit, she understood the situation instantly, calling incantations until her white spirit hammer formed in her hand. With several swinging arcs over her head, she bludgeoned the coffin. A huge hole crumbled through several layers of material.

The mermaid-oil lamps' wavering light shone down on Qin Shi Huang's actual, two-thousand-and-two-hundred-year-old bones. They were dressed in impeccable black-and-red robes, the silk slick and shiny as if they'd been tailored yesterday. It was weird that his flesh had rotted away while everything else was frozen in time. But then Zack remembered the story of how Qin Shi Huang's death bed betrayers had kept his death a secret while they worked out their schemes, causing his body to rot in his carriage, and they had to put it with a bunch of pickled fish to mask the smell. He must've been nothing but bones by the time the betrayers had finally put him to rest.

Zack couldn't decide if he felt bad for him. But he also couldn't deny what he was looking at—the bones of a legend.

Hands shaking so hard he could barely move them, Zack reached into the hole and grasped Qin Shi Huang's skull.

Magic *crashed* into him. A storm of power blew him through a lifetime of memories. Every story Qin Shi Huang had told about himself and every story others had told about him, more vivid than ever. From being a lost prince abandoned in an enemy kingdom to fighting for power through a vicious court that saw him as a foreigner to conquering his entire known world so that foreign countries were no longer a concept.

When the memory storm finally slowed down, Zack found himself in a dim bedchamber lit by sparse oil lamps. Lying on the bed was an old Qin Shi Huang—no, not even old. Middle-aged, hair mostly still black. He coughed, blood sputtering from his lips, yet he kept trying to read the pile of bamboo scrolls beside his bed.

Then, different from all memories before, he did a double take on Zack. Like he could actually see him.

Zack looked behind him, but there was no one else there.

"Does China survive?" Qin Shi Huang asked, voice so low it rumbled like distant thunder.

"It does," Zack said between deep, disbelieving breaths. "It will."

Qin Shi Huang's bloody mouth crooked with a smirk. "Then let them say what they want."

His eyes fell shut. The bamboo scroll slipped from his fingers. It landed on the cold stone floor with such an impact that Zack jarred back to reality.

He was staring into Qin Shi Huang's empty eye sockets— he'd taken his skull out of his coffin. Wu Zetian and Tang Taizong were shouting at him while using their weapons to take down creatures. The army had changed course and surrounded them. The Yellow Emperor hollered commands from the bottom of the dais.

But Zack eyed the sea of soldier statues throughout the burial chamber and knew exactly how to get out of this. Exactly which legend to invoke.

Zack raised Qin Shi Huang's skull over his head and shouted, "*The First Emperor unifies China!*"

His voice echoed supernaturally through the entire cavernous burial chamber. Then, at once, every mermaid-oil lamp snuffed out.

Several moments later, they reignited with eerie blue-and-white flames. A cold magic Zack hadn't felt in so long gripped his bones like ropes of ice, hitting him so hard that he crumpled into a low crouch. His meridians turned pure black, and he knew his eyes had blackened as well. The next breath that left him was as icy as winter air. Qin Shi Huang's skull crumbled into black, smoky *qi* and wreathed around Zack's arms and body, briefly flaring behind his back like wings—the wings of their black bird ancestor. Zack gasped for air, his shoulders rising and falling, his hands stiffening like claws. The rainbow aurora from the portal darkened and burst out like a shock wave through the burial chamber, through the army of statues. Their painted eyes turned black, as if infected with ink. The phantom sound of marching and a low chorus of singing haunted the chilly mausoleum air. Everyone, including the creatures, looked around in bewilderment.

The clay soldiers scraped and creaked to life, brandishing their weapons.

Archers dropped to one knee and fired crossbow bolts at the creatures. Infantrymen swung long swords and dagger-axes. Chariots charged into motion, carrying more archers, who took down any creature that got too close to Zack and the emperors. The noise of war filled the colossal chamber.

Heaving out a long, cold, forceful breath, Zack straightened himself, arms lifting to his sides. His blood and veins turned black as well, looking like decayed tree branches between the angular lines of his meridians. Black *qi* surrounded him like an aura of death. Step by weighted step, he went down the dais, staring right into the Yellow Emperor's glowing eyes.

Terror crossed the Yellow Emperor's similarly meridian-lit face.

"Bear your sword, my king!" Wu Zetian chanted behind Zack, racing down the dais as well.

"Bear your sword, my king!" Tang Taizong joined in.

The Tai'e sword gathered to shape as a length of extra-dense coldness against Zack's back. He drew it and swung it over his shoulder. It parted the air with a visible warp.

With a snarl and a wave of hand, the Yellow Emperor summoned a parade of creatures to protect himself. He turned around and broke into a run.

Zack tried to give chase but couldn't move any faster. His body was too strained by sustaining his army of resurrected soldiers. The Tai'e sword dissipated as the emperors stopped chanting.

As if picking up on what he needed, one chariot charged toward him with a metallic jangle. The charioteer, six horses, and carriage were made of thousands of intricate bronze pieces.

"Get on, Ziyang!" said a voice as faint as wind.

Zack recoiled. *"Dad?"*

The charioteer's mouth didn't move, but he turned his bronze head to stare at Zack with his pure black eyes as he pulled up in front of him and the emperors.

Zack was so stunned he stood rooted in place.

"Come on, kid!" Tang Taizong dragged him onto the chariot. Wu Zetian gave him a push on the shoulders.

"D-dad, is that you?" Zack gripped the chariot's bronze edge.

No answer. Had he imagined the voice?

The charioteer simply lashed the bronze reins. The six horses lurched into motion, chasing after the Yellow Emperor, who'd gotten on top of a winged creature. They galloped through the war zone and splashed through the mercury river leading out of the bronze mountains. Metal-scented wind tunneled past them.

At the blast hole of a doorway, they passed the bodies of the other tomb raiders.

"Don't worry—they're just unconscious!" Tang Taizong said.

"Our hosts knocked them out with the same gas used to kidnap them!" Wu Zetian added.

Right now, Zack didn't care. He focused on the radiance of the Yellow Emperor's creature dithering ahead in the tunnel. However, as hard as the chariot raced, they couldn't catch up. Flying was too big of an advantage, and the farther they strayed from the burial chamber, the weaker Zack's magic became. His consciousness lolled. He was definitely going to pass out again. Simon, Melissa, and the emperors had better make sure he didn't get mobbed and killed by myth creatures, or he'd come right out of that portal and haunt them for life.

Soon it became less about catching the Yellow Emperor and more about making it out of the mausoleum in one piece. Zack doubted he could handle a fight anymore. The tunnel was impossibly long. Hot tears and popping spots filled his vision with the strain of keeping the chariot alive, especially the charioteer. He wanted to talk to him. He had questions. But he no longer had the strength to even move his lips.

The moment a hint of morning light washed over them, it was all over. Zack collapsed, his mind plunging into a deep, heavy darkness.

It's okay, Ziyang, a voice may or may not have drifted by his ears. *I'm proud of you.*

How Everybody Sucks and Nothing's Over

WHEN ZACK NEXT OPENED HIS EYES IN AN UNFAMILIAR ROOM, Simon and Melissa rushed over to him yet didn't say anything, looking at a loss for the proper words.

But of course. How were they supposed to *begin* addressing everything that'd happened?

A million questions flailed in Zack's mind, but his throat was so dry that he could only get out the shortest one: "How long?"

"Four days," they answered in sync.

"Huh." He shielded his eyes from the sunlight streaming through the window. "New record."

"You *did* raise an army of the dead." Melissa grimaced, quirking a brow. "You really are surprisingly hard-core."

"And you don't have the seal anymore, so you recovered slower," Simon added with a sympathetic look.

"Mm." Relief lapped through Zack like the waves on Qinhuangdao's beach, a sense of freedom from horrible temptation.

He almost asked if they'd heard the charioteer say anything

during their escape but decided not to. It didn't matter. All he needed was to believe it himself.

Thanks for the assist, Dad.

After Simon passed him a much-needed glass of water, Zack wiggled up in the bed while gulping it down.

"We're still in Xi'an, by the way." Melissa brought over a second glass. "And we're really sorry to spring this on you, but we need to check if you still have your water magic."

Frowning at her urgent tone, Zack flicked his hand over the glass. The water whipped out, slicing through the air to his will, reaching all the way to the other end of the room.

Simon and Melissa breathed in relief.

"You managed to absorb all of Qin Shi Huang's *pò* from his body." Simon followed the darting water with his eyes. "Thank God. You're as powerful as he could've been if he'd possessed you properly."

Unease edged into Zack. "Was the portal not sealed tight enough? Did we . . . fail?"

"No, but the emperors fear that could change," Simon explained.

Melissa's brows tightened further. "The flow of spirits during the Ghost Month doesn't come all at once. It slowly increases until the Zhongyuan Festival in the middle of the month. That's in eleven days. The portal might still get busted open."

Zack's mouth contorted. He stamped the glass onto the nightstand. "Seriously? Then what are we supposed to do? The Heirloom Seal doesn't exist anymore!"

Simon and Melissa looked at each other, and then Simon took Zack's portal-lens out of his pocket and held it out. *"He left something for you."*

A sharp ache twisted in Zack at the reminder of Qin Shi Huang. "That was mine to begin with!" he spluttered.

"No, I mean—just put it on."

Zack took it and did so. Something trembled in him when he definitely did not feel any magic.

Yet Qin Shi Huang appeared in his portal view.

Just as Zack jerked against the bed's headboard, the construct spoke, "Hello, Zachary. Do not panic. I am not alive. I am an artificial intelligence program created by Qin Shi Huang to provide you further guidance through your journey, which I am afraid is not over."

"We're calling him Qin Ai," Melissa said somewhat awkwardly. She and Simon were also wearing their portal-lenses. "It's a pun on 'sweetheart' in Mandarin, which is *qīn ài*." She pronounced the second *qin* in a slightly different way.

"My programming suggests I should be deeply offended by that name." Qin Ai's tone remained flat. "But given that I do not experience emotions, I do not care."

Zack touched his fingers to his temples, feeling like his head was close to exploding. "He . . . he . . . he *made an AI*? The two-thousand-year-old tyrant-emperor *made an AI*?"

Simon blinked. "You still get surprised by this stuff?"

"All right, fine!" Zack threw his hands up. "Qin Ai, what are we supposed to do next?" he said in the tone of summoning Siri.

"Before he vanquished himself, my creator's last belief was that the situation can only be salvaged if a new plug is made for the portal. His original plug was made from the five-colored stones, the same material by which the creator goddess, Nüwa, mended a hole in the sky." Qin Ai waved his wide robe sleeve. Polygons swept out a virtual map of China beside him, lit up with glowing markers. "Now you must journey across China to gather more of these five-colored stones to create a new plug within eleven days."

Zack stared at the map, a muscle twitching under his eye. "Great. Another timed mission."

"Also, I should warn you that my creator might become your enemy this time. His spirit will gather again, and soon, but he will not be the same. He will only remember what's been preserved in the cultural consciousness, which means he'll have no memories of what he's done as a legend spirit, no memories of the portal since that did not go down in history, and no memories of you. But he'll be able to sense that you were born with a piece of his lightweight *hún* spirit, which he'll want to absorb. By killing you."

Zack's blood iced over. "Please tell me you're joking."

Qin Ai's expression didn't change. "I am an artificial intelligence. I do not joke."

Zack ripped off the portal-lens, dropped it on his covers, and slumped against the headboard with his face in his hands.

". . . Zack?" Simon touched his arm.

"Gimme a minute," Zack said, muffled against his palms.

"Man, I still can't believe Qin Shi Huang actually did that to himself," Melissa said. "Basically giving up everything that he was."

"None of us can," Simon said in a smaller voice. "Which means the new him that's going to pop up won't be someone who would do that. Tang Taizong's pretty shaken up about it. 'Over two thousand years of emotional development down the drain,' he said. He'll come back as bad as everyone thinks he is."

"Okay, I get it!" Zack dropped his hands from his face, snarling.

Simon and Melissa flinched.

Guilt bled through Zack. *God*, what was he becoming?

You can either let this journey crush you, or let it transform you into someone stronger, Qin Shi Huang had once told him. But this wasn't the transformation Zack had wanted. He may have wished to be stronger, but he refused to get that strength by becoming a jerk hated by everyone, doomed to die alone.

No. He was not Qin Shi Huang. And neither was he Jason Xuan, nor was he Shuda Li. Zack had spent so much of his life looking up to idols, trying to become someone different from himself, but they had all turned out to be shams with much bigger messes going on in the background than their glorious images suggested. He was done following others. He was Ying Ziyang, Zachary Ying, and from now on, he would find his own way.

"Sorry." Zack lowered his head, touching his clasped hands to his forehead. "We'll just deal with him like we deal with everything else. Cross that bridge when we get there. But, most importantly—" He looked at Simon while trying not to come off as too mean. "Did you restore my mom's spirit yet?"

Simon's mouth opened and closed. "Zack, we're so, so, *so* sorry about everything that happened with her. Honestly."

"It was wrong for us to keep you in the dark like that," Melissa added, wringing her hands.

Zack shoved down his irritation at how Simon clearly hadn't taken the trip back to Maine. His head throbbed. Memories of how he had acted while having the seal assaulted him like slaps. He really didn't know how much of it was the seal and how much of it was himself.

Zack wasn't innocent. They'd wronged him, but he'd wronged them back.

He dragged a hand over his face. "Just restore her spirit as soon as possible, and we're even."

"Um—" Simon bit his lip.

Zack tensed, alert yet again. "What?"

"Okay, uh, Zack, please don't get mad at us."

"Oh, he's definitely going to be mad." Melissa's wide-eyed gaze slid aside, but she wrenched it back to Zack. "But we promised no more secrets."

"No more secrets." Simon nodded with a solemnity like he was going off to war.

"What is it?" Zack threw his covers off and staggered out of bed.

"So . . ." Simon gulped, backing away. "We got a message

from Yaling. The hospital had contacted her. They said your mom had recovered and checked out."

"But—" Zack started.

"But Tang Taizong summoned Li Jing, who said her spirit's still in his tower."

Zack's heart pounded louder and faster. "Then . . . then who—*what's* using my mom's body?"

"That's the problem, Zack." Simon shook his head with a haunted look. "I'm so sorry. We have no idea."

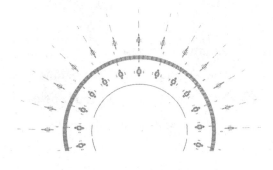

Acknowledgments

I'M GONNA BE HONEST—I HAVE ABSOLUTELY NO IDEA HOW I pulled off this book. Even when I was three chapters till the end, finishing it seemed like an impossible task. This may have been a wacky book, but I wrote it during a very tense time in my life. I had just graduated from university when the COVID-19 pandemic began to grip the world. I had my *Iron Widow* book deal on hand, but even then, my family didn't believe in my aspirations of being an author because it had taken so many years for me to score that first deal. "You've already won the lottery once, what are the chances you'd win it again?" they asked me. They wanted to know my *real* five-year plan for myself. They thought I was childish for being absorbed in fiction and my "hobby" of writing instead of pursuing a conventional career like an actual adult. I had many major fights with my parents, but I couldn't even move out of the house because of the pandemic raging in full swing outside. During those months, I poured my everything into *Zachary Ying*. My obsession with Chinese history, sci-fi concepts, and *shonen*-anime-esque adventure stories, combined into one bonkers book. I couldn't even describe it to my family without sounding ridiculous. Miraculously, the gamble paid off. This book sold at auction. My unexpected YouTube career took off around the same time, and now my family are the "Weird Flex But Okay" family at their Asian friend group gatherings. So thanks to them for eventually believing in me 😄.

I don't entirely blame my parents for not having faith in me from the beginning, though. After all, how many young Asian authors are publicly visible successes? It's hard for immigrant parents to accept a gamble when they don't see people like you winning. But as more of us break into the publishing industry with stories unapologetically inspired by our own cultures, I believe the attitudes of our elders will change as well. Shout-outs to the authors who inspired me: Joan He, Kat Cho, Elizabeth Lim, Julie C. Dao, Chloe Gong, and many more.

Thankfully, I was far from alone in my journey. My deepest gratitude goes to Rebecca Schaeffer, who convinced me to try my hand at writing middle-grade books on a Skytrain ride and then dealt with my months of whining years later as I powered through this book. And of course, it would not have seen the light without my brilliant and thoughtful agent Rachel Brooks, who was as excited as me about the book the moment I first pitched the concept to her. She landed it at such a loving home at Simon & Schuster Margaret K. McElderry Books. I can't gush enough about my editor Sarah McCabe, who understood exactly what I was trying to do with the book, and challenged me to take it to the next level. Special thanks to the whole team at McElderry Books: Justin Chanda, Karen Wojtyla,

Anne Zafian, Bridget Madsen, Elizabeth Blake-Linn on the editorial and publishing side; Lauren Hoffman, Caitlin Sweeny, Alissa Nigro, Lisa Quach, Savannah Breckenridge, Anna Jarzab, Yasleen Trinidad, Saleena Nival, Nadia Almahdi, Jennifer Jimenez, and Nicole Russo in marketing and publicity; Christina Pecorale and her sales team; Michelle Leo and her education/library team; and of course, Karyn Lee for the cover design and Velinxi for the cover illustration that I have NOT been able to stop thinking about. Seriously, I had a document full of ideas for the cover, and Karyn and Velinxi brought to life EVERYTHING that I wanted, from the water dragon to the underwater palace city to Zack and the emperor in action poses on the front in the correct outfits 😭.

More thanks to the beta readers of this book: Rebecca Schaeffer, Francesca Tacchi, Marco Malvagio, Tina Chan, Carly Heath, and Kate Foster. Your cheers and challenges were what kept me pushing this book toward its final form!

To new friends in the Ultraman fandom—Emcee, Taya, Cubee, Tri, Klenda, Gun, Tori, Mike Dent, Ori, and so many others for giving me a stable online home amidst the absolute chaos that is my influencer/author life.

To my assistant Trisha Martem, for helping to tamper that chaos.

Finally, to Kazuki Takahashi, for inadvertently shaping so much of who I am as a person by creating *Yugioh*, and to LittleKuriboh, for the unforgettable legend that is *Yugioh the Abridged Series*.

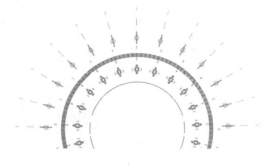

About the Author

XIRAN JAY ZHAO IS THE #1 *NEW YORK TIMES* BESTSELLING author of the Iron Widow series. A first-gen Hui Chinese immigrant from small-town China to Vancouver, Canada, they were raised by the internet and made the inexplicable decision to leave their biochem degree in the dust to write books and make educational content instead. You can find them @XiranJayZhao on Twitter for memes, Instagram for cosplays and fancy outfits, TikTok for fun short videos, and YouTube for long videos about Chinese history and culture. *Zachary Ying and the Dragon Emperor* is their first middle-grade novel.